KELLEY ARMSTRONG

This special signed edition
is limited to 2000 numbered copies
and 26 lettered copies.

This is copy 1551 .

A Twist of Fate

A Twist of Fate

Kelley Armstrong

Subterranean Press 2021

First Edition

ISBN
978-1-64524-052-5

Subterranean Press
PO Box 190106
Burton, MI 48519

subterraneanpress.com

Manufactured in the United States of America

ONE

HERE ARE TWO things I do before I leave the house that night. Two snippets of time to be preserved in the amber of memory, polished until they gleam sun-bright.

After August falls asleep, I slide from our bed and pull on the riding dress I secreted away before we retired. He groans, and I go still, my heart hammering. At a thump behind me, I turn, barely daring to breathe. He's on his back now, eyes closed, sound asleep.

I exhale. As I do, clouds shift beyond the window, and moonlight hits him. That sliver of light plays across his bare chest and face, and three years seem to disappear, and instead, it is our wedding night and I'm looking at my new husband, my breath catching as the moon glides over him.

I will never be this happy.

That is what I thought. I'd been almost shamed by my joy, as if I did not deserve it. I'd been afraid for it, too, wanting to swaddle it in wool, lest it shatter.

How did I get so lucky?

I'd thought that, too. August Courtenay was the third son of an earl, and for a young woman like me—with a good name but nothing more—our marriage should have been the achievement of a lifetime. His family and his fortune meant nothing to me, though.

 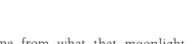
Perhaps, then, my joy should come from what that moonlight revealed: a man with the face and body of a Greek god. I'd be lying if I said I didn't thoroughly enjoy the sight of him. Yet again, that wasn't the source of my happiness.

If anything, August's wealth and good looks had been detriments to our union, sending me fleeing his early pursuit. Only a fool falls for a man like that. A fool who thinks she'll win more than a few nights of passion and a cheap bauble for her finger instead of a wedding band.

No, my joy in that moment, waking beside my bridegroom, was the happiness of finding that most elusive of romantic prizes: love. Love from a man who saw to the core of me, past all my rough edges and idiosyncrasies. And I saw everything in him and loved him back. Loved him beyond imagination, beyond measure.

That was three years ago. Now...?

I have a secret passion for Gothic tales, and I know how this one should go. Penniless girl weds an angel and finds herself shackled to a demon instead. There is nothing demonic in August. Just something small and frightened that I desperately want to soothe, and I cannot.

In each of us, we carry a shadow of the child we were, and August's is a very sad and lonely boy who is certain every woman he loves will leave him. One would think that marriage, and then a child, would cure his fear, but the more tightly we are bound to one another, the more fearful he becomes, that fear manifesting in an anger and a jealousy that has begun to frighten me.

I picture the bride who woke beside her husband three years ago. I imagine what she'd think if she could see herself now, slipping from bed, pulling on a riding gown, preparing to sneak back to Thorne Manor and retrieve her wedding band, innocently left in the kitchen as she helped the housekeeper fix an uncooperative bread dough.

That bride would laugh at her future self. Why all the intrigue? August knows she helped with the dough. He'd understand her removing her ring. What else would he think? That she'd taken it off for a tryst with

the owner of Thorne Manor... August's oldest and dearest friend? How absolutely preposterous.

That is the extent of my husband's jealousy. The sick and sorry truth of it, that I have done nothing to ever give him cause for concern. I *would* never do anything, still being as madly in love with him as I was on our wedding night. Yet he cannot rest his watchful gaze when I am around other men, even his most trusted friend, who has treated me like nothing but a dear substitute for the younger sister he lost.

And so I must slip from bed to ride through the night and retrieve my wedding band while praying—*praying*—my husband does not wake to find me gone.

As I rise, I watch August, and my chest tightens with love and with loss, and with the determination that we will get past this. We must. I won this incredible man, and I will not give him up so easily.

I ease from the room to the second thing I will do before I leave. The second memory I will unknowingly create. I tiptoe into the room beside ours, where I creep to a bassinet. Our son—Edmund—sleeps as soundly as his father.

I bend and inhale the smell of him, his milky breath, his sweet skin. I cannot resist brushing my lips across his head, already thick with his father's curls. One light kiss, and then I slip away, whispering a promise that I will be back before he wakes.

Escaping the house is not easy. It is the Courtenays' ancestral estate, a "country home" that would fit five of our London townhouses. Having grown up in London, I'd shuddered when August first invited me to his family's Yorkshire estate. Afterward, he joked that I very coincidentally fell in love with him on that visit, and it was the countryside that truly won my heart. Not so, but Courtenay Hall ignited a fierce passion for *place* that I'd never experienced before. It is, of course, his eldest brother's estate, yet the earl abhors the countryside, and we are free to summer here.

A house of this size, of course, requires staff, and I must exit as stealthily as any burglar would enter. At one time, the staff was accustomed to their

young mistress creeping out for a moonlit ride. I'd gallop under the stars, across the estate's vast meadows and through its game forests, and never encounter a single person who felt obliged to tip his hat or who looked askance at my windswept hair. I'd return after an hour or so and crawl into bed, drunk on moonlight and freedom, and August would sense the cool draft of my night-chill body and roll over to greet me with lovemaking.

Last month, when we arrived at the summer estate, I'd slipped away for a ride, and August had followed. He'd stuck to the shadows, and when I caught him, he insisted he'd only been concerned for my safety. If that were the case, he'd have said so and ridden with me. No, he'd been following me.

So while I do not fear being stopped by staff, I do fear them innocently mentioning my moonlit ride to August. Yet I am prepared, and soon I am on my horse, riding from the estate without attracting any notice.

Thorne Manor is not, unfortunately, over the next hill or down the next dale. It's nearly seven miles away. I am only glad that I have a young and healthy gelding and that the roads are empty at this hour.

When I near the village of High Thornesbury, the sound of voices drifts over on the breeze. Drunken male voices. I skirt the village at a quieter pace and then set my mount galloping up the hill to the manor house.

The house is dark and empty. William had business to tend to in London, and so August insisted he take our coach. Yes, a lord, particularly one with William's income, should have his own coach, but our William is even more eccentric than I. As for household staff, he has only his aged housekeeper and groom, and he gave them two nights off to stay with their adult children in High Thornesbury.

I don't stable my horse. I'll give him a quick grooming before the return journey. For now, I leave him at the water trough and then slip in through the kitchen door, which never quite locks properly and needs only a certain lift-and-pull to open it.

My goal is less than ten paces from the door, where I'd helped the housekeeper, Mrs. Shaw. Baking is my passion. It had also been my

salvation when my parents died and left their three daughters with a comfortable home and a small income but no money to bring into a marriage. As the oldest, I considered it my responsibility to provide that for my sisters. There'd been an easy and acceptable way: marry one of several rich suitors. Or a difficult and scandalous way: open my own bakery. Naturally, I chose the latter.

My wedding band is exactly where I left it, tucked behind a canister of flour. I'm putting it on when a scream sounds overhead, and I jump, my riding boots sliding on the kitchen floor.

Eyes wide, I press myself into the shadows as something thumps on the floor above. I hold my breath and measure the distance between myself and the door. Another thump, and I turn instead to a hanging meat cleaver.

I ought to run. That is the sensible thing to do. Yet I keep imagining that scream. A high-pitched screech like that of a terrified woman.

William is away, and most of High Thornesbury will know it. How many also know about that broken kitchen door? For a man with William's dangerous reputation, one would think he'd be far less trusting. Or perhaps he expects his reputation will keep invaders at bay.

There is another possibility. Not burglary, but a man luring a woman to this empty house.

I touch the handle of the cleaver before thinking better of such a sharp and unwieldy weapon. I take a poker from the hearth instead. Then I creep, sure-footed, to the stairs.

I'm halfway up before a sound comes again, and it stops me in my tracks, my mind struggling to identify what I'm hearing. It's hollow and haunting, half yowl and half keening, raising the hairs on my neck.

I climb slower now, poker gripped in both hands, gaze straining to see in near darkness.

I reach the top, and the sound comes softer, hauntingly desolate. I swallow and continue until I reach an open door. Moonlight floods the small room. A child's room, yet I've stayed in this house often enough to

know it's William's. His childhood bedchamber, which he inexplicably insists on retaining.

The sound comes again, but there is no sign of anyone within. The noise seems to emanate from the vicinity of the bed. Could someone be prostrate and injured on the floor behind it? I grip the poker tighter and take two steps before my ears follow the noise instead to the box at the end of William's bed. A storage chest.

Am I hearing a trapped child?

One hand still wielding the poker, I heave up the heavy lid of the box to see a calico kitten trapped within and yowling piteously.

"Who put you in there?" I whisper, and I'm about to throw the lid completely open when—

The box disappears. One second, I'm gripping the half-open lid, staring at a kitten, and the next, the lid disappears, leaving me staggering. I stumble forward and catch myself on the foot of the bed.

I push up sharply, shaking my head as I hold the foot of...

The foot of a bed that is not William's.

TWO

HE BED IS but an empty steel frame, listing to one side, in a room that stinks of disuse. The moon shines through a curtainless window.

I look around. It is structurally the same room, yet entirely different in its furnishings. There's a narrow bed frame and an odd white-painted chest of drawers. A vanity sits to one side, its top scattered with jars, all of them coated in a quarter-inch of dust.

I walk to the vanity and lift one bottle. It looks like red glass, but the material is like nothing I've seen before, lightweight and covered with glossy printed paper that has faded with age. Big letters proclaim "Sun In," and the picture... Is that a photograph of a young woman?

I turn the bottle into the light and nearly drop it. The photograph depicts a naked woman. I blink and stare. No, she's not entirely unclothed, but she might as well be, dressed only in scraps of blue fabric over her breasts and nether regions. She's at a beach, holding some sort of ball-like sphere, and I can only stare in horror and fascination.

I gingerly set down the bottle and pick up a tiny tube made of the same strange material. It bears the words Dr Pepper. Some kind of

remedy, then? I open the cap to find a waxy sweet-smelling stick. A third container is white with a bright pink lid. The glossy paper is covered in lips and hearts, and the typeface screams "Teen Spirit" and proclaims it to be something called deodorant. A deodorizer? I have heard of such a thing to cover the scent of manure. As for "teen spirit," I know what spirits are—either alcohol or ghosts—but whatever is a teen?

Clearly I am sleeping. I only dreamed that I awoke and rode to Thorne Manor. I've never been an imaginative sort—my sister is the writer—but some latent talent has arisen in this fantastical dream.

I set down the "deodorant" and walk from the room. It does *look* like Thorne Manor. Pictures line the hallway, but it's too dim for me to see them, and I don't pause to look closer. Downstairs, a clock strikes the hour, and it is unmistakably the same clock.

I reach the front door, and that, too, is the same, or so it seems until metal glints, and I notice an odd locking contraption above the knob. When I turn the handle, a metal bolt slides back. The doorknob itself has also changed, but after a few tries, it opens with a click.

I pull the heavy wood door to look out at a front lawn so wild and overgrown it would give Mr. Shaw heart failure. I walk down steps to a laneway that now runs to the stables instead of circling past the house.

There's no sign of my horse, but by now, I don't expect to see him. This is clearly a dream, and I am exploring it out of curiosity. When I wake, it'll be a delightful story to tell August.

Should I share it? What if he wonders why I am dreaming of Thorne Manor? My heart thuds. Is this how it will be forever now? I cannot even share my dreams with my husband for fear he'll read something untoward in them?

No, we will overcome this obstacle. It may take time, but he will see he has no cause for jealousy.

I cross the lawn to find a wider road than I remember. At the foot of the hill, High Thornesbury glows with an eerie light, a dome of it cast over the village.

Entranced, I hike my skirts and make my way down the hill. It is not a short walk. Not an interesting one, either. Everything seems exactly as I recall until I round a corner to find a metal signpost. It seems to be warning of a sharp curve, which makes me laugh. Any fool can see the curve. It's not as if a horse will come careening around and miss the turn entirely.

A sheep bleats in the distance, and a cow answers. I smile. That, at least, has not changed. Nor have the brambles along the roadside, already thick with red berries that will turn black and sweet in another month. The air smells of heather, the scent of the moors. There's something else, an acrid scent I don't recognize, but the heather is stronger, along with the less pleasant odor of sheep droppings.

I'm nearly to the bottom of the hill when thunder rumbles. I peer up, but the night sky is clear, moon and stars shining bright. The sound grows closer and becomes like the growl of some wild beast. I stagger backward as lights appear from nowhere, two blindingly bright orbs bearing down on me faster than a horse at full gallop.

It is, of course, my imagination. A new fancy from my dream. After that initial moment of terror, I fix my feet in place, determined to see what my mind has conjured. I am curious. Yes, that is an odd reaction to a creature barreling toward me, growling and shrieking as it rounds the corner. But I want to see it. I want a tale to tell August and a tale to tell my sister Miranda, one that might inspire a fresh tale from her pen.

At the last moment, my resolve cracks. This creature—a low-slung carriage-sized shadow—is charging me at demonic speed, its eyes blinding my own, and a tiny voice whispers, "What if it is not a dream?" I throw myself to the side, diving through a tangle of hedge and bramble as the beast screams to a stop.

Through the thorny vines, I watch as the beast sprouts wings that disgorge two men. The one closer to me is dressed in blue trousers that fit as tight as riding breeches. Over his chest, he wears a shirt without collar or sleeves or buttons or cravat. He looks like a vagrant, unshaven with wild and uncut hair.

"What?" His shadowy companion throws up his arms. "Are we stopping for hallucinations now?" His voice is thick with the local accent, but it's not quite right.

"I saw a girl in the road," the other says. "A blonde in a blue dress."

The first man snickers. "Like the one who shot you down tonight? Had one too many pints, and now you're seeing her everywhere?"

"That was a purple dress. This one was blue. A long, old-fashioned dress."

His companion gasps. "Oh, my God, you saw her!"

"Saw who?"

"The ghost of the moors." The shadowy figure waves his hands. "Whooo! She's coming to get you!" The figure starts climbing back into the beast. "Get back in the bloody car, or you're walking home."

The other man returns, and the beast roars off. I watch it go...and then I run.

I race back to Thorne Manor, up the stairs to that strange and empty room, where I wait to wake up.

I do not wake up. At some point, I sleep, instead, drifting into a fitful dream of hearing my son's cries and being unable to find him. Then I wake from that to find myself on the floor of that bedroom, in a house that is and is not Thorne Manor.

I investigate. It is all I can do, short of sobbing in a corner, which would hardly solve anything. The house is empty. Long empty, although furnishings suggest it has not been abandoned. And those furnishings... the strangeness of them, like the house itself both familiar and not.

The kitchen is filled with devices I do not recognize, cannot fathom the purpose of, mingled with ones so familiar I find myself stroking them like talismans that will carry me home. The entire house is like that—things I know and things I do not. Somehow that is worse than if it had been entirely unfamiliar. It's like seeing a portrait of my parents that does not quite look like them, teasing me with grief and longing and frustration.

I find water, and I find food, and I ponder my situation for a day and a night before coming to the only conclusion that makes sense. I have passed through time.

Later, I will laugh at how long it took me to realize what would seem obvious to any modern denizen of the world. Time travel is so deeply embedded in modern storytelling that it is almost cliché. Yet I come from a world that has not yet birthed H. G. Wells and his time machine. I have read both *Rip Van Winkle* and *A Christmas Carol*, which lightly touch upon the concept of moving through time, but that is nothing like what I experience.

And yet I *have* encountered the concept, in a way, which might be the only thing that keeps me from declaring I've gone mad.

It happened on my honeymoon. August and I were on a ship bound for Italy. It was our second day into the voyage, and we'd only left our stateroom for food. That morning, we were stretched out naked on our bed, the sea breeze drifting through the open porthole. I remarked on how incredible it was that we could travel to Rome in a few days, and I mused on how much faster it might be for our great-grandchildren.

"You should ask William about that," August said, cutting an apple and handing me half. "I believe he may have secret knowledge of the future."

"It certainly seems like it, with his gift for investing."

"Not a gift at all. As I said, secret knowledge." He slid closer and lowered his lips to my ear, as if we were not alone in our stateroom. "I believe he once knew a girl from the future."

I sputtered a laugh. "The future?"

He rolled onto his back. "The summer we were fifteen, he became incredibly, irritatingly distracted, with scarcely any time at all for me."

"No time for you? Or your youthful shenanigans?"

"Shenanigans? True, I was a bit of a rascal, getting myself into this bind and that."

"Bind," I murmured. "Now that is a word I have never heard used to refer to a lady's private parts."

He choked on a bite of apple, sputtering as he coughed it out. He waggled a finger at me. "I was a very proper young man, Rosie, who saved himself for his marriage bed."

That had me laughing hard enough that someone rapped on our door to be sure we were all right. August assured him we were.

"So William shunned your company," I said. "That summer you were busy falling into binds, and he did not wish to join you."

August shook his head. "I will not rise to your bait, only saying that your opinion of my youth is very wicked. Not inaccurate, but still wicked. So William spurned me, and being mildly jealous—"

I cleared my throat.

He gave me a look. "All right. *Very* jealous. A man must have one flaw, and that is mine."

"*One* flaw?"

"Others have more. I have but one." He coughed to cover my laugh. "And so, to resume my tale, I became jealous and resolved to learn the reason for his distraction. It was a girl."

I gasped. "Truly? A young man distracted by a young woman. What a twist in the tale!"

He rapped my bare bottom with one finger. "You mock, but William was not me, and I had never seen him display more than mild interest in the fairer sex. Yet there he was, enthralled by a secret love. Even more remarkable was the girl herself, who dressed and spoke in the oddest way."

"Because she was"—I gripped his arm, my eyes mock wide—"from the future!"

"Well, no, at first, I thought she might be French. Or American. Or perhaps some fae creature from his beloved moors. After that summer, William fell into the darkest brood, and I realized the affair had come to an unhappy end, and I resolved not to tease him about his mysterious buxom brunette. Then, years later, when his mother passed and he realized the family coffers were near to empty, he began making the maddest gambles, investing in newfangled ideas that seemed destined to failure."

"Yet they succeeded, and thus he filled the family coffers to overflowing. And somehow that is proof that this girl was from the future...?"

"She gave him information *on* the future. On inventions yet to come."

"So William Thorne fell madly in love with a girl from the future, who broke his heart but shared secret knowledge of her advanced culture." I peered at him. "Are you sure she wasn't French?"

He laughed and pulled me to him for a kiss. And that was the end of the conversation as we resumed our honeymoon and promptly forgot everything else.

I still do not leap on August's speculations as the obvious answer. Yet there is another aspect to the tale that forces me to consider it.

August hadn't merely raised the possibility of traveling through time as a hypothetical fancy. He'd been talking about William Thorne, who'd met a strange girl at Thorne Manor, a girl with odd dress and odd speech, whom William kept hidden, a girl August believed came through time.

A girl who came through time *at Thorne Manor*. Where I opened a box and tumbled into the dusty and abandoned bedroom of a girl.

It is then that I remember the kitten. I return to the bedroom and, in the light of day, clearly see tiny feline tracks on the dusty floor. Tracks that lead to the foot of the bed and disappear.

A kitten from the future, who somehow passed through time and found herself trapped in a box that doesn't exist in her world. She cries for help, and I come running, only to pass through time in the other direction.

That is both perfectly sensible and perfectly ridiculous. Yet if time travel exists perhaps it is like yeast, an inexplicable but proven chemical reaction. Add yeast to the right ingredients, mix in the right environment, and you can make dough magically rise. Add a portal to a house, mix in the right circumstances, and you can blink through time.

Someone in the distant past discovered that yeast makes dough rise. For centuries before that, people ate unleavened bread. Was it not possible that I had made a discovery of my own? One made before me by a girl

who met a boy from another time, loved him and then disappeared back to her own realm?

The solution then is obvious. Recreate the circumstances and return to my husband and child.

I plant myself in that spot, matching my dust-cleared footprints exactly. And there I stand through four hourly chimes of the clock below.

I had arrived shortly before the grandfather clock struck three in the morning. Perhaps timing is the key then. That night, I stand on that spot from one until five. I repeat this every night for a week. Then I think perhaps the moon matters, and I wait for it to be in the same portion of the cycle and try again.

I wear the same dress. I position myself as if opening an invisible box. I arrange my features in some semblance of surprise, as if seeing a kitten. Nothing works.

For six weeks, I try to get home. When I need food, I forage or raid village gardens at night. Days and weeks come and go, and I stay. I stay in an empty house, crying myself to sleep, dreaming of my husband and child, becoming a mere ghost of myself.

I stay, and the kitten does not return, and when six weeks have passed, I begin to understand what that means.

I am here, and I am not going back.

That leaves me two choices. Fade away with wanting, drifting into madness as I haunt this empty house. Or make a life for myself here. Make a life while never giving up hope, while never stopping my efforts to return to my family.

I stay until the second change of the moon brings me no closer to home. Then I dry my tears and walk out of Thorne Manor.

THREE

MIGHT NOT BE the writer in the family, but I could pen an entire novel on my first year in the twenty-first century. It would be an adventure, a mystery, a tragedy and a farce, and at times, a tale of horror.

In a terrible way, it is my parents' untimely passing that allows me to survive in this new world. We may have had little money, but our parents made sure their daughters wanted for nothing. Our mother educated us. Our father hired tutors when we had the extra funds. I was given free rein in the kitchen, even when I ruined a small fortune in ingredients, testing new recipes.

We were spoiled in other ways, too. Relatives breathed a sigh of relief when I neared marriageable age. Here, clearly, lay the solution to my parents' financial woes. I might be an odd girl, but smitten young men already penned odes to my fragile beauty. I could be married off soon and married off well to a wealthy bridegroom who would extend his generosity to my sisters and help them make equally good matches.

A sensible plan. But if my parents had been sensible people, their daughters would not have been dowryless. My parents were not fools. Nor were they spendthrifts. They were something even less acceptable in society. They were romantics.

My father was the second son of a baronet, whose only chance at a gentleman's life had been to make either a good marriage or a good career. Instead, he became a physician and married his mentor's daughter. While he was an excellent doctor, he shared his wife's charitable heart and—like her father—insisted on charging patients according to what they could afford. We were far from penniless, but my sisters and I were often the only girls at a party wearing last year's fashions. Worse, we weren't the least bit ashamed of it.

My parents married for love and found wedded bliss, and so that would be my dowry: the freedom to marry the man of my choice. And I had been in absolutely no rush to do so.

Had they lived until I wed, I'd have gone straight from their home to my husband's, never needing to worry about the myriad concerns that come with independent life. If I'd been that girl, I doubt I'd have survived my first year in the twenty-first century. Instead, I'd lost them when I was nineteen, alone and unwed, with two younger sisters to care for.

Even with that experience, in this new world, I am like a baby taking her first steps, putting each foot down with care and deliberation, constantly assessing and analyzing her environment. Oh, I suppose there are babies who fearlessly rush into ambulation, accepting the bumps and bruises as an intrinsic part of the process; I was not that child, and I am not that adult. I consider, consider and then consider some more.

That first year is an excruciatingly slow process of learning about my new world. I raid gardens for months while I determine the best and safest way to gain employment. I live in sheds for months more until I have the money and knowledge to rent a room. Others would move faster, but my careful deliberation allows an easy transition. I do not make mistakes that mark me an outsider. Mistakes that might have landed me in a psychiatric ward.

I assimilate. That is the word used for newcomers to a land, and that is what I do. Slow and careful assimilation, all the while telling myself it is temporary.

I return to Thorne Manor every month, matching the moon cycle. With each failure, I fortify my defenses against despair until the day I arrive to find the house occupied. Seeing that, something in me breaks. The change is not unexpected—I noticed a caretaker had been preparing the house in the last month. It is not even an unmovable obstacle—the new owner doesn't change the locks, and I had a key copied from one found in a kitchen drawer. Yet as the house moves into her new phase of life, it draws back the shroud on a mirror I've kept carefully covered, refusing to acknowledge the reality reflected there. The reality that I am not moving forward in my own life. That two years have passed, and I am no closer to home than I was that first night.

That mirror also shows a woman two years older. A mother with a son who will now be three years old. A wife with a husband who...

I've tried so hard not to finish that sentence. Not to wonder what August thinks happened to me. I tell myself that perhaps time is frozen in their world, and when I return, it will still be that same night. My years away will have been an adventure during which I grew and learned so much. I will return no longer the young bride, cowed and confused by August's jealousy, but a twenty-first-century woman with the skills and the confidence to correct the problem. To save my marriage without losing myself in the process.

A glorious fantasy. The reality? The reality is that my gut tells me time has not stopped in that world. My infant son is a young boy now and almost certainly has no memory of me. My husband will have thought I ran away, abandoned him, his worst fears come true.

I've refused to face these things because they loose a wild, gnashing, all-consuming terror inside me. I've been forgotten by my son, reviled and hated by my husband, and there is naught I can do about it.

Has August moved on? Found a new wife for himself and a mother for Edmund? The thought ignites outrage. His wife is alive. Edmund's mother is alive. Yet when I consider it in the cold dark of night, I must face an equally cold and dark truth. I almost hope August has moved on. For his sake. For Edmund's.

I do not want them to mourn me forever. I do not want that place in their life vacant forever. If I cannot return home, I want August to have found a woman who makes him happier than I did, a woman who can silence his demons, a woman who will love my son as her own.

And where does that leave me? Does the woman in the mirror stay frozen forever, aging but unmoving? Subsisting and existing but never truly living? Alone and lonely, the exact fate I would never wish on August?

Is it time for me to move on? More than a year will pass before I'm ready to answer that question.

IT IS year four. My son has just turned five. My husband will turn forty soon. I myself have celebrated my thirty-first birthday. Time passes, and I stay still, and I am, in this very moment, facing that as I've never faced it before. I stand in my bakery, looking at a man who could be part of my future.

He could or he could not, and either seems equally likely. I do not know him that well. We may realize we are not compatible. Yet it isn't about *this* man so much as it is about taking *this* step.

Eight words. "Would you like to go for tea later?" Even if nothing comes of it, by speaking the words, I am acknowledging that I may never return to August and Edmund.

The man—Noah—has no idea what I'm contemplating. He's pretending to choose two macarons. For over a month now, at precisely one o'clock each afternoon, Noah stops to pick up macarons for his afternoon tea. I'm not even sure whether he eats them. The first time, when he'd come wanting sweets for his mother, he'd declared he wasn't much for pastries himself. That, apparently, was before he tried my macarons.

They're decent macarons. Not my finest pastries. The delicate almond cookies sandwiched with ganache are currently in vogue, and I do them well enough. My minuscule bakery in the Shambles has won awards for

my cannelés and my jam tartlets, but the tourists want macarons, and apparently, so does Noah. He's just never certain what flavor he wants on that day, which is an excuse to linger and chat with me, and I am fine with that because he is an excellent conversationalist.

Do his visits remind me of August's wooing? Of how my husband wandered into my shop looking for a gift—for a lover, of course—and left nearly an hour later with a basket of pastries, none for his lover? Do I compare and contrast August's visits with Noah's and find the latter lacking? Excellent conversation, to be sure, but bereft of the charm, the spirit and the sheer overwhelming Augustness of August that finally won me over.

It is not the same. Nor do I want it to be. I look at Noah, a handsome divorced thirty-five-year-old with a steady office job and a good flat and a kind manner, and I know that if I'm to take this step, he is an excellent man to take it with. He is safe.

I will not say he is boring. I will not. On a scale of one to ten, with one being deathly dull, Noah rates a perfectly respectable seven. It's not his fault that August was a twelve, and really, if I'm being clear eyed with myself, honestly remembering the tumult and heartache of our last year together, perhaps I would, in the long run, be happier with a seven. Just as August, if he has found new love, has hopefully found someone more conventional, able to placate his jealousy in a way I could not.

Noah leans over the counter, dark hair tumbling forward as he peers through the glass at the jewel-toned cookies below. "They're all too good, Rosie. That's the problem."

"I should suggest one of each, but I'm a terrible salesperson."

He smiles. "And as much as my stomach would love that, my waistline would not. You need to start offering only two types a day, so I don't need to choose."

"Is that what you'd like?" I say. "Grab two and be on your way?"

Rosalind Courtenay, are you flirting?

Yes, I am, and when Noah lifts his eyes to meet my dancing ones, his cheeks color. "No, I suppose that isn't what I'd like at all."

I wait for him to say more. He won't. His gaze slips to the wedding band on my finger, and that is enough. He knows I claim widowhood, but as long as I wear that ring, he is respectful of my grief. If a step is to be made, I'm the one who must make it.

We speak instead of local politics and an upcoming festival where I will have a booth. I'm debating what to sell—in addition to macarons, of course—and I ask his advice, and we chat until a queue forms and my shop girl—ahem, *sales associate*—cuts me a look that politely begs for help. Noah sees it and chooses swiftly, as considerate as ever.

He's barely out the door when I make my decision. I will ask him to tea. Today. Now.

I serve one quick customer and then apologize to my assistant and promise to be quick. Apron off, I'm out the back door, ducking down the narrow alley to intercept him.

He's moving fast, his tall and lanky frame expertly weaving through tourists milling through the Shambles. Tourists. I owe them my success. As lauded as my pastries might be, it's my key location and those tourists themselves who allow me to pay the rent on both my tiny shop and flat. And yet, well, I'd be lying if I didn't admit there were times when I cursed them, muttering that the lack of tourist hordes was one thing definitely better about the nineteenth century.

With his height and his sharp suit, Noah easily cuts through the crowds. I'm a five-foot-tall, slight-figured blonde in a sundress. No one moves for me. No one even notices me. Well, yes, some men do, sadly, but not to move out of my way.

I'm weaving through the crowd when a child's screech catches my attention. Children—particularly young ones and particularly happy ones—always have that effect on me. I'm like a pointer hearing a game bird. I stop whatever I'm doing as if that joyous cry might somehow come from my son.

This time, it's not even a boy. It's a girl of perhaps eighteen months. She's spotted a bright-colored toy in a shop window and nearly launched

herself out of her father's arms, reaching for it. That makes me smile, even as a pang shoots through me.

I'm about to turn away when the father's voice cuts through the surrounding burble of tourist chatter.

"Yes, yes, Amelia, that is a toy. A lovely toy, and we shall return for all the required closer examinations once your mother has shown me this magical bakery, which is apparently, even more magical than all the other bakeries she adores."

The first thing to catch my ear is the name. Amelia. I've always liked that name. Then I notice the man's tone. It's oddly formal…and yet not. Almost a mockery of the speech of my own world, like an actor well-versed in older language, using it to humorous effect. Both of these, however, would not hold my attention if it were not for one more thing.

That voice.

I know that voice, and on hearing it, I turn slowly, my lips parting in a whispered, "William?"

While he's facing the toy shop, his figure matches that of William Thorne. Dressed as I never saw Lord Thorne dressed, of course—in a casual shirt and trousers, with a zebra-striped baby bag over his shoulder—but he's tall and broad shouldered with dark hair that curls at his neck nape. And the woman beside him, angled sideways from me?

I remember August's words from that night in our stateroom.

I resolved not to tease him about his mysterious buxom brunette.

The woman with William is tall with chestnut-brown curls and a full figure. She's also pregnant, and though I can't see her face, her figure nudges at my mind. I'm chasing that nudge when she smacks her husband on the arm.

"If you're going to mock my love of bakeries, William, perhaps you shouldn't bring treats to the flat every evening."

"Mock? Did I mock? Never. I happily indulge your passion for pastries. I simply wish that if you were to discover the most magical of all magical bakeries, it could be located somewhere other than *this*."

He turns to look meaningfully along the narrow cobbled road with its cutesy shops and gaggles of tourists. I have to smile as he shudders. His companion rolls her eyes, her response swallowed by passing college students in Harry Potter robes, shouting, "Expelliarmus!"

It is only then, as the students pass, that I realize William has turned. That I see his face, and that it is, beyond any doubt, *his* face. And the woman with him is his "girl" from the future.

The latter might seem wild conjecture. After all, *buxom brunette* is hardly an uncommon descriptor. Yet I see her face now, and I am, for a moment, back in twenty-first-century Thorne Manor.

I might have lived there for two months, but I'd never paid much attention to the house itself. I'd paid particularly little attention to the objects that make a house a home. The books on the shelves, the photos on the walls, the papers on the desk. Those were all reminders that I was trespassing on another's property, invading another's most private place. Yet when I see the woman's face, I cannot deny that I've seen it before. An old photo at Thorne Manor, one of a young girl with her parents, all of them in modern dress.

This woman was once a girl with a connection to Thorne Manor. A relative of those who owned it in the present. That was how she met William, how she'd passed through time to spend a teenage summer with him.

More than that, I know her. Not the girl, but the woman. I see her face in full, and recognition strikes like lightning. She has come to my shop thrice in the past week. We've spoken on the last two occasions, but even on that first one, I'd noticed her.

I can picture her, standing in my shop, eyeing the pastry display, her daughter on one hip. I noticed her, not because she was beautiful or unusual. I noticed her because she was happy. A mother perhaps nearly a decade older than me with a baby on one hip and another in her belly. A mother glowing with contentment and joy. I saw her, and I'd retreated into the back. As I did, our eyes met, and hers widened, and I'd thought it was because she realized I was backing away.

When she came two days later, I made a point of serving her, shamed by my first reaction. She'd asked questions in an accent I'd mistaken for American. As we talked, I learned she was a history professor from Toronto, married to an Englishman. They had a summer house in North Yorkshire, but her husband was in York for a horse show, and they were spending the week at a holiday flat.

When she'd come by yesterday, I'd found myself smiling, happy for the excuse to chat. I even offered her my card and said the shop shipped throughout Yorkshire. We don't ship anywhere, actually, but I'd felt the urge to reach out. I've come to realize I've omitted one very important part of a satisfying life: companionship. So I was seeking that, whether with this woman or with Noah. Baby steps toward a fuller life.

Now, seeing the woman with William, I know exactly why her eyes had widened that first day. Why she'd returned twice more and made a point of talking to me.

She knows who I am.

She has seen a portrait or photograph of me in my world. Her husband was August's best friend. She would know his wife had vanished, and she might even know my former profession. One day, she walks into a bakery in York, and who does she see? She cannot believe her eyes, quite literally, and so she comes twice more, striking up conversations as she continues her assessment. When she has decided I am indeed Rosalind Courtenay, she brings William to confirm.

I watch them. Her face is turned up to William's, his own countenance as joy bright as hers. Tears spring to my eyes. I could not be happier for him. He is a dear friend and a good man, yet there has always been a shadow in him. Now it is lifted, and he glows with its leaving, and I want to run to him and throw my arms around his neck.

William. Dearest William. It is I. Rosalind.

Yet my feet do not move. I only stare, and that moment of joy on seeing him freezes in my gut as one tear trickles down my cheek.

William.

I want to run to you. Throw myself at you. Beg you and your lovely new wife for help. You are here, in my world, and you can take me home.

Tell me you can take me home.

What if you cannot? What if you are trapped here, too? Only for you, it would be a blessing. You have your wife. You have your daughter and another child on the way. You have your home and even your beloved horses. You will miss August dreadfully, but otherwise, there would be nothing tying you to that other world.

Even if William and his wife can move freely between worlds, that does not mean they can take me back. What would we do then? Have William return to tell August that I'm trapped forever in the future?

As I watch, William and his wife continue toward my bakery, and my feet remain rooted to the cobblestones. They are nearly past the alley when William half turns, frowning. My breath catches, but his gaze only slides across the shadows before he continues on.

I wait until they are gone, and then I run. It is time to go back to Thorne Manor. Back to that spot that brought me here, in the hope—the wild hope—that seeing William means I can finally return home.

FOUR

Y DINNER HOUR, I'm climbing the hill to Thorne Manor. I have texted my shop clerk to let her know I was called away on a family emergency, which is not untrue. She will close the shop doors in my absence, and I have scheduled her weekly pay deposit for the next two months. I will make long-term arrangements through William. That presumes I *will* cross over, but I cannot think of any other possibility and therefore will act as if it is a given.

Once at Thorne Manor, I slip in the back door and race up the steps, as if the portal is a door already closing. Yet even as I pass through the rooms, I take more notice than I have during my last few visits, and I marvel at how truly single-minded I must have been to have missed the changes.

When I dart into the tiny bedroom, now an office, I see a photograph on the desk that has me stopping, shoes squeaking on the wood floor. It's a shot of William holding his daughter on a pony. Leave it to William Thorne to teach his daughter to ride when she can barely walk. What gives me pause is the clothing. It clearly comes from my time. The picture, though, is taken with a modern camera.

They can go back. Take a camera, snap a photograph and return.

That's when I notice the other two subjects in the picture. A man and a boy. The man stands back a step, laughing, as the boy sits behind young Amelia, his hands firmly on her waist. The boy could be holding the child in place, but his expression suggests he's holding on for dear life, as if this baby will save him should the horse bolt.

I look at the boy, and my tears well, and in a single blink, they're streaming down my face. The preschooler is the spitting image of the man behind him, the laughing, impossibly handsome man with dark blond hair and green eyes.

"August," I whisper. My fingers move toward him, but instead, they slide to caress the face of the boy. Of my son.

"Edmund."

My knees buckle, and I fall against the desk, heaving for breath I cannot find. I knew my son was no longer a baby. Rationally, I understood that. Yet I held fast to the hope that time had not progressed in their world. Here is the proof that denies that dream. My son is no longer a baby. He is a boy, one who has never known a mother.

Never known *a* mother? I have no reason for saying such a thing. As soon as I disappeared, August would have had women queuing up on his doorstep, offering to mother his abandoned infant.

My son has almost certainly known a mother. It just wasn't me.

I take deep, shuddering breaths until I'm able to slowly straighten.

My husband may have a new wife, and that will cut me to the core, but I will accept it. My son may have a loving mother, and that will cut just as deep, but I will accept it, too. There will still be room for me. Living in this world, I've seen families with more than two parents, children raised in an abundance of love.

I'm turning from the desk when a shape appears at the door. I jump, yelping. A cat fixes me with the most disgusted glare, tail swishing as she comes into the room.

A cat. A calico cat.

The kitten from the box. Not a kitten anymore, but a full-grown feline. One who has crossed and come back again just like William and his daughter and wife.

I take the photograph from the desk. Then I lift my bag and stride to the time-portal spot. I clutch the picture of my family as I fix my gaze on the cat. One is a sign of where I need to be, the other proof that such passage is possible.

I close my eyes and picture this room in William's house. I let my son's and husband's faces hover before me, a tether to that world. The time is right, and the way is open, and by God, I will pass if I need to ram through time itself.

I clutch the photograph and focus on my family and on the cat. If she can cross, I will, too.

I will, I will, I will.

I do not. Even with my eyes closed, I know nothing has happened. The room feels no different. Sounds no different. There's a meow, and fur brushes my bare legs as the cat rubs against me. With a sigh, I open my eyes, and I'm staring at that same desk. Even the picture still sits there, in its silver frame...

The picture sits on the desk.

The same picture I have in my hands.

I blink, and I see it is not the same photograph at all. Or it is the same pose, yet it is in black and white, with the sepia tone of a Victorian photograph.

I stare at that picture, and I throw back my head and laugh. Yes, it's the same desk...because they had one made for both homes. The same photograph, too, using a sepia filter to look as if it belongs in my time.

In my time.

In *this* time.

My chest tightens, stealing breath. What if I'm wrong? Perhaps there was a second photograph, and that's what I'm seeing. When I look about the room and discover I have not passed through time at all, it will destroy me.

In these four years, I've broken down more times than I can count. Those moments where I no longer wanted to live in a world bereft of every person I'd ever loved. Yet those black hours were spots of mold on a loaf of bread that I could not afford to throw away. Cut them out and move on.

That's what I've done. I've made the new world my own. I've allowed myself to see the beauty in it. I've allowed myself to marvel and revel at technological advances. I've allowed myself to marvel and cheer at social advances. But even then, in the back of my mind, I wasn't only thinking of how wonderful it was to walk the streets at night and not be thought a strumpet, to run my own shop and not be thought a harridan. I learned everything I could, all the while only thinking how wonderful it would be to take this knowledge home with me.

I could help August understand how his jealousy felt like control. I would ask—no, *insist*—on resuming my trade in whatever form wouldn't dishonor his family. I would tell my sisters to pursue their passions, and I'd help them do it and never let anyone tell them they were fragile things in need of a man. I'd known all this in my heart before, but being in the new world gave me the confidence to push harder for what I believed in.

What happens if I look around now to see that I did not cross and must accept finally that I will never cross?

I don't think I can bear it.

I will, though. For four years, I've kicked my fears from the darkness and soldiered on, eyes on the horizon even as my heart stayed in the past. I will do the same now if I must.

I slowly turn my gaze and…

The thick-cushioned recliners are gone, replaced with deep arm chairs. The shelves remain the same, but the books on them are different, old titles still gleaming new. While the structure of the desk remains the same, it holds a very different collection of goods. A jeweled inkwell and pearl pen in place of a silver writing set. A stack of writing papers where there had been a stack of printed pages. No laptop cord snakes from a wall socket. There are no wall sockets at all.

I take it all in, and then I collapse atop my bag. I grip that bag tight as sobs of joy wrack my body.

Then I realize where I am. On the spot that holds the portal.

I scramble up, gasping and clawing and stumbling until I'm safely away from the spot. At a rumbling meow, I look up to see the calico cat watching me with disdain, rolling her feline eyes at this foolish human, making such a fuss over something as small as stepping through time.

She stalks off, and I rise, wiping my eyes and then grabbing my bag and...

I stop midstep. Where exactly am I going?

Back to August, of course. To my son. To my life.

No. I cannot. Not like this.

On the trip to Thorne Manor, I'd realized that if I did cross, I could not run pell-mell back to August. Unless he was at Courtenay Hall, I'd need to take a train or coach to London, which required not only Victorian currency but also a bit of time to acclimate to this new world, lest I be thrown into Bedlam for my bold and odd actions.

Yes, perhaps that shouldn't matter. I ought to run all the way to Courtenay Hall, and if he's not there, run to London itself. That is the impulsive and romantic solution. It is not mine.

I'm finally back, and I will not end up in a ditch, dead of exhaustion. My heart wants to fly to my husband and son. My head counsels pragmatism and caution.

There is also the strong likelihood of August having remarried. For everyone's sake, I must know his situation in advance, lest I bring unnecessary turmoil and heartbreak to a difficult situation.

The answer is simple. William's wife said they were in York for a week. Her first visit had been six days ago. That means they'll be home tomorrow. I need only to settle in and wait.

THREE DAYS have passed with no sign of William or his family. I'm certain they travel between the worlds. There is ample evidence of a child in residence here in the nineteenth century.

Yet the house is shuttered tight, and the longer I wait, the more I must accept that William's family may pass between worlds, but that does not mean they do so daily. It would be easier, if they were in York for the week, to shut up Victorian Thorne Manor for longer and give the staff a proper holiday.

I've noticed a local boy coming to tend the horses, but otherwise, I haunt Thorne Manor unbothered. And I do haunt it. I pace like a fretful ghost. With each passing day, I ask myself how much longer I'll wait. How much longer I *can* wait.

I search through their correspondence for hints about August's whereabouts and, yes, his marital status. I discover that William's wife's name is Bronwyn. I discover that he's retained his London townhouse, but his solicitor still needs to beg him to return, even briefly. I discover that, with marriage, William has become slightly more sociable, but that only means they accept the occasional invitation from country neighbors. All this is lovely…and does not help me one whit. If there is personal correspondence, it is not retained.

As the fourth day dawns, I make the only choice I can. Or, perhaps more accurately, the only choice I can without going mad. I must find my husband and negotiate this situation without the aid of a friend who can confirm my outlandish story.

I am already prepared to depart. I did not sit on my hands for three days. I discover to my relief that William has allowed his housekeeper to continue storing secondhand gowns here for her side business. In guest room wardrobes, I locate two traveling dresses and a day gown with all the required undergarments. As I don a dress that morning, I unreservedly admit that of all the things I missed in my world, the complexity and discomfort of the undergarments is not one of them.

My bag contains several items accumulated for a very specific purpose: to allow me to affect a disguise. I knew years ago that I might require one when I returned, and so I had all the accoutrements in my flat.

Two years ago, I cut my hair to shoulder length. The style flatters me and is much easier to care for. Yet it is not the hair of a Victorian woman. So I require a wig. I'd chosen one of long dark hair, thicker and straighter than my own. I also have contacts to change my blue eyes to brown. Modern makeup allows me to shade my skin and alter my cheekbone structure, as well as covering my freckles and adding a birthmark. Yes, I watched far too many YouTube makeup videos—being in a strange world with no social life meant I'd had plenty of free time on my hands.

I've lost weight, too. I've always been slight of build, and Victorian friends had teased I was a poor advertisement for my pastries. Since leaving that world, my appetite has dropped to nil, and I've grown unhealthily thin. It does help me now, though, along with a stuffed brassiere to alter that aspect of my figure. Add a pair of spectacles, and I look so little like Rosalind Courtenay that August himself might not even recognize me. I do not, however, intend to deceive him. I simply need to make inquiries about August—to determine his current whereabouts—without arousing suspicion.

Next, I steal Victorian currency from William. Of course, I have every intention of repaying him, and so *borrow* would be the correct term even if it feels like theft. I know from experience that he keeps money in a kitchen drawer for Mrs. Shaw to pay whomever requires paying, William not being fond of purchasing on credit. I open the box, expecting to discover a handful of shillings, perhaps even a full pound. There are shillings, and there are *also* pounds, for a total of nearly twenty guineas.

Really, William? You leave this unlocked in the kitchen drawer?

If asked, he'd say that no one dares steal from him. True, perhaps, if Mrs. Shaw found the box empty, William might rage in public, but in private, he'd say what my parents did when we came home one day to find our house burgled.

I trust that whoever took it needed it more than we did.

While I consider taking only part of the money, practicality wins out. I can guarantee the Thornes full repayment from my funds in the twenty-first century. To be safe, I'll take it all. I leave a note apologizing for the theft and promising it will be repaid with interest. I do not sign it.

One last look around the house. One last peer down the lane in hopes I'll see Mrs. Shaw coming to open the manor, presaging her lord's imminent arrival. All stays still and quiet. I take a deep breath, lift my bag and walk out into this new-old world.

I WALK to Whitby. It's a brisk autumn morning, the wind blasting over the moors as I cut through them. It's a shortcut to the seaside town, letting me take the bridle paths that cross the open fields, but it also means I can avoid people, particularly those who might notice I wear white shoes emblazoned with the name of a Greek god. When I draw close to Whitby, I replace my Nikes with far less comfortable footwear.

I have chosen the Whitby train because a coach from High Thornesbury to York would have prompted questions for a Victorian woman traveling alone. If anyone asks, I'm a governess on my way to a new position. My appearance fits the stereotype of the part—an unflattering, ill-fitting but quality dress; spectacles perched on my nose, and soft hands and clear skin that suggest I'm not accustomed to manual labor.

Catching a train in the busy seaside town means I will attract little notice on my journey. Once in York, I will make inquiries regarding August Courtenay. He had a son, did he not? Of age for a governess? All my questions about his current abode and marital status will seem innocent enough then.

When I board the train, it seems I will have a compartment to myself. Yet after the journey begins, a young woman pops her head in, takes a look at me and enters with a sigh of relief.

"Please tell me that seat is empty," she says, gesturing at the one across from me.

I smile. "It is."

She collapses into it with another deep and dramatic sigh. "I was nearly trapped with two gentlemen who drank far too much gin in town." She wrinkles her nose. "And ate far too many fish. From the smell, I almost wonder whether they were rolling in both."

"You are safe here," I say. "If they bother us, we will fend them off together. I have a very sharp shoe in my satchel."

She laughs and slumps in the seat to catch her breath. We sit in companionable silence for a few moments before she asks where I'm headed. I practice my story on her.

"A governess?" Her eyes widen with such delight you'd think I claimed to be a princess. "My sister is a governess. In York, no less. I must give you her address. Let me find my notebook."

As she rummages in her bag, she asks more questions, and I answer, happy for this excuse to test my performance. Nothing in my story—or my speech or behavior—strikes her as odd, which is an incredible relief, and soon we're caught up in conversation, the notebook forgotten.

The young woman—Emma—is traveling to York to fetch an aged aunt back to Whitby, where she's staying with several elderly relatives enjoying a seaside visit. Emma was supposed to travel with another aunt to pick up the newly arrived one, but that aunt took ill, and so she is making the trip alone, and she is delightfully giddy at the prospect.

I try to picture a modern girl being so thrilled at a solo voyage. It would more likely be a chore. For Emma, though, it is as dangerously and scandalously thrilling an adventure as a solo flight across the Atlantic, and I'm thoroughly charmed.

We arrive as the sun is dipping behind the horizon. I'm quiet for the last half hour of our journey. Emma is busy writing in her notebook, and I'm contemplating where I'll spend the night.

"Oh!" she says, slapping shut her book and tucking it aside. "We're here!"

I startle, so deep in my thoughts that I didn't notice the train slowing. She leaps to her feet as only a girl of her age can, fairly clapping her hands in delight. As I gather my things, her fingers clasp mine, and I look up into round eyes shadowed with worry.

"What if she's not here? My aunt was supposed to arrive from London an hour ago, but what if her train has been delayed?"

"Then I suppose you'll have an hour to yourself. One last gasp of freedom."

I smile, but worry darkens her face, and she looks out the window. "It is much busier than Whitby. Do I wait in the station? That's safest, don't you think?"

I want to tell her it's fine to go out and find supper, perhaps a spot of late tea. Yet the sun is dropping, and she is right to be nervous.

"If your aunt is not there, I will wait with you," I say.

She gushes her gratitude, and shame prickles in me. While I'm happy to help, I'm also aware of how this could help *me*. She will introduce me to her aunt, who will ask where I'm staying, and I will admit I do not have a room yet. While I don't expect an invitation to share theirs, it will be much easier to rent a room if I'm accompanied by a respectable elderly woman.

We disembark while Emma cranes her neck to look for her aunt. I'm no help at all. At my height, all I see are men's cravats.

"We should check whether her train arrived," I say.

Emma nods. "I'll speak to— Oh, there's a station clerk. I'll ask him."

She zips through the crowd, and I'm about to follow when I notice her bright yellow carpetbag on the ground. Good thing the color blazes like sunlight on the dingy platform.

I clutch both our bags as people jostle past.

"There you are!" a voice booms.

A hand clasps my arm. I turn to see a stout middle-aged woman, sharp nosed and sharp chinned, with a gaze that skewers me like a mouse in a hawk's sights.

Her grip tightens, and she propels me ahead of her.

"Thank goodness for that hideous bag," she says. "I would never have found you without it."

"Bag?" I glance back at her. "Oh! You must be—"

"Mrs. Landon, of course." She glowers at me. "Did the voyage addle your brain, child? Come along. The coach is waiting."

This must be a companion or lady's maid of Emma's aunt. She's mistaken me for the girl. Either she's nearsighted, or she's never met Emma, because the only thing we share in common is dark hair and dark eyes.

I try again to protest, but the woman is surprisingly strong for her age. The train whistles, drowning me out. I look around and—

There is Emma, atop a grassy rise less than twenty feet away. She's looking right at me, her expression calm, and I decide she clearly does not recognize me. I wave madly to get her attention. She still doesn't react. She just looks at me. Then her lips part.

"I'm sorry," she mouths…and then scampers into the gathering dark.

FIVE

'M HAULED ALONG another ten steps before I fully comprehend what has happened. Before I understand I've been duped. Emma left her yellow carpetbag at my feet because someone was looking for a dark-haired woman with a yellow carpetbag. Now that someone is dragging me toward a waiting coach.

In London, I'd heard this story many times. Even in the modern world, I heard variations on it. A young woman, on her own, met by someone who promises her a position and then bustles her off into a waiting coach or car, beginning a journey that will end in horror and despair. A young woman forced into service, where indentured servitude will be the best of the options laid before her.

My journey will not end that way. I'm no innocent and naive girl, no helpless chit to be meekly propelled into a coach to hell.

I do not fight, though. I simply right myself, getting my balance. I'll play along for a few moments as I walk toward the—

The coach.

It's shining black with matching horses whose harnesses bear a family crest. The coach of a wealthy family. That is not, however, what stops me. It is the crest emblazoned on the side.

"Courtenay?" I whisper. "This is the Earl of Tynesford's coach."

"Yes," the woman says. "The earl's own coach, come to take you to Courtenay Hall. I hope you appreciate that, girl."

I stand there, blinking, as the door opens, and I turn to see the man holding it for me, and I blink again. It takes me a moment to place the face. It's been four years, and he was but a boy when I last saw him. The head groom's son, Hugh. My mouth opens, his name on my lips, and I snap it closed.

I get into the coach. I do not leap in. Nor do I need to be prodded.

Hugh takes my bag and then reaches for the yellow one, but I collect myself enough to murmur that I require something from it and keep it clutched as I climb into the coach.

I move as if in a sleep trance. I *am* in a sleep trance. I must be. This is what dreams are like, are they not? A young woman bursts into my train cabin. She abandons me with a bright yellow bag, which causes me to be identified and bustled into a coach heading to my husband's family estate.

Disjointed and dreamlike circumstances culminating in the thing I want most. To go home.

I fell asleep on the train, and I'm dreaming. So I follow the fantasy, climbing into the coach with its leather-trimmed seats and fur blankets, the smell so familiar it makes my eyes well with tears.

The woman—Mrs. Landon—talks briefly to Hugh, her tone curt and perfunctory.

I rouse from my stupor enough to open the yellow carpetbag before she climbs in. What fanciful treasures will it contain? A flight of doves, perhaps?

No, this is my fantasy, and so it will contain magical recipes straight out of a fantastical novel. Apple pies that taste of crisp autumnal days. Ginger biscuits that taste of Christmas morning. Candied tartlets that taste of a carousel ride. And, of course, a fairy eager to help with the cleanup.

I smile, open the bag, and then laugh under my breath as I do indeed find a piece of paper. Then I open it and stop smiling.

Dearest train companion,

By now you will find yourself in quite a pickle, and I do apologize, but it is hardly my fault. The fool was so desperate for a governess that he offered the first quarter's wages in advance. Naturally, I could not ignore such an opportunity.

Imagine my delight on learning your trade. It is as if Fate herself led me to that train compartment. I went in search of a dark-haired woman who could pass for a governess, and what did I find? An actual governess!

I would advise most strongly against attempting to correct the misunderstanding. The earl's housekeeper knows only that I am dark-haired, carrying a yellow carpetbag and coming from Whitby. If you protest, you will surely be arrested for theft. That is why I did not simply abscond with the forwarded funds. If you must flee, I would strongly suggest, from experience, that you do it under cover of night.

The position is yours if you wish it. Of course, you will not receive payment for the first quarter, but food and lodgings in an earl's hall should compensate adequately. I even considered taking the position myself, but as my mum always said, while I'm a good little actress, I'm not ready to take the stage.

Admittedly, and I warn you of this because you seem such a lovely woman, the fact that the earl's brother has been unable to retain a governess suggests the boy is an absolute terror. You do seem a capable sort, though. Perhaps you can manage it, reminding the child that such behavior might be acceptable in an earl's son, but not in the child of an earl's second son.

Best of luck!
Emma

PS Feeling rather more guilty than I expected, as you do indeed seem lovely. I have enclosed ten shillings, which should allow you to flee on the next train if you must.

PPS Oh! I ought to tell you your name. It is Clara. I do not recall the boy's name, but I am certain you'll learn it soon enough.

I stare at the letter. My gaze fixes on two words. *The boy.*

Emma had been hired as governess to a boy at Courtenay Hall. Edmund.

In that moment, I forget that I've already labeled this a dream. I hesitate, fingers touching those two words.

The boy.

Is it a dream? That's a rather blithe explanation with little substance to support it. I had not been tired when I boarded the train. I certainly was not fool enough to sleep while alone in a compartment.

I'd deemed it a dream because the situation made no sense. With this letter, it does.

Emma said it was Fate. Obviously, that is a selfish young woman plastering a good face on a bad deed. Yet it could be Fate, could it not? The hand of the Almighty at work? I have suffered, and I know not what sins I suffered for, but now I return, and my suffering has won me this gift of Fate, to be on that train, to be found by that young woman, to be brought home—*home*—to my son.

As the housekeeper—for I presume Mrs. Landon to be such—enters the coach, I read the letter again, and I do not fail to miss the point about my charge being the child of the former earl's *second* son. August is his third. But that is an error easily made.

I tuck the letter away and settle my hands in my lap. "I wish to apologize, Mrs. Landon, for my reticence on the platform. The journey was taxing, and I was not accustomed to the crush of people. It set me quite off balance. I appreciate your guidance in seeing me to the coach."

She sniffs. "If you are so easily unbalanced, this might not be the job for you, Miss Smith." She passes a critical eye over me. "You're a tiny thing. I don't know what he was thinking, hiring you sight unseen. I told him that the boy requires a sturdy governess with a firm hand. He also requires his *father* to be at home, not gallivanting about the countryside."

"The master has an active social calendar, I presume?" That would describe August, though my heart sinks at the thought of him ignoring our child. He had been a far more attentive father than most.

Mrs. Landon sniffs again. "He has almost no social calendar to speak of. He works. Works, works, and works some more. It is most unbecoming of a man in his position." A brief pause before she grumbles, "Even if it is the family business."

The family business?

No social calendar?

That would be August's brother, Harrison, who is indeed the second son. Harrison has three children, but only one, by his second wife, is young enough to require a governess. A son I remember as a little hellion, exactly as both Emma and Mrs. Landon have suggested.

As I deflate, I stop and reconsider. Is this not the better scenario? It sounds as if Harrison isn't even at Courtenay Hall. If his son is living there, though, that suggests Harrison has made it his residence, which means August will be elsewhere—the brothers do not get on.

Harrison's son will not recognize me. We've barely met. While there will be staff, such as Hugh, who were around in my time, the turnover at Courtenay Hall had always shocked me. Growing up, my family managed to employ a housekeeper and part-time gardener, and our parents instilled in us the value of long-term relationships with staff. That was not an attitude August's father—or his brothers—shared. August would quietly supplement wages, but that was not enough for many, who also had to contend with poor treatment from the rest of the Courtenay family.

As governess, my primary contact would be with Mrs. Landon, whom I do not know. Might I not, then, tarry a while at the hall? Play the role of Clara-the-governess while I obtain the information I need?

It is a better plan than mine, and I have a young con artist to thank for it.

Enjoy your ill-won gains, Emma, and if I ever see you again, you shall receive my gratitude, how little you might deserve it.

With that, I smile and settle in for the rest of the ride.

SIX

URING MY TIME in the twenty-first century, there were things I never did. Things I dared not do. One of them was looking up historical records of August and Edmund.

I suppose, in hindsight, if I were the truly pragmatic person I believe myself to be, this natural step would have saved me all this subterfuge now. I'd know whether August had remarried and possibly even where he spent his summers these days.

Yet if one researches anything about a person from the Victorian era, one will get their birth and death date appended after their name as a matter of course. I would see the year my husband had died. The year my son died. Perhaps some hearts could handle that. Mine could not.

It wouldn't matter if they'd both lived to ripe old ages. It would be a reminder that they were dead and dust, buried and forgotten, their fading graves mere curiosities for cemetery walkers.

Still, I had spent over four years living mere miles from Courtenay Hall, which was a historical building, occasionally open to the public. I could not resist visiting. Not the house itself—that risked learning the family history and those dates of death. Instead, I'd wandered the grounds.

I'd visit early enough in the day that most tourists were roaming the house ahead of the crowds. So I had the grounds to myself and fantasized

that I was in my own world, just out for an early walk, August still abed, Edmund sleeping after his morning feeding.

Now, as I approach in the carriage, I realize just how desperate I must have been if I could have convinced myself I was back in this time period. Yes, the layout has changed little. To my left is the fountain, the tinkle of water filling the quiet evening air. To my right, the hedgerow maze, dotted with dark lanterns to be lit for a party on a summer's eve. Gardens everywhere, immaculately tended by a small army of gardeners. Far to my left, if I squint, I can make out the glitter of the moonlight on the man-made lake with the pond closer to the house. And farther still, the endless darkness of my favorite place—the hunting woods and its delightful follies, waiting to be explored anew.

The differences go beyond sight. It is smell and sound and simply the *feel* of the place. In this time, there is no stink of diesel fuel. No whir of mechanical fans. No distant roar of traffic. With the faint smell of horse and horse by-products, perhaps no one would call the air *fresh* and, yes, not all those "by-products" come from horses, but it smells clean to me, sharp with the crisp tang of autumn, the chill in the air and the scent of woodsmoke promising warm fires beyond the walls.

Those stone walls loom three stories high. A grand mansion that took a half century to build. The Courtenays were never known for cutting corners, at least not when it came to their standard of living. The house had been designed in the eighteenth century by the most famous architect of the day. Then it'd taken sixty years for the family to accumulate the funds to finish the structure until it stands as it does today with two massive wings, a dozen bedrooms and a main hall that will seat fifty for dinner—a hundred if you don't mind moving tables afterward for dancing.

I'm gaping up at the house as the coach pulls to a halt. I rise, but a lifted finger from Mrs. Landon stops me. She's spotted a very nervous maid hovering on the doorstep, and she steps out to speak to her, closing the door against my exit.

When she returns, it's to throw open the door with, "He's gone. Again." She scowls my way, as if I bear full responsibility for this. "Seems he wasn't keen to meet his new governess."

"I presume you mean my charge," I say mildly. "Has he had poor experiences with my predecessors?"

"None of them stayed long enough for that," murmurs Hugh.

"You'll have to find him," Mrs. Landon says. "Consider it your first duty, Miss Smith."

"I'll help her," Hugh says. "I know where the young master likes to—"

"You'll do no such thing because you will be otherwise occupied, carrying Miss Smith's bags to her room and then putting away the coach. If Miss Smith cannot find her charge, then she is hardly equipped to tend to him."

Hugh slips me a sympathetic look. "It ought to be simple enough, miss. The young master is fond of the Greek temple, which is…" He turns, shading his eyes against the gaslit lanterns.

"Up the hillside," I say with a smile. As soon as the words leave my mouth, I duck my gaze to say shyly, "I came here on a holiday when I was a girl. The grounds were open for a Christmas bonfire. I recall the temple, and I shall search for the young master there."

As I leave, I slow my steps, lest I betray my anticipation. I certainly do know how to find the temple. It's where August proposed. To hear him tell the story, he'd had no intention of asking for my hand on that trip. He'd already done so a half-dozen times, and so he left the ring in London. Then he'd watched me fall in love with the estate, and he'd found a ring in his mother's old jewelry box. He'd proposed in the Greek folly under the stars of a summer night. And I'd finally accepted.

Once I'm past the house, I jog up the hill as fast as my skirts will allow. The temple sits at the top. It's a miniature replica of the Temple of Athena in Athens and dates from the late eighteenth century, when it'd been fashionable to display your knowledge of the world by rebuilding it on your estate grounds. A Greek temple, an Egyptian pyramid, even fake Roman ruins were scattered over the property.

In the moonlight, the white stone glows atop the grassy hill. As I approach, my gaze scans the horizon for Harrison's son. What was his name again? Damn it, I should know that.

I also need to remember to keep my cursing to myself. My rare words of profanity amused August. They would hardly amuse Mrs. Landon, and I've grown too accustomed to the occasional mild oath in public, perfectly acceptable in the twenty-first century.

Was the boy's name Edward? No, that was Harrison's second son. James? No, that was his firstborn. What was—?

The breath in my lungs disappears, as if I've stumbled into a vacuum.

August is at the temple.

It is not August, the thirty-year-old man I first met. Nor is it the thirty-five-year-old one I lost. Nor even the thirty-nine-year-old one he will be now. Instead, I see a ghost of the August I never knew, the one who lived before I first drew breath.

In Courtenay Hall, there is a painting of August as a boy. The first time I saw it, I mistook it for some cousin who closely resembled my husband. Surely, that somber, big-eyed six-year-old was not the vibrant, laughing man I knew. In that portrait, I caught my first glimpse of the boy August hid so well. The boy whose beloved older sister died shortly before that portrait was painted. The boy whose father paid him no attention, seeing him only as the child whose birth killed his wife. The boy who grew into a young man whose fiancée—William's sister—had left him without a word of explanation.

It was here, at Courtenay Hall, that August first introduced me to his difficult past. He'd joked about "haunting" the halls and fields and forest, a quiet child I surely would not recognize, in the years before he met William Thorne, when he'd truly been alone. One of his favorite places had been the temple folly, and he'd spent hours imagining elaborate scenarios with Greek monsters, himself as the conquering hero, saving the maiden.

When he then proposed to me there, I could not help but accept. I saw the lonely boy he must have been, and I wanted to be the maiden to his hero.

No, I wanted to be the *hero* to his lost boy, the woman who would not leave.

Only I had left, hadn't I?

When I crest the hill, this is the August I see—the boy from that portrait, pensive and quiet, sitting on the edge of the temple and gazing up at the stars. My throat closes, even as I know I'm imagining the scene before me.

Then the boy half turns and gives a start, his gasp audible. He is twenty feet away, bathed in moonlight to my shadow. His eyes widen, and they are not August's eyes at all. They are my own.

"Edmund," I whisper, the word no more than breath.

He dives from the base and darts into the forest. I race after him, his name on my lips, refusing to come as more than a gasp. Bushes crackle and crash, and I follow, pushing into the thick forest, his figure no more than a will-o'-the-wisp glow.

Edmund! It's me! Your mother!

That's what wells up inside me. But it stays in there, common sense pinning it down.

I don't care about common sense. This is my son. My *son.*

All my plans flit away like bats in the night. This is my child, and I must get to him, must gather him up in my arms and hug him and cry over him, and tell him it is me.

Yet I cannot get a word out. Not even his name.

How many nightmares have I had of this? Of catching a glimpse of my son on a city street and giving chase, of trying in vain to shout his name as he runs ever farther away?

In my heart, I know he isn't fleeing me—not fleeing his mother—but simply running from a stranger. It doesn't matter. In that moment, all the guilt rushes forth, the dam of denial shattered.

Yes, I didn't leave on purpose. Yes, I've spent years trying to get back to him. But there is still guilt, *so much guilt.*

I should never have ridden off that night. What a silly thing to do, such an inconsequential worry. Even if August had found me without my

wedding band, if I had admitted to removing it at Thorne Manor, it would have been only a bump in our relationship. He would have seen the logic in my explanation.

I never feared a beating or even a slap. I just… I'd hit the point where I found myself going to ridiculous lengths to keep the waters of our marriage calm, and in the last few years, I've realized that was not my responsibility. As a couple, we needed to confront his insecurities, not buffer him from them.

I made the wrong choice, and my family suffered for it. My son suffered for it most of all, and seeing him flee, I *feel* as if he's running from me, and I tear through the forest, vines lashing my feet, brambles cutting my flesh. Logic screams that I'm only terrifying him more, but I cannot stop.

When I spot the bobbing light of a lantern, I race toward it, clawing vines and branches out of my way until Hugh appears. He lifts the lantern and falls back, as if seeing a ghost. Then he blinks and hurries toward me.

"Miss!" he says. "Did you fall? Are you injured?"

I brush my skirts and push back strands of wig hair. "The boy. I startled him, and he fled, and now I cannot…" I gulp a breath. "I cannot find him. Please help. It's dark, and he cannot see the way, and there are ponds and cliffs and—"

Hugh lifts a hand, cutting me short. "The lad is home, miss. That's what I came to tell you. He's abed, and you had not returned, so I came to search."

I blink, orienting myself. Edmund is at the house? How long have I been out here, running about like a madwoman?

"You needn't worry about the lad," Hugh continues. "He knows the grounds, day or night, and his father may spoil the child, but if he caught him near the ponds alone, he would earn himself a right punishment." Hugh glances at me as we walk. "Mr. August's sister drowned there when she was but a lass."

Yes, of course. The first time I'd seen August in a panic was when he found me dipping my toes in the east pond. That was where his

sixteen-year-old sister died when he was a child. He'd made me promise never to go near the ponds or lake alone.

Then I realize what he's said. Mr. August. Yes, "Mr. Courtenay" would be correct, but the more familiar variation is a way for staff to specify among the various male Courtenays. That's not what catches my attention, though.

Hugh said August is my charge's father. That means there is no doubt who I saw.

My son.

I need to tell him. Speak to him. Explain.

No, my heart might be a wild thing, clambering in my chest, but I must proceed with caution here. Establish my true identity with others and obtain their assistance in breaking the news to Edmund. Otherwise, I'm a mad stranger claiming to be his mother.

But who do I enlist? William is the obvious choice, yet he's a hundred and seventy years in the future. August? Clearly, my husband ought to know the truth before our son, yet he's not at home. Do I tell the staff? Put the burden of establishing proof on them? What if they drive me out? What if they have me committed as a madwoman? Or jailed as a fraud? This isn't the twenty-first century. I could be locked up and never have the chance to prove myself.

What is the alternative? Pretend to be Edmund's governess? Lie to him? *Get to know him*, a voice whispers. *Prepare him.*

And then say, "Surprise! I'm your mother!"?

Hugh interrupts my rumination. "I am sorry our Edmund led you on a merry chase, miss. He is an odd little lad."

I must stiffen at that because Hugh cuts me a worried look before hurrying on, "I don't mean that as it sounds. He's a sweet child. Good-natured and kind, and if he has his odd ways..." He shrugs with a half laugh. "The gentry are entitled to their odd ways, aren't they?"

"How is the boy odd?"

Another shrug. "He's like a little ghost, flitting about, at least when his father isn't home. Mr. August brings the child from his shell. You won't

find a more devoted father. Mrs. Landon grumbles about that, but Mrs. Landon grumbles about most everything."

"I got that impression," I murmur.

He grins. "She's the earl's hire, and so we are stuck with her, I fear. She thinks the little master a right spoiled child, too fearful by half, and his father scandalously affectionate. One can hardly blame Mr. August for that. He had to be both mother and father, with young Edmund's mother dying when the boy was still in his cradle."

It takes all my strength to force out a strangled, "What?"

He glances over, brows raised. "You haven't heard the story? How Mr. August's beautiful bride went for a moonlit ride and perished in the sea?"

"Perished in...? No, I-I have not heard it."

"Then you must not be from these parts. I thought I detected an accent in your voice. I remember Lady Rosalind. She was very kind. And very pretty." He winks at me. "I was a boy of fourteen and quite taken with her."

I'm glad for the darkness so he won't see that I don't smile—my heart is thudding too hard.

Hugh continues, "Lady Rosalind loved to ride, especially at night. My father always said he could tell when she'd gone out, and he'd quickly tend to the horse on her return so no one would know and give her trouble for it. After Edmund came, there'd been no moonlight rides, but that night she could not resist. The next day, the house was in a frenzy, searching for her. Her horse was found washed up on the shore. It must have plunged from the cliff at night and drowned them both in the sea."

My stomach lurches, and I clap my hand to my mouth.

Hugh nods gravely, thinking I'm affected by the plight of this poor stranger. My first thought is for my horse, the darling gelding I always rode at Courtenay Hall. Then I realize the rest of what Hugh said.

Everyone thinks I'm dead.

I'd been nowhere near the sea that night, but I hadn't tied my horse at Thorne Manor. He must have been spooked and run and ended up at

the sea, falling to his death. Finding him there, everyone would presume I was dead.

My husband would presume I was dead.

My son would grow up presuming I had died.

"Are you all right, miss?"

"Y-yes, I'm sorry. I just… I had no idea. How horrible for the family. I fear the information I received was scant, and I looked no further than confirming their good reputation. So forgive what may seem a question to which I ought to know the reply. I was under the impression that August Courtenay has a wife. Did he remarry?"

"Not yet, miss." He walks a few more steps and then clears his throat awkwardly. "If I may be impertinent, might I suggest…" Another throat clearing. "The master is said to be a handsome man. He comes from a good family and is…well situated financially. There have been— That is to say, some of the governesses…"

"Set their hat on him?" My laugh is genuine. "I would have thought ladies of my profession had more sense than that."

"Several were from very good families, no better than his wife's, and so perhaps their hopes were not without merit."

"True enough. I know better than to have designs on my employer. I am also no longer a young girl who might be wooed by promises of a ring."

Hugh's eyes widen, and as he stammers, I curse myself. I chose my words with care, but they were still not proper sentiments for a Victorian spinster.

"Mr. August does not—" he begins. "He is not that sort of man."

"Good," I say. "If young Edmund's governesses left because they failed to earn a promotion to mother, then you will have nothing to worry about with me."

He goes silent, and I count out five more steps before saying, "Is that why they left?"

"That…that may be the answer, miss." He straightens, his tone hearty with false conviction. "Yes, I am certain it is."

SEVEN

A T Hugh's suggestion, I manage to avoid Mrs. Landon by coming in the side door. He directs me to my room in the nursery. As in many grand houses, the nursery is far from the master bedroom. That would horrify twenty-first-century parents, but it is how August grew up. He hadn't even received another room as he grew older. He'd been kept apart from the rest of his family, as if he were a bastard child.

When I'd made it clear that I expected our son to sleep in the adjoining room, August had been quick to agree. His family whispered that this was what came of marrying a girl without breeding. When we visited the hall and they refused to allow our infant son to share our quarters, we slept in the one adjoining his, a cold and cramped room given to guests one hopes to discourage from long visits.

When I enter Courtenay Hall now, the house is in near darkness. Memory lets me pass through the maze of halls with ease, and soon I'm climbing the stairs to my destination.

Having seen the bright and cheery children's bedrooms of twenty-first-century acquaintances, I now truly recognize how ghastly a place my husband grew up in. In Courtenay Hall—the hereditary seat of a family

who would rank among modern billionaires—the nursery is the worst part of the house. The hallway is dark and narrow, and it smells of mildew and the stink of wet stone. Worse, in a grand manor house like this, the nursery is not merely where the children sleep. It is also where they eat and play and spend most of their indoor time.

I pause outside August's old room, arguably the best in this wing and where I suspect my son sleeps. I'm tempted to peek in on him as I did when he was an infant, poking my head in his cradle nearly every hour just to watch him sleep. But there is a vast difference between a mother checking in on her baby and a governess checking on her charge, especially when they have not been formally introduced.

I continue walking down the hall.

It is only now, returning from the twenty-first century, that I can smile at the odd quirks of Victorian decorating. Rooms stuffed with furniture and bric-a-brac, all of it chosen for its individual attractions. Establishing a common decorating theme is hardly a concern, unless you want to be truly fancy and put all your Middle Eastern–themed items in one room, your Egyptian ones in another and your Asian ones in a third.

A house like Courtenay Hall will always be more austere, hearkening back to the Regency period, as if that is a sign of taste. Rather like the modern wealthy styling their homes Colonial or even faux Victorian.

Even with the pared-down decorating, Courtenay Hall is still far too full of "stuff" for my newly ascetic tastes, like the hallway I'd just passed through, lined with Greek and Roman busts on pedestals, the bane of staff forever terrified of knocking into one.

The governess's room is another matter. It is austere. Empty. Even desolate. One would think, for a tiny room with a sloping roof, it'd be all too easy to cram it with basic furnishings. Instead, the narrow bed and single dresser look lost in the emptiness, and my two bags sit forlornly in the middle of a bare floor. The bed bears a coverlet so threadbare I wouldn't donate it to charity.

"Well, Emma," I murmur. "Let's hope you packed blankets in that yellow bag."

A throat clears behind me, and I spin to see Mrs. Landon in the doorway, holding a tray. I apologize and reach for it, but she keeps her hold on it.

"You did not speak to me when you came in," she says.

"I did not wish to bother you, ma'am. I entered through the wrong door, and someone said Master Edmund was already abed, so I asked for directions to my room." I nod at the tray. "It is very kind of you to bring me supper. I know I arrived late, and so I did not expect a meal."

"I did not expect to be bringing it myself," she says. "From now on, you will speak to me before retiring for the evening."

I half curtsey and bow my head with murmured assent.

As she relinquishes the tray, I glance down at a gristly cut of beef and congealing gravy with a chunk of bread that looks as if it could hammer nails. Good thing I ate a hearty meal in Whitby.

I thank her, and she informs me that the young master rises at seven, and I shall join him in his rooms at seven-thirty, where we will dine together.

"I will be looking forward to it," I say.

Her sniff calls me a fool, but she only lifts her skirts, as if to avoid trailing them on the dusty floor, and she leaves me to my cold supper.

✦

I FALL asleep as soon as my head hits the pillow. I am in Courtenay Hall, and my son—my son!—is in the next room. My bedchamber could be as dank as a debtor's cell, and I would not trade it for a penthouse suite. I crawl under that scratchy coverlet, and my entire body collapses into the lump-riddled mattress.

I am home. I can rest.

Finally, I can rest.

And so I sleep until I'm woken by the scrape of branches against glass. I manage to prop open one eye long enough to peer at the deep-set

window. Shadows shift over it as a tree sways in the wind. When the scratching comes again, I cover my head with my pillow and flip over to face the wall.

I'm halfway to sleep, caught in that sweet state of half slumber, when a voice whispers, "Leave."

I go still, eyes opening in the darkness.

"Leave," the voice whispers. "Leave or be lost."

I leap up and reach for the bedside light, instead hitting an oil lamp. I steady it, the oil sloshing. Then I light it, and a sickly yellow glow fills the tiny room.

"Hello?" I say, already feeling foolish. The room is so small I can tell at a glance that I'm alone. Still, I gather my courage and say again, a little louder, "Hel—"

A gust of ice-cold air blows out the flickering lamp. I freeze, wide eyed in the darkness, before giving myself a shake and relighting the lamp. When the cold air hits, I quickly put the lamp on the far side of my bed. Then I turn.

The window is open.

It had not been open when I went to bed.

Another sharp shake of my head. I'm being foolish. The window has blown open. It's a breezy night, and those branches scraping the window pushed it ajar.

As I rise from bed, I pause, looking down at my bare feet, scant inches from the pitch blackness that is "under the bed." I laugh softly, but it's a little ragged, and I do take the lantern and bend to peer under like a brave child checking for monsters. There are none.

I laugh again, more confident now, as I shake my head at my foolishness. What did I think it was? A ghost?

I should follow that by saying there are no such things as ghosts, but that would be a lie. The Second Sight runs in my family. My grandmother saw ghosts, and my sister Miranda does, too. I, however, do not, which means that voice whispering in my ear was the wind entangling with my imagination.

I cross to the window. The latch hangs unfastened and barely attached, the screws rusted. Mystery solved. A strong gust snapped it open. I could ask for a repair, but I don't mind an open window at night, not when the breeze is so exquisitely scented with autumn. I *may* ask to have that tree outside trimmed. For now, I'll snap off whatever twigs I can reach.

My hand extends through the opening, prepared to grab the offending tree branch. The nearest one is a good ten yards away.

I poke my head out and crane it around, looking for hanging vines that might explain the sound I'd heard. The stonework is immaculate, though, without so much as a rogue tendril of ivy.

Hmm. That's odd.

Perhaps *odd* shouldn't be the word. I woke hearing a scratching at my window, and there is nothing there to scratch it. Yet this is the advantage to knowing that ghosts walk our world. It normalizes what might otherwise induce horror. If you ignore ghosts, they don't realize you can see them, and so they go about their business, flitting past, paying you no mind. As harmless as moths.

What happened to me here isn't proof of a haunting. It's proof of a brain that is at once exhausted and exhilarated. When Miranda had been about Edmund's age, she'd spend all of Christmas Eve racing about, eating pastries and sugared almonds, and eventually she'd reach the point where her mind simply quit, and she started spouting nonsense, furious when no one could understand her. That's what happened to me, my overtaxed brain spouting nonsense, imagining voices at my ear and scratching at the window.

I close and latch the window. Then I stand there, looking out at the lake, the moonlight like a child's paper boat floating over the windswept waves. I focus on that patch of white and follow it up and down, up and down. When I'm too drowsy to watch any longer, I drag myself back to bed and fall into it, and I'm asleep within moments.

I WAKE in what is clearly another dream, with William's calico cat on my bed, staring down at me. I groan and flop out one arm to pet her. She jumps, the look on her face making me chuckle, as if I've tried to plant a kiss on the cheek of a society matron. I'm closing my eyes again when I stop.

This isn't William's calico cat. This one has black spots on its face. I blink and lift my head. My wig shifts, and I groan again, reaching to straighten it. I really ought to have dyed my hair and made up some story to explain the shortness of the cut. Now I have to wear this damnable thing to bed, lest the maid see me jumping up with blond locks.

"Are you awake, miss?"

I jump, hands going to my wig. Edmund sits at the foot of my narrow bed, facing the opposite direction. He rises with his gaze still averted.

"Mrs. Landon told me to fetch you," he says. "I did not think it was proper, but she said I must. You have overslept."

I blink, not at the words but at his voice. His diction is higher than children I met in the modern world, but I can no longer recall whether that is normal for this time. I suppose it might be for an only child surrounded by adults. It's the tone that throws me more, each word clearly enunciated but emotionless, as if he's reading from a script.

Then I realize what he's said. I overslept. On my first day.

"Sorry," I say as I scramble up. "I forgot to set my alarm."

He goes still, head cocked, and while I can't see his face, I can imagine it screwed up in thought as he tries to figure out what I just said.

Set my alarm.

In a world where one cannot simply set an alarm on one's phone or even bedside clock.

I give an awkward laugh. "Sorry, that's what we said in my last position. The little girl I looked after had the funniest ways of phrasing things. Setting the alarm, as if a screaming bell would wake us at the appointed hour."

"May I leave now, ma'am?" he asks, and the laugh dies in my throat. "I ought not to be in your bedchamber."

"I will ask a maid to wake me in future. Or, if Mrs. Landon insists, you can simply send your cat in to do the job."

I say it lightly, trying to coax a smile from him, but he stays motionless.

"I will be in my playroom," he says. "Our breakfast is served there."

He rises, and still without looking my way, scoops up the cat and slings the beast over his shoulder. I tense, ready for a meow of indignation, but the calico lies there as limp as a fur stole. She lifts her head to fix me with a baleful look and then rubs her head against Edmund's neck as they leave.

EIGHT

 DRESS AND REPLACE my makeup disguise. So far, the only person I've seen who might recognize me is Hugh, and he obviously does not. Yet I must be careful. There is bound to be a portrait of me somewhere in this house, and I don't need Mrs. Landon taking too close a look at it and then at me.

I find Edmund in his quarters, sitting upright at a small table, mechanically eating his breakfast. At his side, the cat fixes me with a glare as I enter. Edmund glances over, but his gaze passes without focusing as he dips his chin in a nod far too solemn for a child of five.

"Good morning, miss. Your breakfast tray is here."

"And how is breakfast on this fine morning?"

I wince. My voice is so cheerful it sounds shrill.

He murmurs something I don't hear and returns to staring out the window.

"So," I say as I sit across from him. "What shall we do this morning? It looks like a lovely day. Perhaps a walk?"

"If you wish."

"What do you normally do in the morning?"

He pauses, as if the question requires great thought. "If Papa is not home, I am sent outside to play."

"By yourself?"

He looks at me then, frowning. "There are no other children here, miss. If Papa is at home, then we play together."

"And your governesses do not play with you?"

His frown deepens into a wary look that wonders whether I'm mocking him. When he speaks, the words come slowly. "They are busy preparing for my lessons and conducting their own business."

Their own business is playing with him. A Victorian education hardly requires a half day to prepare lessons. His governesses had used it as an excuse, pushing him out the door for fresh air and exercise so they'd have time to themselves.

"Well," I say. "I understand you may not wish to play with quite such an elderly lady as myself."

I pause, hoping for a smile, but he only regards me solemnly, and I resist the urge to add that his father is nearly a decade my senior and apparently a spry playmate.

I continue, "But for today, let us walk about the gardens and yard and take our exercise that way."

✺

BY THE time we finish breakfast, I've convinced myself that reticence is simply Edmund's nature. He is a solemn and thoughtful boy, little given to smiles. That pains my heart, but it does not mean there's anything *wrong* with him. While I remember a rambunctious and curious infant, there'd been a quietness to him, too.

It's not me; it's him.

I steadfastly cling to that until we leave the nursery and come into contact with other people. We pass a couple of maids cleaning the house and Hugh in the yard, and the moment Edmund sees them, he lights up, not exactly bouncing with puppyish enthusiasm but happy and cheerful. They speak to him with obvious affection, and he happily returns their

smiles and basks in their gentle teasing. As soon as we pass them, though, that light winks out, and he is once again an automaton of a boy, moving in stiff and dutiful silence.

It *is* me.

My child does not like me.

He is uncomfortable in my presence, and I get the distinct feeling that he's silently praying I'll decide it's too chilly and retreat inside, leaving him to his own amusements.

I'm trying too hard. My voice is pitched too high like someone ill accustomed to interacting with children. I *am* ill accustomed to interacting with children. I avoided them in the twenty-first century because they reminded me of my lost son. And now here is my lost son, and I've turned into a woman who makes me cringe. High-pitched singsong voice, forced humor, the stink of "trying too hard" wafting from my pores.

Relax. Be yourself.

But what if he doesn't like the real me, either? What if I reveal the truth on August's return, and my son is disappointed?

This is my mother? No, there must be some mistake.

I cannot worry about that. I can only be more myself and hope that helps the situation. So on that walk, I relax, and my voice returns to normal, and I do not force jokes on him but simply ask questions to which I genuinely crave answers. And his demeanor changes not at all.

It's warmer today, and the walk is a pleasant one. I talk about that. I talk about the changing colors and the science behind it. I talk about the animals we see scurrying across our path as they make ready for winter. He answers dutifully and nothing more.

We're circling the fountain when I say, "It must be difficult having a new governess. You were likely very fond of your previous one."

His look makes me sputter a laugh.

"Or not?" I say.

"No, she was fine," he says quickly. "Only she left after a few days."

"The one before her then?"

"She left after a week."

I press him and discover that August has been living at Courtenay Hall for almost a year now and has not kept a governess longer than six weeks.

Edmund expects me to leave, too. He is already preparing for that departure by withdrawing behind a wall of polite indifference. I do not understand why the governesses failed to stay—did August's lack of romantic interest make the isolation untenable?—but Edmund is aware this isn't normal.

Does my son blame himself for this carousel of caregivers? I'm certain August would not allow him to think so. Still, Edmund has decided that I will not remain long, and so there is no point in getting to know me.

I want to tell him that I will be different. I *know* I will be. I'm his mother—I'm not going anywhere unless dragged off kicking and screaming, and then I'll fight my way back until Edmund himself tells me to leave.

Yet to him, I'm merely another governess, one he has just met. To make any promise to stay will sound, at best, blithe and careless, and at worst, well, creepy. So I change the subject and vow to take less personal offense at his cool reception. Perhaps it really isn't me *or* him. The fault lies with a parade of inconstant governesses. I may not know why they left, but I'm certain it has nothing to do with Edmund.

WE'RE BACK in the nursery by late morning. Time for lessons. I pull a book from the shelf and turn to see him frozen there, panic in his blue eyes, and his reaction twinges old memories.

I set down the book and open it to the first page. "Let's start by testing your reading."

He says nothing.

"You don't need to read the whole page," I say. "Just tell me which words you recognize."

Silence. Then, before I can speak, he blurts, "I cannot read. I am not"—he swallows—"not clever."

Indignation flares, hot as molten lead. "Who told you that? I hope it wasn't your father."

His eyes widen. "Oh, no. I mean that I heard my governesses talking to my father. They say I ought to be reading by now. Papa says I only have a little trouble with my reading, as my mother did, and she *was* clever."

My eyes brim, and I blink back tears. In his face, I'd seen that flash of panic and humiliation that I remember so well. Now, as he speaks, the memories rush back of my own childhood self listening to conversations I, too, was not supposed to hear.

I recall a tutor hired with money we did not have, my parents desperate to help me overcome my reading difficulties. That tutor telling my mother that I was simply not very intelligent, that some girls were not, and they were lucky that my younger sisters were already reading. My parents should take comfort in that and plan a less strenuous academic future for me.

On hearing that, my parents fired the tutor and devoted themselves to teaching me. While I will never devour books at my sisters' pace, I'm comfortably literate enough to read for both work and pleasure.

"What do you see?" I ask as I crouch beside Edmund, book open.

He says nothing.

"May I tell you what I see?" I ask.

His thin shoulders shrug, too despondent to even manage his usual polite response.

"I see letters in the wrong order," I say. "For example, I know this must say 'breakfast,' but I see 'breafkats.'"

"Breaf-kats?"

I nod. "I've come to understand that the word is breakfast, but I have trouble *seeing* it. I also have trouble sounding out words. I remember my tutors getting so frustrated with me. If I can read *cat*, why can I not sound out *catch* or *bat?*"

"Nor can I," he whispers, his voice barely audible. "I know my letters, but…"

"It doesn't help you read them. It feels like two very different things."

He nods.

I push down my skirts to sit on the floor beside him. "I was nearly eight before I could read, and yet now I'm a governess." I look at him. "Do you think that means I'm not clever?"

His eyes round, as if he voiced the insult himself. "No, ma'am."

"It's Clara," I say softly. "My name is Miss Clara, and I could not read until I was nearly eight. People didn't just say I wasn't *clever*. They said I was stupid. I'm not, though. I just have trouble reading like some people have trouble seeing or trouble walking. Do you know anyone like that?"

He nods. "The woman who brings our milk and eggs in the city cannot walk without a cane."

"Do you think the less of her for it?"

He shakes his head. "She must work harder than others, which means we ought to appr—" he says, struggling with the word, "appreciate the milk and eggs even more. That's what Papa says."

"He is correct. The same is true of you and me, Edmund. We must work harder to do what others do easily. That is all."

He listens solemn-eyed. Then he looks at the book, and the fear seeps back in. "We're going to practice my reading, aren't we?"

I snap the book shut. "Later. For now…" I push to my feet. "Do you like stories?"

His gaze slides to the bookcase, his expression still wary, expecting a trick.

Do you like stories? Then here's one you can read.

"I love stories," I say. "Before I could read, my mother read to me every night, and my youngest sister made up tales just for me. It helped me *want* to read—so I didn't need to rely on others for stories. Would you like me to tell you one?"

He nods.

I move to the shelf of toys, seeking inspiration. "Let's see. I know a story about a boy who lived locked away in a tower. One day, a calico cat came with an invitation for him to attend..." My gaze slides over the toys and notices a prominently displayed collection of metal knights. "Knight school."

"Night school?" Edmund frowns. "School at night?"

I pick up a toy. "No, knight school. But it also took place at night, for secrecy. Knight night school."

A smile slips out at that one, and I launch into a tale.

I don't just tell Edmund a story, though. As I'm describing the castle-school, I suggest we draw a map of the area and a blueprint of the structure. Then I need to divide the students into groups, which requires a visit to the library to look up heraldry. We stay in the library to research medieval food for the opening night banquet.

After lunch, it is out into the yard with wooden swords because I need us to act out the first fight scene so I might properly describe it in my story.

We're clashing swords when we gain an audience—Hugh and another young groom whom I do not recognize.

"That is not how you hold a sword, miss," Hugh calls as they both snort with laughter.

"You dare question my technique?" I hold the tip under his throat. "Fie on you, lad."

His eyes widen, and I pause, wondering what I've done wrong. Then I remember the Clara Smith he met last night, the meek and quiet governess.

Damn.

I tone it down, choosing a demeanor midway between that Clara and myself as I say, "I suppose you can do better."

"I think even the young master can do better," the other groom says, earning an elbow in the ribs from Hugh, even as Edmund giggles.

"All right," I say, holding out the sword. "You may take my place, and I will observe."

As I watch Hugh lead Edmund in a sword fight, I will admit to being more than a little pleased with myself. I've managed to sneak everything

from geography to history to exercise into my "story." I even got a little reading when I'd misread a word and Edmund corrected me.

I suspect he doesn't struggle with it as much as I do. He's just embarrassed to struggle at all, and therefore he refuses to read. We'll work on that. My son is everything I hoped he'd be—inquisitive, kind and sweet natured. The dyslexia is but a small obstacle and one I'm well equipped to help with.

I do not fail to notice that, while Edmund has relaxed as the day wears on, he relaxes even more with Hugh. That is to be expected. I'm glad of the opportunity to see Edmund's true self coming through, unfettered by anxieties.

Hugh himself has matured into a lovely young man though I will admit it is odd to come back to this time, when a boy of eighteen is truly considered a man, fully assimilated into the working world. I suspect many a twenty-first-century teenager would be delighted to have Hugh's independence—a steady job with a decent income and his own quarters—but I cannot help but be saddened by the reminder of how quickly youth is banished here.

The swordplay ends with a cat. Edmund's cat, to be precise, appearing from nowhere to demand her young master's attention. I haven't seen her all day—she must have been off mousing—but when she wants petting and cuddling, Edmund must drop what he's doing to obey, or she'll trip him by winding around his legs. I have to smile at that, reminded of the cats I'd had as a child.

As we head inside, calico slung over Edmund's shoulder again, I ask her name, and he looks at me with a frown. "How do you know she's a girl?"

"Because she's a calico. It is not impossible for a male cat to have that coloring, but it is extremely unlikely."

He purses his lips as he considers the matter. "I think you are correct. Her mother is a calico, and so is her sister. Her two brothers were not."

"You knew her mother then?" I ask because I believe I know the answer to this.

He nods. "She is my Uncle William's cat. Pandora, because he found her in a box." He looks up at me as we walk. "Do you know that story?"

"The one about Pandora and the box? I do indeed."

I know both—the myth *and* the story of how Pandora-the-cat ended up in that box, crossing time to find herself trapped there. I cannot, of course, tell him that. Not yet anyway.

"Aunt Bronwyn—that is Uncle William's wife—has Pandora's other girl kitten. She named her Enigma because she found her in a locked room and had no idea how she got there. That is what *enigma* means: a mystery."

"It does indeed."

Edmund pets the cat draped over his shoulder. "When I saw Pandora's kittens, I said I should like one, but Uncle William said they all had homes." A shy smile. "That was a trick. She did have a home—Papa had already picked her out for me. So when he brought her to me, she was a surprise. That's what I named her. Surprise."

"It's a good name."

His nose scrunches, and in the sunlight, I see a smattering of freckles over it, just like my own. "No, it's rather silly. I was only a baby. I call her Surrey. I think that's a better name."

"Both are lovely names. Fit for a lovely cat."

His lips twitch. "Mrs. Landon calls her an orange devil. That's because she doesn't like cats very much, so when she tries to shoo Surrey off the furniture, the cat scratches her."

"Animals know when they aren't wanted."

A solemn nod. "That's what Papa says. He also says that cats often have a person they like best, and they do not like others very much. I am Surrey's person. She lets Papa pet her and, sometimes, Hugh and Violet, but no one else can pick her up."

He glances my way. "If you like cats, you may try to pet her, but if you do not, you shouldn't." A pause. "Even if you do like them, she may not allow it."

"I will attempt it once she knows me better, and if she draws blood, I cannot say I wasn't warned."

NINE

E TAKE TEA in the nursery. My dinner last night had been a poor representation of the cook's abilities—a meal meant to be hot is never good when served ice cold. For both breakfast and lunch, I received far better fare. I will not lie and call it excellent, but it was quite good...with one exception: the cook is very clearly not a pastry chef.

Last night's bread had been barely edible, and this morning's toast had been dry and heavy. The other food had compensated, but now tea is a plate of pastry goods—sandwiches, scones and tartlets—and I can do nothing but nibble and drink copious amounts of tea and mourn the fact that the former cook must have retired.

When the maid—Violet—comes to clear the plates, she notices the amount left on mine.

"Was it not to your liking, miss?" she asks.

"No, it was excellent. I overate at lunch and was not hungry."

When she leaves, Edmund scoops up Surrey and, without lifting his gaze from her, says, "It is a sin to tell a lie."

I tense. "What?"

"You said the food was excellent, and it is not. It is horrid. That's what Papa says. Mrs. Beechworth cannot make a proper tea."

"I wouldn't call it *horrid.*"

"It is not excellent, though. You called it excellent."

"I was being kind."

Solemn eyes lift to mine. "But if you tell Cook it is excellent, then she has no reason to do better. Papa says we ought not to say it's horrid. That's rude. Because she is new, you could say that there is room for improvement."

I laugh. I can't help it, the sound burbling up as I lower my voice to whisper, "Yes, 'room for improvement' is quite correct. However, it's one thing for the master—or his son—to say that to Mrs. Beechworth. It's quite another for a new governess to say it. You are right, however, that I went overboard, calling it excellent. Has your father encouraged Cook to develop her baking skills?"

He shakes his head. "No, he does not eat that part of tea. My mother was a baker, and he says that anyone who tasted her scones or tea cakes could never enjoy anything else." He strokes Surrey's head. "I never tasted hers. She died when I was a baby."

The wind rushes from my lungs, and I cannot draw breath. He isn't looking at me, and I've never been happier of that. I open my mouth to say I am sorry, but I cannot form the words. They would be devilry and deceit.

What I am doing is devilry and deceit.

I ought to...

Flee? Yes. I ought to leave, but it is too late for that now. I should have done it last night before I met Edmund. If I'd gone then, I could have returned as myself without the disguise, and no one would have recognized me as Clara Smith, the governess who disappeared in the night.

If they *did* recognize me, I could have explained the situation, and it would have become something to laugh at in future, how I'd been tricked by Emma and mistaken for the governess.

I've lost that chance. Perhaps I could flee now and return as myself, unrecognizable as the former Clara Smith. Is that fair to Edmund, though? He will think yet another governess abandoned him and on her first day, no less. If he recognizes me, I will have lost any modicum of trust I've gained thus far.

I've made a mess of this. Damn Emma. Damn William, too, for not returning to Thorne Manor before I grew impatient and left.

That's silly. I know it. The fault is mine for being impatient. For not talking to William in the twenty-first century. For not waiting longer at Thorne Manor after I crossed. I might say I'm not impetuous, but I've been nothing but impetuous since I saw William and Bronwyn in York. Making bad choices and entrenching myself further in this mess.

Yet I look at Edmund, and there's part of me that whispers it might not be a mess. I am getting to know my son. He is getting to know me. I will be honest with him as soon as I can. I will never pretend I was not Clara Smith. I will explain, and I will be honest with both him and August.

I was afraid. Afraid you'd remarried, August, and I would be an unwelcome intrusion. Afraid to admit the truth to others and be thrown in an asylum or prison. Afraid to reveal myself before you were here, August.

I may have made a mistake, but I did not do it to hurt anyone.

Expressing sympathy for Edmund's loss would be wrong. Instead, I only ask whether his London cook is a better baker.

"Papa says she is ad-ad-adequate. Aunt Bronwyn is better, but she has gone away for a fortnight. She promised she will bake cookies when she returns."

"Cookies?"

"That is what she calls them. She is Canadian and uses funny words."

"Does she bake good cookies?"

He nods. "She says my mother's would have been better. Papa agrees, but he says Aunt Bronwyn's are very good. They have chocolate in them." He lifts his eyes to mine, and a light twinkles in their depths. "Do you know what that is?"

"Chocolate? I believe I have tried it a time or two."

That light turns to a mischievous gleam. "Would you like some? Aunt Bronwyn keeps a box in the pantry, and sometimes I sneak down for a piece."

As a proper governess, I should refuse. I should also include a few stern words about pilfering from the kitchen. But I'm not a governess. I'm a mother who is catching the first glimpses of her son, of the real boy lurking within an overly polite and serious child.

"On one condition," I say. "If we are caught, you must allow me to say it was entirely my fault, that I said I wished a taste of chocolate, and you were simply accommodating that wish."

His shy smile breaks into a grin, and he's on his feet and out the door before I can even rise from the table.

Even before we open the kitchen door, the smell of baked ham makes my stomach growl. I really ought to have choked down a tartlet with tea. Perhaps I can grab an orange or banana from the kitchen.

I stifle a laugh even before the thought passes. There will be no bowls of tropical fruit in this kitchen. I might find apples, and only if they've been set aside for baking.

Edmund cautiously opens the door and peers through. Then he beckons me forward, and we creep in like thieves. I pause to let my gaze drift enviously over the kitchen as it always did when I came to Courtenay Hall. The sheer amount of space made my baker's heart sigh with longing. Of course, coming back now, I do not fail to look at the coal-fueled stove and remember how much easier it'd been to cook on a gas one. Then there'd been the microwave for melting butter or chocolate at lightning speed. Also, the electric choppers and mixers and blenders...

There had been times, as I set my mixer to cream butter and sugar, that I marveled at the technology and the ease it brought to baking. But there were times, too, when I would put aside the gadgets and immerse myself in the experience of doing everything by hand, to revel in the connection and the control it brought to my craft. The only thing I will miss unreservedly is the breadth of ingredients, such as the one we're here to pilfer.

We slip into the pantry, which again brings sighs of envy. Yes, I believe I would happily give up my microwave if it meant having a pantry like this with the space to arrange every instrument and ingredient just so.

I will certainly give the new cook credit here. She might not be able to bake bread, but she can certainly organize a pantry, and as Edmund scampers on ahead, I linger, tracing my fingers over gleaming pots and labeled canisters, sighing with satisfaction and envy, the way another woman might walk through a perfect shoe closet.

That's when I see Edmund climbing up a shelf, and I dart over with a gasp. He answers my fear with a withering look, plucks a canister from the shelf and hops down.

"Cook keeps putting it higher," he says. "As if I do not know how to climb."

When he rolls his eyes, he looks so much like his father that I smile even as my heart twists.

"Perhaps she is only ensuring there is chocolate left when your aunt wishes to bake," I say.

"I am careful," he says. "I only take two pieces a day."

He opens the top, and the smell of chocolate makes my stomach growl anew. I glance in, and I have to laugh. It doesn't just contain chocolate. It contains chocolate chips. Clearly, someone is smuggling in goods from the twenty-first century.

He hands me one chip. I put it onto my tongue, expecting the overly sweet taste of cheap chocolate, but it seems William's wife seeks out a higher quality, and I nod in satisfaction.

"Is it good?" Edmund asks.

"Very good."

"Cook says it does not taste like proper chocolate. She says they make proper chocolate in York, but I prefer this."

I smile. Yes, one day, York will be the chocolate capital of England, but for now, trade in the sweet treat is only just beginning, and it is not the chocolate enjoyed nearly two centuries later. It's rough and grainy, and it'll

be another two decades before someone invents the machine that refines cocoa to create the creamy texture modern people enjoy.

"Do you know how to bake?" he asks as he puts the lid back on the canister.

I give a start at that, but only say, carefully, "I did a fair deal of it in my youth."

"Were you good at it?"

"I...was told that I was."

He scampers off into the kitchen. I follow to find him riffling through a drawer. He pulls out a handwritten page and hands it to me, and as I skim it, my lips twitch.

The page is labeled Bronwyn's Biscuits, but it's clearly the Toll House cookie recipe. It reminds me of modern bakers laughing about the number of people who "inherit" their grandmother's prized chocolate-chip recipe only to discover it is, word for word, the Toll House recipe.

When I opened my shop, I'd attempted other variations, but the one that sold best by far was the original with only a few tweaks. The Toll House recipe is the taste of chocolate-chip cookies, the sensory experience of youth, and a baker messes with it at her peril.

I'm holding the recipe when I see Edmund beside me, his upturned face fairly burbling with hope and expectation.

"You...would like me to bake these for you?" I say.

"Yes!" He tempers his enthusiasm with lowered eyelids and a quiet, "If you would, Miss Clara."

With that, I swear I hear the softest click. What is the saying, that the way to an Englishman's heart is through his stomach? Perhaps not entirely true, but one look at my son's face tells me that I've unlocked a box here, the way into his good graces, and it is laughably simple, almost too simple. He wants me to do what I do best: bake for him.

I don't hear the door open. I see only Edmund's eyes widen and feel his hand tug at my skirts, mouth opening—

"What do we have here?" a high voice trills.

I turn to see a woman in her fifties, gray haired and ruddy cheeked. Bright blue eyes fix on Edmund as she plants her hands on her wide hips.

"Sneaking into the pantry, were you, boy?"

Her face is fixed in a terrible glower. Too terrible for the transgression, and her twinkling eyes tell me she's teasing. The obvious affection in her eyes warms me instantly.

"I'm sorry, ma'am," I say, inclining my head in a nod of respect and chagrin. "Edmund mentioned you have chocolate, and when I expressed my surprise, he brought me down to show me. I ought not to have entered the kitchen without your permission."

She waves a hand and says, in a broad North Yorkshire accent, "Oh, I am not one of *those* cooks, all fussy about her kitchen. You are welcome in it when you wish, miss. It's this boy who ought to be banned."

She waggles a finger. "Banned, I tell you. Him and his chocolate."

She rolls her eyes. Then she sees what I'm holding and lets out a dramatic groan. "Is he asking you to bake those horrid biscuits?" She walks over and points at herself. "I am the cook. I cook." She points to me. "That is the governess. She governs. If you want those dreadful things, I shall make them for you."

Edmund turns a plaintive look at me.

I clear my throat. "Actually, I was going to ask whether there was any chance I might borrow your kitchen tomorrow to bake these with him. As part of his lessons."

Her brows shoot up in a look of horror. "Baking lessons? For a boy?"

"Not baking lessons," I say quickly. "A real-world application of academic principles. Ways to incorporate learning in everyday life. Baking these would allow me to teach him lessons on weights and measurements and science."

"Science?"

"The combination of ingredients and the chemical effect of those combinations. Also, if I transcribe this in a more legible hand, Edmund can practice his letters by reading it as we work."

She thinks this over and then nods slowly, "That is a very different way of teaching, but you are welcome to use the kitchen tomorrow if you'd like."

We're in the midst of arranging a suitable time when Edmund's head jerks up. He goes as still as a hunting dog scenting game. I frown, hearing nothing. Then comes the faintest clop of a horse's hooves on the lane outside. I turn to speak to Edmund, but he's already tearing out the door.

The cook cocks her head, as if just catching the sound. She looks toward where Edmund's footfalls echo through the halls. Then she shakes her head.

"No warning," she mutters. "No warning at all."

"Unexpected guests?" I say.

"Unexpected master of the house," she says.

I stiffen. "The earl?"

She laughs softly. "No, lass. It may be the earl's house, but he isn't here often enough for us to call him master. There's only one person the boy runs to like that."

My mouth opens, but I can't get out the words, and she says them for me.

"His father. Mr. August is home."

TEN

UGUST IS HERE.

I don't remember leaving the kitchen. I'm not even certain I bid Mrs. Beechworth farewell. My feet move of their own accord, carrying me up the main stairs and through the library to the parapet that overlooks the front lane.

With fumbling hands, I open the balcony door. The sound rushes in before I see them, Edmund's shrieks of delight, sounding like a five-year-old child for the first time since I've come home. Then a voice that makes me grab the doorway for support. The laughing contralto of my husband.

I force myself to slide out into the shadows. Gripping the balcony wall, I inch forward, following their voices down until I can see them.

The horse appears first, a big bay that Hugh is already leading away. Then Edmund in the air, being whirled around, his face glowing. And, in a swirl of light and shadow...

"August," I whisper.

I remember the first time I heard him called that. I thought I'd misunderstood. August was a perfectly respectable name, an old name, an emperor's name. Yet when I heard it, I thought of the month, and the man before me had embodied that word as surely as if he were the

personification of it. Hair the color of summer wheat, eyes as green as grass, and a lazy late-summer smile that warmed everyone around him.

August.

I grip the wall to keep from falling to my knees and weeping in relief. As he speaks to our son, I hear his voice, his laughter, his teasing words, and I choke on a sob.

Four years. Four endless years of desperately fighting my way back.

Now I'm here and…

And what?

In the modern world, I was quite fond of movies, particularly the romantic ones. I know what should happen next. I'll throw off my wig and spectacles. Cast aside my contacts. Rub the makeup off as I bolt through the house, startling everyone who sees me. I'll run until I'm out the door, and he'll turn and see me. Shock will render his face immobile for a split second before his lips part in my name, and he'll shift Edmund to one arm, opening the other as I race to him.

That is the final scene in the movie, right before the closing credits roll. Our heroine has fought her way back through time, and when her beloved husband returns, she discards her disguise, and they are a family again.

This is why I love stories…and why I cannot tell them myself. Even this morning, with my knight's tale for Edmund, I had to shamelessly borrow. Otherwise, I'd have constructed a boring but realistic tale, devoid of magic and flights of fancy.

I can imagine the fairy-tale scene for this moment, yet when I picture it, I see the reality instead. Me running through the house, shedding my disguise, racing out the door…and August backing away, our child clutched to his breast as he demands to know who the bloody hell I am. Some madwoman impersonating his wife, surely, because Rosalind is dead and gone four years, and this is a cruel, cruel trick to play.

Chaos then, as I try to explain, while being dragged off by the grooms, poor Edmund confused and frightened.

Oh, I'll eventually get my story out, but by then, the damage will be done. Edmund won't see me as his mother, won't even see me as the governess he was coming to trust—he'll see me as the shrieking madwoman who had to be dragged away kicking and screaming.

No, I must get this right, and getting it right means speaking to August alone. He will summon his new governess, and if Edmund is there, I'll ask for a private audience. Until then, I'll keep to the shadows—my disguise surely will not fool my husband. Then, once Edmund is out of earshot, I'll tell August everything.

It is not the ideal situation. That would have been speaking to William and Bronwyn first and then orchestrating a meeting where William could broach the subject before August saw me, giving August time to assimilate the information. Just when he thought his friend had gone mad, I'd come in.

Is that cowardly, wanting someone else to tell August? It's certainly not the romantic option, but it would have been the practical one. August will know nothing of William's time-travel trips, which will make this a very awkward conversation and may very well end badly.

Yet Bronwyn knows the truth. If all else fails, I have her. A stranger I've met three times in my life holds my future in her hands. She knows where I've been, and William will believe her.

So I return to the nursery and wait for the summons. When I glance out the window, I see August playing with Edmund, racing about in the yard, and I tuck into the shadowed window to watch the glorious sight.

Minutes tick past. Then an hour. When I finally hear footsteps, I fly to the door and yank it open to Violet's startled face as she holds out my supper tray.

"Oh, miss," she says. "You do not need to wait in the nursery. The young master will be with his father for the remainder of the day. They are at dinner now, already making their evening plans."

"Oh. I thought Mr. Courtenay might wish to speak to me. I was hired by mail, and I expected he'd like to meet me in person."

"I am certain he will. He takes a great interest in the young master's care and education. Yet when he returns from business, he will think of nothing but his son until morning." She notices my expression. "I could tell him you wish to speak to him."

"Yes, please. Tell him it will be brief. I do not wish to interfere with his evening. I'll wait in the library, should he decide to see me." I pause. "Would you also please ask him not to bring his son? This ought to be a private conference."

Violet stiffens. "Is there a problem with the lad, miss?"

"Not at all." I hope she cannot fail to see the genuine warmth lighting my face. "He was very quiet and reserved this morning, but I had glimpses later of a delightful child. Clever and inquisitive and unfailingly polite."

She relaxes at that, and I continue with, "I simply find it best to occasionally meet solely with a child's parents in case there are concerns either side needs to raise. I have none myself. I do know, though, that Edmund struggles with his reading, and I would prefer he need not endure a discussion of that."

Violet nods. "Yes, he need not. He is a good boy. A very good boy."

Is her tone a little too earnest? Perhaps, but given the turnover in governesses, I can understand why she'd be quick to defend her young master. I thank her and then sit in front of my supper tray, staring at food my roiling stomach will not allow me to eat. As soon as enough time has passed, I'm on my feet and out the door, hurrying to the library to meet my husband and put an end to my ordeal at last.

I'M STILL wearing my disguise. I must in case I'm spotted on the way. I consider removing the wig once I'm in the library, but someone could still come in before August. It won't matter anyway. August is my husband. He knows every inch of me. Makeup and a change of coloring will not fool him.

I find a book and pretend to read. Footsteps pass in the hall, but I do not even set the book down. I know August's footsteps, and these are not them. And then finally, they come, footfalls so familiar my chest squeezes away my breath.

I snap the book shut and straighten, and I catch my reflection in the glass and laugh softly. I look like Edmund when he heard August's horse, his ears as attuned to that sound as mine are to August's footsteps.

I rise as the door opens, and his name is on my lips, but I hold it back, instead murmuring, "Mr. Courtenay."

My lips quirk even as I say his name. He will know my voice, and his head will jerk my way, eyes going wide.

"Miss Smith," he says brusquely as he walks in.

I try not to deflate. After all, it has been four years, and he expects a stranger. He'll know me once he looks over. He steps into the room, and something catches his eye, and he glances the other way, giving me one split second to gaze at him first.

I do gaze at him, and I remember how the second time August came to my shop, I pretended not to recognize him from his first visit. As a shopkeeper, it was in my best interests to pay attention to my customers, especially one who'd spent as much money as he had. He should have walked in and had me greet him with a welcome and ask whether he'd like more of the spice tarts he'd bought the first time. That is good customer service, and I practiced it religiously.

So why pretend I didn't recognize him? Because August Courtenay was the kind of man one could not fail to notice, however brief the encounter. A face that belongs on a marble statue and a body to match. The clothing didn't hurt matters. Everything August wore was stylish and flattering and perfectly tailored. Clothing was his one true area of indulgence. It was like drizzling butter-sweet caramel on the perfect slice of modern cheesecake, making it irresistible but also just a little too much of a good thing.

When August walked into my bakery, I could not help but notice him. It was like Apollo himself striding in, the sun god casting everything else

into shadow. A practical woman turns away from the dazzling glow. She does not wish to be blinded. She understands that a man like that knows *exactly* how good he looks, and he expects to be remembered, and so she shall not feed his ego.

But August is no longer a stranger in my bakery shop, and there is no danger in looking. In fact, as his wife, it is my prerogative to look, and as much as I've enjoyed it in the past, it is nothing compared to this moment. During years of separation, one might paint a rose-tinted veneer on one's lover, only to see him again and be disappointed that he does not gleam quite as brightly as one remembers. I had subconsciously done the opposite.

In my memories, I had doused August's glow because that was not the part of him I grieved for. It was like those early days in the bakery when I shielded my eyes to his brightness until I could see the man beneath. What I remembered of my husband was not how the sight of him weakened my knees with lust, but how much I missed our conversations, his laughter, his irrepressibly vibrant personality. I remembered the parts I loved best, but here, faced with his presence, I see the rest, and I'm a giddy girl inside, unable to believe that this man is mine. He has not remarried, and he is still mine.

He turns then, and I'm positively quivering with expectation. He will see me. See me and...

His gaze passes right over me, as if I'm furniture, and it settles somewhere over my shoulder, his eyes unfocused in a way that I know so well. It's the same look I'd see whenever he was summoned to speak to his brother, Everett, the earl. In August's mind, he's already finished this meeting, and he's back with Edmund, enjoying their evening together. Now he just needs to physically get past the interruption he's already mentally dismissed.

"You're settling in well, Miss Smith?" he says.

"Y-yes."

Look at me, damn it, August. Just look.

And then, as if I spoke the words, his gaze moves over my face...only to continue on as he walks to the window and gazes out.

"I am sorry to interrupt your evening, sir," I say.

He waves a hand over his shoulder, dismissing the apology. "I am always available if you need to speak about my son. Well, when I'm at home, I'm available, which is less than I'd like since my brother passed."

"Bro—" I begin and then stop myself. As his wife, I could ask for more. As a governess, that is not my place.

But I'm no longer the governess, am I? That's why I'm here, to unmask myself. Yet I cannot help thinking of what he's just said.

His brother is dead. That wouldn't be Everett Courtenay, the earl of Tynesford. Others have spoken of him.

I remember then what Emma said, calling August the second son, and Mrs. Landon saying he was handling the family business, and me thinking that was Harrison's job. That is why I'd first concluded that my employer must be Harrison.

No, my employer is August, who is now the second son and in charge of the family's holdings because Harrison has passed.

Oh, August, I am sorry. I know you did not get on with Harrison, but he is still family. I also know you wanted nothing to do with managing the family's holdings. You had your own business, your own interests.

August continues, "I am home as often as I can be, though. That is important for Edmund."

And here is my opening. I seize it before I can reconsider.

"It is," I say. "It must have been difficult, raising him alone. It cannot have been easy for either of you, with your wife...gone."

His fingers tighten on the windowsill, his shoulders tensing.

August, turn around. Just turn around.

"A boy needs his mother and—"

"And you may stop right there, Miss Smith. My wife is not a source of discussion in this household."

"I am sorry, sir, but—"

"No, Miss Smith. I have very few rules, but that is one of them. Do not speak to me of my wife."

"I understand it must have been difficult—"

"No, Miss Smith. You do not understand at all." He turns sharply, his gaze still unfocused, and I expect to see grief in those eyes. Instead, they blaze with a fury that makes me stagger back. He doesn't seem to notice, just strides toward me, voice lowering.

"I'm sure it makes a very romantic tale for you, Miss Smith. The tragic death of a young wife and mother. That is the story I tell for my son, but it is not the truth."

No, August. You are correct. It is not the truth. Let me tell you—

"The truth, Miss Smith, is that my wife deserted us."

I blink, but he isn't looking at me, doesn't see me. When I open my mouth, nothing comes.

"We were having difficulties, and she decided she could no longer remain my wife, and so she left. Abandoned us."

Left? Left? How can you—?

I can't even finish the thought. It is as if I've fallen into a nightmare. One where I return and August doesn't know me. That is exactly what's happening here. Not that he doesn't recognize me—at this moment, that means nothing. But the fact that he could, for one second, think I would abandon him and our infant *son.*

He turns sharply on his heel. "That is more than I intended to say," he says gruffly. "I am out of sorts this evening, and I do not know why. It is as if…" He looks around the room, his hand rubbing his mouth.

As if you sense your wife here, August? As if you hear her voice?

Yet you do not hear me at all, do you? Because you do not know me at all.

I loved you, August, loved you with all my heart, and I would know you if forty years had passed. I would know your voice, your laugh, the barest glimpse of you would be enough to set my soul racing.

I thought you knew me the same way. Inside and out. The woman who loved you and our son unconditionally and would never—never—abandon you.

I want to run. Run to my room and slam the door and fall onto the bed sobbing.

No, I want to take him by the shoulders and shake him until he sees me and ask how, how in God's name, those words could have left his lips.

The one thing I don't want to do, though? Flee from this house.

It takes only a split second for horror and confusion to give way to anger and resolve.

I will not be frightened away so easily. If I have lost you, August, as much as that may rend my soul in two, I will not give up my child.

I am back, and back I will remain.

"If we are done here, Miss Smith…" August says.

"Oh, yes, I believe we are quite done here, *sir*."

Something in my voice makes him give a start, and he turns, and for the first time since my arrival, he meets my gaze. Meets it, and his eyes widen.

You see something you recognize, don't you, August? Something you know and yet do not know at all, and that confuses you.

I had been so certain he'd know me. He'd look into my eyes, past the spectacles, past the colored contacts, and he would know me. This is the true delusion I've fostered through my four years of exile. I remembered a man who knew me as no person has ever known me. A man who knew me, heart and soul and mind, and *loved* me. Loved me as I loved him.

You did not know me, August.

You were so pleased that I saw past your handsome exterior and loved the man, and I'd been so pleased that you saw past my exterior and loved the woman. I was a fool.

This is the moment when he could change that. When the confusion could fade into piercing recognition.

Rosalind?

Or, barring that, he could pursue the confusion, that flicker of recognition.

Do I…know you?

If he said those words, I would reveal myself. Instead, he looks at me with one flash of confusion that hardens into dismissal.

You see something that you recognize, August, and you choose not to pursue it.

He turns on his heel, muttering something I do not catch, and I lift my chin and walk from the room, not as a governess but as the lady of the house.

That is what I am, August. A lady now, a lady before I met you and a lady heretofore. The mother of your son. You may not be ready for that, but it remains indelible fact. I am returned, and I shall not be denied.

ELEVEN

 MARCH TO MY room, head high, startling one of the maids, who stares as if seeing a stranger.

Ah, twenty-first century, you have not solved the problem of British classism, but you opened my eyes to it, and I will always thank you for that.

While I'd been aware of the issue—my progressive parents made sure of that—I'd never truly understood the depth of it until I returned. I saw people being treated with lowered gazes and subservient nods, and I'd wondered what they'd done to deserve such deference. Nothing, I'd realized. They were simply members of the upper class, their very bearing signaling that. Now I affect the same bearing—the one I grew up with— and this poor maid stares after me in shock.

I continue to my room, close the door and stand there, head held not in defiance but in uncertainty. Frozen in place by the looming question of "what now?"

What now indeed.

What do you do when your husband doesn't recognize you? When he accuses you of something so heinous that you'd be less shocked if he claimed you'd butchered a stranger in the street?

He thinks I abandoned my husband and child. Like a feckless child who decides she is tired of her toys and throws them away. When I *was* a child, I could not bear to part with my most favored dolls and books. Even gifting them to another would have felt disloyal.

How could he think I would do that? How could the notion even enter his mind?

The answer whispers deep inside me.

It's not you, Rosalind. It's him. His experience. His mother. His sister. His fiancée. You need not forgive him entirely, but you cannot honestly be quite so shocked.

I will address that later, when I'm ready. I will give measured consideration to his words in light of his past. I will also cry. I will sob uncontrollably in my bed, bereft and broken. Yet those must be future reactions. For now, I'm angry, and I will not deny myself that anger.

So, what am I going to do about it?

March back in there and reveal myself?

I dare not. I am no longer a beloved dead wife returned from the grave. I am a…

Say the words, Rosalind, as much as they hurt.

I am a hated fiend.

I saw that in his eyes. If I tell him the truth now, I do not know what he will do.

I'm sorry, August, but I do not trust you. I cannot, after that.

Do I flee then? Sneak out and return to Thorne Manor to await William and Bronwyn's return?

That is the practical answer, but right now, I care less about pragmatism than pride. I will not retreat at any cost.

No, that is a lie. I *would* retreat if my staying hurt my son. I might even retreat if it hurt my husband, but I will not think of that. I'll pretend that, in my fury, I am a woman scorned and I would gladly hurt August as he's hurt me.

For now, the question is only this: what path harms Edmund the least?

My heart tells me that it would be worse to leave. My heart hears August's voice, spitting those ugly words, accusing me of abandonment, and it hears the lost little boy. The boy whose mother died, sister died, fiancée ran off. It hears a child who felt abandoned by every woman he loved.

I will not do that to my son.

Oh, I'm not foolish enough to think Edmund loves me. He barely knows me. But so many others have left him that it had been a huge risk to open himself, even a little, to me. What if I leave him now, only to return in a week or two as his mother?

I am here, Edmund. Your mother returned to you. I will never leave you.

Well, yes, I did leave that one time when you were a baby, but that wasn't by choice.

And, er, yes, I did leave last week, by choice, but that time I was very, very angry with your father.

I won't do that to my son. I will stay and be his governess and get to know him until William returns to Thorne Manor, whereupon I will depart for as brief a time as possible and only after forewarning Edmund with a promise of my return.

Edmund said the Thornes would be gone for a fortnight. That must almost be over. In the morning, I shall post a letter for Bronwyn Thorne and entreat her assistance as soon as possible.

My course of action resolved, I stride to the bed and let myself fall on it and…

A smell wafts up, and I wrinkle my nose.

As I turn, my hand presses down on the bed, and a dampness rises through the thin coverlet. I look down to see red suffusing the dingy white.

I yank back the covers, and there is blood. At first, that's all I see, and I presume what women often presume, seeing blood in their bed. Yet I'm not menstruating, and it is entirely the wrong spot, up on my flattened pillow. There is also hair. A hank of blond hair in blood, and my hand flies up to my wig, but I know it is not mine.

I'm lifting the pillow for a closer look when a voice says, "Cook asked me—"

And then a scream with the percussion clatter of a dropped silver tray. I turn to see Violet in the doorway, a tea tray on the floor, her dark eyes fixed in horror on the bloodied pillow in my hands.

I can only imagine how it looks, the new governess holding a bloodied pillow up, as if in offering to some unseen demon.

I drop the pillow and rush to her, saying, "It's all right. I only found it."

I expect her to recoil in horror from my touch, but she just keeps screaming and then launches herself at me, arms going around me as she buries her face against my neck. I stand there, utterly bewildered by her reaction. She's crying now, sobbing something about governesses and ghosts.

"What's going on here?" a voice says.

Mrs. Landon rounds the corner and stops so sharply you'd think she caught us in a very different sort of embrace. She realizes Violet is crying and continues her strides forward.

"Come now," she says. "What's all this?"

"It—it's back," Violet says, lifting her head and moving away from me. She points at the bed.

"I found that," I say as Mrs. Landon strides toward the pillow. "It was under—"

"Who told you?" she says, spinning on me, fury rising in her eyes. She glances at Violet, who lets out a squawk and backs up, hands rising.

"I did not say a word, ma'am," Violet says. "I would not. Ever."

"Well, someone told her." She advances on me. "Not even here a full day, and you're already finding that, are you?"

"I have no idea what *that* is. I came into my room after speaking to Mr. Courtenay, and I noticed the smell." I pause and inhale. "You do smell it, do you not? It isn't the blood."

"Sulphur." Mrs. Landon spits the words. "You know very well what it is. Someone told you about this nonsense, and you're already taking advantage of it."

"I have no idea what—"

"It was one of them, wasn't it? One of those wretches who came before you. That is how you learned of the position. They told you the story, and you accepted the position and demanded a quarter's wages in advance. Then you did not even wait two nights before planting this... this *thing*."

"You think—" I sputter. "I have no idea what 'nonsense' you mean nor what other governesses might have told me, had I spoken to any, which I did not. As for the quarter's wages—"

Footsteps in the hall cut me short. Those footsteps I know so well, bearing down on my room with, "What the devil is going on here?"

August appears. There's no anger on his face, just the irritation of having been disturbed. His gaze crosses us, and his mouth tightens, and he looks every inch the master of the house, annoyed at having his evening disrupted by the histrionics of his female staff.

I reach for the pillow. Then I see a movement behind him. The hall is too shadowed for me to make out Edmund, but I know he is there, particularly when August reaches a hand behind him to gently warn the boy back. I step in front of the pillow before my son sees it.

"There was something distressing in my bed," I say. "Violet saw it and became understandably distraught, and that brought Mrs. Landon. We were discussing the matter."

"Discussing?" One brow shoots up. "That was a very heated discussion, Miss Smith."

"It's that nonsense," Mrs. Landon says before I can respond. "The nonsense that frightened off her predecessors."

August deflates, lines appearing at the corners of his mouth. "What is it now?" He glances back to where Edmund obviously waits. "No, tell me tomorrow, Mrs. Landon."

"She believes I planted the thing that I found," I blurt as he turns to leave. "She believes I heard about this 'nonsense' and am attempting to fabricate an excuse for fleeing with my quarter's wages. I have no

idea what she's speaking of, sir, and I wish to assert, while you are here, that if—for any reason—I leave before my paid quarter, I will return the wages advanced to me."

His brows rise. "That is a generous—but perhaps hasty—offer, Miss Smith."

I lift my chin. "I know that, but I believe it is the only way to defend myself against the charge."

He looks at me. Really looks at me. Until now, his gaze has been distant, as if he's already moved past this domestic squabble. Now he meets my gaze and there is a second, one split second...

You see something, August. Damn you, I know you do.

He steps back abruptly with a gruff, "Understood. Mrs. Landon, please handle this matter without accusations and without *discussions* loud enough to force my investigations. I am spending the evening with my son, and I do not wish to be disturbed again."

I half curtsey and nod, but he's already gone.

Mrs. Landon does not leave immediately. She orders Violet to replace my sheets and pillow, over my protests that I can take them to the laundry myself.

"You think that's clever, don't you?" she says after Violet is gone.

I bite my tongue. Anything that comes out of my mouth right now will not help my cause.

"Oh, Mr. August is pleased enough," she says, that raptor-sharp gaze piercing me. "He's an honorable man, and so he expects honor from others. If you say you'll repay him, he'll believe it. But all you need to do is flee in the night like the others, and then how will he get your wages back?"

I march to my bag and pull out my money pouch. I have a third of my remaining money in there, the rest secreted away. I dump the contents onto my bare mattress.

"Seven pounds," I say. "That will cover a month's wages, yes?"

"A month, not a quarter."

"I have the remainder banked," I say. "I have one day off per fortnight. At my next one, I shall visit the bank in York and withdraw my unpaid wages, which you may dole out as needed. I was unaware of the situation here, and understanding it now, I do not wish there to be any misunderstanding. Please take that money for now as a partial guarantee that I will not flee in the night."

She scoops up the pounds but leaves the smaller change. Then she turns and walks out with a huff. I don't ask for enlightenment on this "nonsense" as she called it. I am curious, bursting with it, but I'm not certain how to acquire the information without giving her claim to say I'm plotting my own early departure.

That problem is solved as soon as Violet returns. She looks out the door, listening for Mrs. Landon, and then whispers, "It isn't nonsense, miss."

I say nothing, only nod and take the sheets to help her make up the bed.

"It's a ghost," she says.

I hesitate, remembering last night, the scratching at the window, the whispering at my ear.

"You don't believe in phantoms, miss?" she says.

I choose my words with care. "I do not *dis*believe in them, Violet. The ones I have heard of, though, are far past bleeding. Or shedding hair."

She gives a tight, nervous laugh. "That's what I thought, too. Until I came to work here. But Cook says there are all kinds of ghosts. Some make noises, like footsteps. Or throw things about. This one leaves..."

She looks down at my bed and shivers.

"So that has happened before?"

She nods. "It always happens to the new ones. The governesses, that is. It usually takes longer, though." Her voice drops with her gaze. "She must not like you."

A chill ripples through me. I shake out the pillowcase to cover it. "The ghost, you mean? She has an identity?"

Violet swallows. "Several, miss. It depends on who's telling the story. Some say she is the earl's sister, who died when he was a young man."

I shake the pillowcase hard and say nothing.

"Some say she is the first governess who left. Margaret. Brought from London when Mr. August came to visit two years ago. She disappeared a week later, all her belongings left in her room. Mr. August should have had them search the pond and lake, but he believed she left of her own accord. Her purse was gone with her money, but we still think..." She swallows. "We are quite certain she drowned. On account of the hair."

"She drowned on account of her hair?"

A half titter. "No, miss. I mean the hair in the beds. It's wet."

I think back to that clump of bloodied hair. To the pink dampness coming through my sheets. Yes, the hair had been sodden, and not simply with blood.

Violet continues as she tucks in the sheet. "Mr. August's sister drowned, and Cook thinks Margaret did, too. But most say it's a different ghost altogether. One bent on scaring off those who threaten her rightful place with young Edmund. One who also drowned."

I go still, my hands quivering. I know what is coming, and I brace myself for it.

The maid's gaze rises to mine. "They say it is his mother herself, come from her watery grave to frighten away any woman who comes near her son."

TWELVE

I DO NOT SLEEP well that night. I'm not certain I sleep at all. It isn't fear of ghosts. Last night, I dismissed any such thoughts with rationalizations for what I heard. Now it is clear that something is afoot, and clearer that "ghost" is not the answer. Ghosts may whisper in ears, and they may even be capable of scratching windows, but they do not leave blood and hair under pillows like some perverse follicle fairy.

Are you certain? a voice whispers inside me. *Absolutely certain?*

I dismiss it. The answer here is clearly a living phantom with a dislike of governesses. I'm not certain how one would scratch at a window on the third floor, but it must be possible. And it is absolutely possible to place that horrid thing in my bed. Hair obtained from a wig shop and blood from a butcher. It's not as if I can send it away for analysis. I only wish I'd had time to examine it more closely.

And the whispering? Who whispered in your ear, Rosalind?

I imagined that. I have grown accustomed to a modern flat, and I heard some ordinary noise in an old and drafty country manor.

I'm unsettled by the thought that anyone thinks the ghost could be me. It makes me want to charge into August's chambers, shed my

disguise and prove that Edmund's mother is not dead, much less a vengeful ghost.

Practicality wins out. I have a plan, after all. Contact Bronwyn Thorne and allow her and William to mediate my return. This is too important to risk for mere impatience.

The main thing is that I now know why the governesses flee. It has nothing to do with my son. They are frightened off, sometimes so terrified that they barely grab their handbag before fleeing. The fact that August has not recognized and resolved the issue only proves his distraction, juggling single fatherhood with managing a business he despises.

I will resolve this myself. I will find whoever is responsible. And, in the meantime, I know what I face: an enemy within these walls, hell-bent on seeing me gone.

I SPEND the morning getting to know the staff better and feeling so disingenuous that I withdraw to my room several times. I would rather be with Edmund, but when Violet brought my breakfast, she passed along August's message that my services would not be required today. He will be with his son.

That leaves me to follow through on my vow from last night, investigating the "haunting." At this early stage, that means first getting to know the staff and forming opinions of their attitude toward the governesses. Doing so makes me feel more like a fraud than ever. I'm feigning interest in my coworkers because I want something from them. In my gut, I know that isn't true. I do want to get to know them. That was my parents' way, and it had always been August's inclination, strengthened when my own upbringing proved his interest in his staff wasn't as scandalous—or middle-class—as his brothers thought.

The problem is that I had not intended to socialize with the staff while I was Clara Smith. I feared that if I did so, when they learned my true

identity, they'd think I'd been wooing them as potential allies in a fight against August.

Fight against August? Is that what I expect? A custody battle? A war to reclaim my very identity as Rosalind Courtenay?

I want to say that is ridiculous. Even had I returned to find him remarried, the August I knew would never have denied me access to my son. But after last night, I fear *that* August was a fictional character in my rose-tinted past. I hope not. Yet I must be prepared, and that does not mean—would never mean—turning his staff against him.

I must follow my natural inclination here and get to know those around me...while recognizing that I'm currently compelled by self-preservation, seeking to uncover the person who wants me gone from Courtenay Hall.

The first step is knowing who has been here since that first governess—Margaret—was frightened off two years ago. I already know Hugh has been at Courtenay Hall since childhood. Mrs. Landon has been here long enough to know Margaret. Same with Violet. Mrs. Beechworth arrived last year, hired after her predecessor retired.

Most of the other recent hires have been governesses. For the past two years, August has spent an increasing amount of time at Courtenay Hall—and Everett spends very little—which has improved staff turnover immensely.

I learn nothing of true interest, but I'm not discouraged. This morning was simply laying the groundwork for deeper probing. As I take a late lunch in my room, I make notes, and I'm so immersed in that I miss the footsteps that announce a visitor until he clears his throat.

I look up sharply to see August in the open doorway. He's poised there, his gaze fixed somewhere to the side of me.

"Miss Smith," he says, his voice as stiff as his bearing. "I apologize for interrupting your writing."

"Not at all," I say, clambering to my feet as I slide the book shut. "I was simply preparing Edmund's lesson plans."

"Making diligent use of your time off."

I force a light laugh. "I would not claim that. I spent the morning meeting my fellow staff and then indulging in a long walk to town." *Where I posted the letter to Bronwyn Thorne.* "Though perhaps I ought to pretend I did indeed spend the entire morning hard at work."

As angry as I am with him, I cannot resist being civil. Being more than civil, even, my tone light and self-deprecating, inviting him to smile or at least relax those set shoulders. He does neither.

"I had intended to spend the day with my son," he says. "But I have been informed he has plans with you."

I blink. "N-no, sir. I would never interrupt your time together. I have no plans with him until the morrow."

"He says you are to make biscuits this afternoon. Edmund is quite adamant on retaining that appointment."

"Ah, I see. Yes, he does love those chocolate biscuits. He undoubtedly fears that any delay might cause me to rescind my promise to bake with him. I will assure him that we can do it another—"

"You will not. That is what I came to say, Miss Smith. You won't be doing that with Edmund. It is not a skill he requires."

I bristle. This is not the August I remember, who would often lament all the skills he did not "require" and was thus unable to learn. The August who would perch on a stool as I baked, much as I had done with our housekeeper as a child, peppering me with questions about the process.

I answer slowly. "It might not be a skill most men require, but it is not something eschewed by all men, either. There are many chefs and bakers—"

"He is the nephew of an earl."

Most would say these words with a twist of hauteur. August's tone carries truth with a twinge of regret. Even if Edmund wanted to become a chef, it wouldn't be allowed.

"Of course," I say. "I only meant that there would be no shame in the lesson. Which truly is intended to be a lesson, sir. A proper academic lesson, not one in baking."

One brow rises, the movement so slight anyone else would miss it.

I hurry on. "As I explained to Mrs. Beechworth, I am attempting to incorporate lessons into activities that Edmund enjoys. Baking is science. I will teach him the scientific properties at work, with the leavening and the combining of liquids and solids. Measurements involve mathematics, and we shall, for example, use a quarter cup measure and determine the number required for a full cup of flour. I also intend to encourage him to read along with the recipe, to bolster his confidence in a nonthreatening manner."

The fact that August does not cut me short shows he is considering my words. That bolsters my own confidence. When I finish, he is silent, and I know he is considering, and I resist the urge to push. A wife might push; a governess cannot.

"I understand," he says slowly, "and I applaud your creativity, Miss Smith. I would encourage you to continue in this vein. But not with biscuits."

"Why ever not?" I say before I remember myself. I lower my gaze. "I mean that while I will defer to your decision, I urge you to reconsider, sir. An interest in baking is not unusual among children, even boys. I also understand that his mother was a baker."

August stiffens, almost a shudder. "Yes," he says, his voice chill. "And he does not need the reminder. His mother left him."

"That is your interpretation of the facts." The words are out before I even realize I've said them. His head jerks up.

I hurry on, forcing my voice to be softer. "That is what you believe, but it is not what he thinks, nor what others think, and I would urge you, sir, not to tarnish the image he has of his mother."

I try to say it as deferentially as possible, but here is where my own class position fails me. While I was not August's social equal when we wed, I never needed to check any impulse to speak my mind, even when my thoughts might criticize his actions. As a governess, though, I should not express criticism even in the mildest of tones.

His green eyes go cold. "I appreciate your opinion, Miss Smith, but I am not a monster who would speak ill of my son's mother, particularly to him. Last night, I misspoke. I had a long journey, and I was not myself."

"I am the one who misspoke," I say. "My zeal for protecting my charge overtook me, and I apologize, sir. I also misspoke if I suggested you had done any such thing. What Edmund has told me of his mother has come from you, and it is all positive."

Silence. Long silence, and I'm replaying what I said to see how it could be misconstrued. Then he says, his voice low, "You have only been here a day, and he has already spoken of her?"

"In situations where comment arose naturally, sir, as with the baking." I want to say more, to parrot what Edmund said, that August no longer took pastries with tea because no one's could compete with mine. I want to nudge those good memories he obviously retained. I bite my tongue against it and say simply, "It is always positive reflections. To him, you think very highly of her and her accomplishments with regards to baking or her own dys—learning challenges."

He glances over. "He told me you share those challenges as well. Is that true?"

Damn it. I hadn't thought of this. I'd acted naturally, sharing my experiences without realizing that might seem odd to August that—like his wife—I am dyslexic.

And is that a problem? If he makes the connection? Perhaps it's for the best.

Or perhaps it is the worst possible thing that could happen at this moment. For August to realize I'm his Rosalind, to use the deception against me.

Then tell him yourself.

Around and around we go, forever returning to this spot. That makes it seem that revealing myself is clearly the best course, yet my head says it is only the most expedient course. The rash and impulsive and dangerous course.

A few days at most. That is all it will take for Bronwyn to get the letter.

"I…told a falsehood, sir," I say. "While reading did not come easily to me, I have taught children with Edmund's condition. I thought he would be more comforted if I claimed their experiences as my own."

August only nods, as if his attention has moved on, and I feel as if I could have said yes, I did not read until I was eight, and my parents tutored me, and my two younger sisters helped, and he still would not have seen the connection. He does not wish to see it, and so he does not.

Or he thinks I'm dead. He might say otherwise, but perhaps that is the small and lonely boy inside, convinced every woman leaves. The adult knows, yet the child only feels.

"You may have your lesson with Edmund," he says.

"My...?"

"The bak—" He cuts the word short, and his gaze swings aside. "You may make the chocolate biscuits. I will send him to the kitchen at three as arranged with Mrs. Beechworth."

I open my mouth, but he's already walking away.

EDMUND AND I bake cookies. As promised, I turn it into a lesson, using measurements and the principles of baking. He helps with the recipe reading and with the baking itself. I stifle any urge to tweak the recipe as I had in my shop. For this, I must follow it to the letter as would a diligent amateur baker. Too many flourishes will suggest I'm overly experienced in the art.

And yet... Well, I cannot resist one tweak, in the guise of scientific experimentation. We make two batches, changing the leavening ingredients so I may demonstrate the difference and also show how a recipe can be adapted to taste, one cookie fluffy, the other flat.

Every parent must dream of sharing their particular passion with their children, whether it is reading or baseball or sculpting. I grew up wanting a large family and imagining how I would teach them all to bake, and if they did not like it, then I would feed them. I would find that recipe they liked above all others, and I would adapt it just for them, and I would make it for their fifth birthday and their fifteenth, and if I was incredibly lucky, all the way through to their fiftieth.

 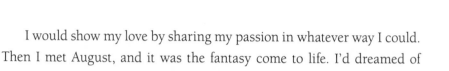

I would show my love by sharing my passion in whatever way I could. Then I met August, and it was the fantasy come to life. I'd dreamed of a husband who would enjoy my baking and encourage it, but he went beyond that, sitting and watching me do it, as if it was the most fascinating thing in the world, not because he enjoyed baking but because I did.

When Edmund came along, August joked that while other parents could not wait for a baby's first step or word, I could not wait until he was old enough to gum a biscuit. Once we reached that stage, I fairly thrummed with excitement, imagining all the stages to come, all the things I could introduce to him as I watched his tastes evolve. Would he like sweets or savories? Nuts or dried fruits or spices? Would he inherit my love of rich creams or his father's weakness for fruity jams? Did early exposure define our tastes? Or associations with positive experiences, like holidays? We were embarking on this incredible journey together, and baking was only the tiniest corner of it, and I could not wait to share it with him.

And then he was gone. Yes, I'm the one who left, but it felt as if he'd been ripped from me. Ripped from my future. All those dreams burned to ash. I was not there to hear his first word. To see his first step. To watch him experience creams or jams or nuts for the first time. As time passed, I began to consider the horrifying possibility that I might miss all of it, and somehow, while other experiences were far more important, this is the one that cut the deepest.

I would never bake with my son.

And now I am, and I could bemoan the fact he doesn't know it's me, but I would never be so petty. I dreamed of this moment, and I thought I had lost it forever, and I do not care whether we are governess and charge. It is glorious.

When we are done, Edmund exclaims over the cookies, telling me—in a confidential whisper—that they are better than even Bronwyn's. I feel a pang of guilt at that. The problem is not that Bronwyn isn't following the recipe. It's that she's had to adapt the recipe for Victorian

ingredients. She's made excellent substitutions, but I'm more accustomed to the peccadilloes of working with a Victorian pantry.

Edmund eats one cookie from each batch—for comparison—and then must, naturally, have another of his favorite.

"And that is quite enough, young sir," I say with a teasing smile. "If you ruin your appetite, Cook shall never let us do this again. We will put the rest away for tea."

"Tea!" Edmund leaps from his stool. "We must bring cookies to Papa for his tea!"

I imagine taking a plate of cookies to August. I remember all the times I would bake something new while he worked in his office, and I'd bring him the first from the oven. That moment of standing there, trying to look casual while feeling as if I were awaiting the verdict of a Michelin reviewer. He would, of course, proclaim it perfect...exactly as our son had done. I would press then, pushing and prodding for constructive criticism to allow me to improve. Improving is a matter of taste. As I demonstrated to Edmund with the two types of cookies, one is not "better" than the other. It is up to the eater to decide which they prefer. With August, it was *his* tastes that mattered, the joy of placing a plate before him and seeing his eyes light up with pure pleasure.

I imagine taking this plate to him, and I know if I did, I could not do it as his son's governess. I would be his wife, on tenterhooks, waiting for his opinion, glowing under his praise. And I would do it knowing that I might never experience this again once he realizes who I am.

I remember August's face as he couldn't even bring himself to say the word "baking."

I set four cookies on a plate. "You made them," I say. "You take them and leave the best part of baking to me."

His brow scrunches. "The best part?"

I wave at the mess. "The cleanup. Now, off with you, young sir, or I shall share the pleasure of scrubbing pans."

He giggles, snatches up the plate and runs off.

THIRTEEN

 PASS THE REST of the day making good on my lie to August. Well, making good on one of them, even if it is perhaps the smallest and least consequential. I told him I'd been lesson planning earlier. That is how I spend the remainder of my day: in my room, composing lessons.

I also spend it fretting and calculating. Fretting about whether I'm doing the right thing and calculating how long I might need to keep doing it before Bronwyn rescues me. There is, of course, the heavy discomfort of realizing I'm treating a near-stranger like a bosom friend. We spoke three times, never even exchanging names, and I expect her to ride to my rescue the moment she receives that letter? She's the mother of a toddler and also heavily pregnant.

I should have written to William instead. That was the obvious choice. Yet I wrote to her, and I can say it's because she's the one who saw me in the shop, but I think it's because she is a mother. Which is ridiculous, really. A father—particularly one as doting as William seemed—would see the urgency of my plight just as easily. Yet I naturally inclined toward sisterhood here. A fellow woman, a fellow mother, a fellow time-traveler, one who will understand what I'm asking and come as soon as she is able.

Once she gets home to Thorne Manor and crosses over and gets the post and arranges to visit Courtenay Hall...

I have calculated she is due to return within days. Yet that does not mean I can expect her here the morrow after next.

And so I fret. Fret, fret and fret some more. I even journal my fretting, as if I might later need proof that I did not make this choice blithely.

See, August? I truly did understand the implications of my ruse, but I feared untimely unveiling more.

I feared you more.

I can tell myself that I fear his reaction, not August himself, but that splits hairs. I fear his pain and fear exploding into a rage that wants me gone, wants me punished.

That night, the "ghost" does not interrupt my sleep. Perhaps I'm simply too exhausted to notice its attempts. That amuses me when I wake the next morning, the thought of whoever is staging this fake haunting scratching at the window half the night, all efforts futile as I slumber.

The next morning, one of the other maids—Bridget—wakes me and is none too pleased at the task. She pointedly notes that I have a window and an eastern exposure, suggesting I have no reason for not waking myself with the dawn as a good servant does. I'll need to condition myself to do so. Failing not only inconveniences the staff but makes me look indolent or, worse, as if I have airs above my station, a woman who does not consider herself mere staff. That is always a danger with governesses. They often come from families not unlike my own, impoverished gentry or upper middle-class.

I take my breakfast with Edmund, who informs me that his father declared the cookies were indeed better than Bronwyn's, but that would be a secret between them, and they would continue to honestly tell Bronwyn that her baking is far superior to poor Mrs. Beechworth's.

This morning, I have Edmund for lessons. His father intends to take him to town after lunch, returning for more lessons until dinner, whereupon Edmund will spend his evening with his father. It is far from the

usual arrangement. Even the best upper-class father might see his children only at meals, their care given otherwise to governesses and mothers. Would August and Edmund be as close if I had not been lost to them? I imagine August would have been more like my father, taking time with his children each day. Yet if I'm to find any silver lining in my absence, I can see it here, in their bond. August knew well what it was like to have a dead mother and a distant father, and he'd vowed our son's experience would be nothing like his own.

The weather is less than ideal this morning, and we wait out morning high winds and bitter drizzle by continuing to develop our "Knight night school" story with all the research and other educational material I can slip in. When we're in the library, I find two books sitting on the table, both with pages marked. One is a collection of Arthurian legends, the other *The Canterbury Tales*. The indicated pages mark stories featuring knights.

Even if the library wasn't reserved for the use of the family, I would know who left these out. The pages are marked with scraps of paper, despite the fact there is a collection of bookmarks on a shelf. I'd been appalled to see August using scraps; he pointed out that the bookmarks, while lovely, had dyes that leached into the pages of the older books.

So Edmund told his father about our project, and instead of August telling me he'd found stories that might interest Edmund, he'd laid them on the table in hopes I would both find them and understand the message.

Are you avoiding me, August?

That seems obvious, and I would like to think it's because part of him recognizes who I am. Yet I suspect there's a much more prosaic explanation. Hugh warned me that August has his own difficulties with governesses, beyond their sudden departures. *Jane Eyre* is far from the first novel to explore the theme of a governess caring for a child and earning the love of the manor lord. Governesses occupy an unusual social stratum. They may be "in service," but many have the respectable family name that would mean a union between a governess and the widowed third son of an earl would be no more scandalous than our own union.

August is avoiding me, and when he must speak to me directly, he avoids eye contact or even looking my way. He is shielding himself against unwanted attention and unprovoked expectations. In this case, while I selfishly wish I could speak to him more, his caution is to my benefit. It ensures he will not recognize me before I reveal myself.

I read one of the stories with Edmund, and I tell him to thank his father on my behalf. I will not use this as an excuse to make contact.

When the sun peeps out in late morning, Edmund and I head out of doors. The weather is better now, the winds dropping, the rain evaporating and even a bright autumn sun popping out to warm the damp air. We begin with a bit of swordplay, which the grooms join in. Then we head off for a walk about the property.

"Do you want to see a special place?" Edmund asks as we reach the main path.

"If it is your special place, then I absolutely do if you do not mind me seeing it."

His nose scrunches, freckles bunching. "I would not say it is mine. It is my uncle the earl's. Everything here is his. It also is not a secret. No one else goes there, though. Well, Papa comes with me sometimes, but it is not easy to reach. He says we could ask the gardeners to repair the path. That would mean others could find it, and we decided to keep it as it is."

"Now I am thoroughly intrigued. Lead on, Sir Edmund."

He scampers ahead, checking over his shoulder only to see whether I can keep up. In this world, women of child-bearing years are discouraged from strenuous physical activity, but the modern world encourages such pursuits in all, and I'm happy to run along after my son.

We head into the forest, which is a relief. If he'd headed close to either the pond or the lake, I'd have needed to rethink the excursion—I won't risk incurring August's mistrust by taking Edmund near any large body of water. It makes sense, though, that it's in the forest if they discussed clearing a new path.

The forest was initially used for game, and it's still stocked for that, but only the gamekeeper uses it and only after warning the family to ensure no one is inside. Mostly, it's another recreational area. In this time period, though, people aren't quite as keen to go traipsing through the forest recreationally. The meadow and waterfront paths are far more enticing. That means many of the old paths once used by hunting parties are long since overgrown. It's one of these trails that Edmund takes me along, and I can see why August struggles to pass. It's thickly wooded, with crisscrossing vines, meaning he'd need to stoop. I must only duck my head.

As I follow Edmund through the thick brush, I hear the burble of water and tense, but when we burst through into the clearing, I see that a narrow stream poses no danger of drowning. Then I see the rest of the clearing and let out a laugh of delight.

It would be difficult, I think, to explain follies to twenty-first-century homeowners. They might have features in their yard, but most are practical—a gazebo, a bench, a birdbath. Oh, there are statues, koi ponds and tiny waterfalls, but nothing quite like a folly, even when they have the money and land for one. For ones like the Grecian temple, modern people would see the appeal, although they'd boggle at the expense and sheer size of such a "lawn ornament." This one would be more confounding.

It's a ruined stone tower, the remains stretching only about ten feet in the air with pieces tumbled throughout the clearing. Perhaps a modern visitor would look on it and see the final remains of a medieval castle. That is what it should conjure. Yet no castle stood here. No tower, either. It was created as a ruin. Faux rubble for visual interest with absolutely no deeper function. And it is utterly delightful.

I did not see this folly on my visits to Courtenay Hall, even in the modern time, which makes me wonder whether, at some point, it was demolished as a safety hazard. I can see why. In the twenty-first century, insurance assessors would look on this and shudder. They'd imagine seniors tripping over the "fallen" blocks, half buried in the ground. They'd

envision children playing in the "remains" of the tower and toppling out. Fortunately, we are not yet in the time of lawsuits, and so the folly remains here, hidden in the woods, for my son to play on.

While August may worry about the water, he must see no serious danger here, and I would agree. Our son is a sensible sort—perhaps even a little too sensible for his age. He still scales the tower like a monkey, but he is careful, and my heart does no more than pitter-patter.

He climbs, and I explore, and we chatter as we do, adding the ruined tower to our knight's tale, imagining terrible fates to explain its current condition. Ridiculous fates, mostly. Meteors and magic and mayhem.

My son lacks playmates. That becomes increasingly apparent by his utter delight at having someone other than his father to play with. I don't blame August. We are not in the age of playgrounds and playdates. Not even in the age of schoolyards for a child of Edmund's standing. He talks about William and Bronwyn's daughter—Amelia—but she is three years his junior and more living doll than playmate.

As I'm thinking of ways to introduce Edmund to other children, he suddenly goes silent. My head jerks up, heart pounding. I'm inside the tower, having climbed the stairs within and perched at the top. Edmund is outside, hopping across the fallen stones. I can see him there, even before I push to my feet. He's looking into the forest.

I squint, expecting to see a deer—or perhaps August himself—but nothing's there. Yet Edmund stares at an empty spot and then lifts a finger, as if telling someone he'll be right there.

"Edmund?"

He spins toward me and lifts that same finger. "Just a moment, miss," he calls. "I'll be right back."

FOURTEEN

DMUND ZOOMS OFF before I can respond, leaving me clattering down the stairs, my damnable skirts tangling. I like dresses well enough, but they are not designed for crawling through ruins.

I race outside, calling, "Edmund?"

I keep my voice neutral, just louder than my speaking tone. My heart might be hammering, but I don't want to race after him, shrieking like a banshee.

I can't see where he ran, and I curse myself for being too panicked to watch where he was going. As I walk in the general direction, the sound of his voice wafts over.

I pick my way through the bushes, moving quietly. The natural answer is that he saw someone from the house and ran to speak to them. So why is my heart pounding? Why is a little voice whispering that isn't the answer at all? Or, if it is, it's not someone I'm supposed to see speaking to him. The latter seems more obvious with every moment I reconsider his actions. He did not summon this person into the clearing to talk. They did not walk into the clearing to join us. This is a secret, and when it comes to children, secrets that involve another person are rarely good.

I can't hear the other voice. Just Edmund's. As I grow closer, his words come clear.

"I know you're here. I saw you."

I creep through the forest, placing each step with care. If he catches me sneaking up on a private interaction, I'll lose the trust I've gained. Yet he's not a teenager, and I cannot say that at the age of five, he's entitled to this sort of privacy.

The other option is to walk out as if I didn't understand that he'd asked me to stay behind. Do that, though, and if someone is there, they'll be forewarned and flee.

"I do not understand," Edmund says, the crackle of undergrowth telling me he is on the move. "Sometimes you speak to me, and sometimes you will not. Is it that you cannot?"

The hairs on my neck rise. I see him now, standing in place and looking about. Then his gaze snags on something I do not see, and he bolts with a cry of, "Wait!"

Edmund tears through the forest, pushing past vines and brambles. He clearly saw something in the distance. No, not something. Someone. Someone who did not always communicate with him. Someone I cannot see.

I can come up with a dozen halfway plausible explanations, but I know the truth. My gut knows it. Just as it knew it was clearly a living person haunting me two nights ago.

Edmund stops, small shoulders sagging, and I know the ghost is gone. I acknowledge that with the same ease I'd acknowledge that a rabbit or deer has fled. That is how I was raised. Ghosts exist, as do deer and rabbits, all of them equally likely to bolt if we pursue.

That is not entirely accurate. Yes, ghosts exist. Yes, most are shy and elusive creatures. Yet they are not like rabbits and deer, there for anyone to see if they have the patience and the interest.

I do not see ghosts.

My son does.

That hits me so hard I grab a tree to steady myself. Then I swallow, square my shoulders and remind myself this is hardly a terminal illness. It is like his dyslexia. He will need to accommodate it and learn how best to do so, and he has been born into a family as equipped to do that as they are to help his reading. I'm here now, and I can help.

The question is whether he will allow it.

I stride forward, making no effort to hide the noise of my approach. "Edmund?" I call in a voice that betrays only a touch of concern.

He turns, and guilt darkens his face as his gaze drops. "I am sorry, miss. I thought I saw a puppy."

He says the lie with such practiced ease that I know it is not the first time he's been caught chasing a ghost. I also know it is not an open secret like his dyslexia.

"A puppy?" I say. "Shall we go find it?"

His guilt flares into panic, and I almost feel bad. Almost. This is like a modern-day bandage, which must be torn off quickly with some discomfort.

When he says nothing, I adjust my skirts and lower myself to one knee in front of him. "There is no puppy, is there, Edmund?"

Mortification now, and I want to wrap my arms around him. Instead, I lay a hand on his shoulder in a reassuring squeeze.

"I… I am sorry, miss. I know it is wrong to lie but…"

"But sometimes, a lie seems like the only thing to say if the truth would not be believed."

His gaze shoots to mine.

I hesitate here. As a mother, I want to tell him the truth about his family. Even if it turns out that I've misinterpreted, he eventually needs to know this secret of ours. Yet I'm not his mother here, and his governess could be summarily dismissed if he told his father I'd been talking about ghosts.

I'm not his governess, though. Not truly, and in the worst scenario, where I'm dismissed, I shall come back with William and Bronwyn and resolve this.

With great caution, I say, "You never need fear being believed with me, Edmund. I am here to listen to you. I cannot promise to keep secrets from your father if I fear you are being harmed, but I will believe whatever you tell me, however strange it might seem."

I pause, and I expect it to only be a pause. This will not be enough. I'll need to push harder and nudge him toward the revelation. Or so I think, forgetting that, for all his maturity, my son is still a boy of five.

"Ghosts," he blurts. "I see ghosts."

"A lot of them?" I say in the same tone one might use to ask whether he sees many butterflies in the meadow.

He shakes his head.

"Do they bother you?" I ask.

His gaze shifts in a way that reminds me of his father, not looking aside but looking within, giving great thought to the question.

"I do not think so," he says. "They are not mean, and they do not try to frighten me. Some are very sad, and that makes me sad."

I beckon him to a nearby fallen tree, where I sit, and he perches beside me. I ask him questions, gently at first, but it quickly becomes clear that he's eager to talk about this. He tells me that he has always seen ghosts though it was only in the last couple of years that he realized what they were.

"When I was very little, I thought they were real," he says. "But then Margaret told me I was seeing ghosts."

"Margaret. She was your governess, wasn't she? The one who came with you from London and then went away?"

His gaze lowers, and his heels thump against the log. "Yes."

"You liked her, I presume."

"I..." A flash of almost wary guilt, and he chooses his next words with very adult care. "She was very nice. I liked that she talked to me about the ghosts. She snuck me sweets and played with me. But when Papa was around..." He wrinkles his nose. "She did not act the same when he was around."

"Ah."

Margaret had set her hat on August.

No, I correct. That is an unfair assumption. My husband is a very attractive man aside from his breeding and personal wealth. He could catch the eye of any red-blooded young governess. That did not mean she had plans to snare him, only that she noticed him and found him attractive and, yes, probably acted differently when he was about.

Edmund obviously liked her enough to entrust with his secret, and she seems to have been kind about it, so I owe her my gratitude and respect for that.

"Who did you see, just now?" I ask.

He hesitates.

"You don't need to tell—" I begin.

"I think it is my mother," he blurts.

"Wh-what?"

At my alarm, Edmund curls back into himself. "It is only a guess," he mumbles.

I take a deep breath. "Can you tell me why you think that?" I ask as gently as I can.

"It is a woman with blond hair, and she tells me she is watching over me."

"Has she said she's your mother?"

He shakes his head.

"Have you asked?"

He squirms. "I have asked who she is, and she says I know, but when I say my mother, she will not answer."

"So you can communicate with her." I make it a statement not a question, and he relaxes, obviously happy to move away from the subject of her identity.

"Sometimes," he says. "Sometimes she talks to me, and sometimes she does not."

"And today?"

"She did not talk. As soon as I saw her, she ran. But she was watching me. She always watches me." He pauses. "It's the good kind of watching, not the bad."

"The bad?"

One thin shoulder lifts. "Papa says that sometimes when people watch children, they are making sure they stay safe. But if somebody watching me feels bad or makes my stomach fluttery, I'm supposed to tell him."

Thank you, August. This is a lesson not often imparted in our world. August had his own troubles growing up as a lonely and handsome boy. Nothing that the modern world would term sexual abuse but certainly encounters that made him wary and anxious.

"So this woman watches over you."

He nods.

"And sometimes—but not always—she talks to you."

He nods again.

"Can you tell me what she looks like?"

His head tilts, so much like his father's that it makes my heart ache. He's giving the question deep consideration, and it is a moment before he says, "I do not ever see her close. She has blond hair, and her skin is very pale. She is not as tall as Mrs. Landon. Perhaps as tall as Violet. She is thin, I think. Like you and Violet."

"She doesn't come close even when she speaks to you?"

More considering, as if this question is more difficult than it might seem. "She comes closer to whisper to me, but it is often at night, and she flees if I turn on a lantern. She comes closer in the forest, but if I try to go near, she flees."

I give all this some thought. I don't do so in silence. I know well that silence in such situations sounds like doubt. As I think, I murmur to him, saying that must be frustrating sometimes, not being able to see or always speak to her, that I can see why it might seem to be his mother, but it is telling that she will not confirm that.

"Does your father know about this?" I ask finally.

He shakes his head. "Margaret said I ought not to upset him. She says he would believe me because I am his son, but it would worry him."

I'm not sure how I feel about Margaret's advice. It is wrong, of course. August should—must—be told. Yet I understand her caution.

I grew up in a family where the Sight was like left-handedness. It happened to some of us and was but a fact of life to be dealt with, not a cause for shame or worry. However, that open-mindedness does not mean we foolishly thought we should be as open with it as with being left-handed. Our parents cautioned us to discuss it with great care and only with those who also believed. Therefore, I cannot fault Margaret for her overabundance of caution. Her family's experience was likely very different than my own, and she did not know August as I did.

"I understand her concerns," I say, "but I believe your father should know."

Edmund tenses.

I continue, my voice gentle. "She said that he would believe you, did she not? Has he shown himself to be anything other than a trusting and reliable father? A kind father?"

Edmund shakes his head.

"Then I propose you allow me to broach the subject with him. I will sidestep into it." I make a little motion with my hand that sets him giggling. "I can be very crafty. I will ascertain his feelings on ghostly phenomena, and if he seems open to it, I will suggest, ever so gently, that you have seen something. If he balks, I'll stop short of sharing your secret. Is that reasonable?"

He considers and then says, "I would like him to know. I do not like keeping secrets from him."

"Agreed. Then I shall approach him on the matter this evening."

FIFTEEN

'M IN THE library awaiting August, and I'm feeling more myself than I have since I stepped through time nearly a week ago. Feeling as if I have my feet planted firmly in this world once more.

In this past week, I've wobbled and weaved, as if I were back on my honeymoon voyage, finding my sea legs. I've thought often of Bronwyn, coming through from the twenty-first century. How foreign it must have seemed to her. As foreign, I suppose, as the day I stepped through and found myself gaping at plastic bottles, blushing at a bikini-clad model. I laugh at myself for that now, particularly the latter. To me, she'd been practically naked. In the modern world, she'd been quite decorously clad, the bottle having been twenty years old.

That bottle had been from Bronwyn's teen years, I realize now. Back when August saw her. Then something happened, and she'd "vanished" from Thorne Manor as surely as I vanished from my old life, all her teen girl beauty products left on that table, gathering dust.

Are my belongings gathering dust somewhere? Have they been packed away? Or thrown into the dustbin as fast as August could throw them, scouring away every trace of his feckless wife?

How in the hell could he think—?

I stop that thought, too, and return to where I started. How strange this would have seemed to Bronwyn. How strange it is to me now, like an old sweater that is blissfully comfortable and familiar but feels just a little too small, too confining.

I have seen more. I have seen a place where I could cross an ocean on a weekend holiday, where I could call someone across that ocean on a whim, and where no one batted an eye at me opening my own shop or walking alone after dark. There, I was no longer eccentric and odd, and that was glorious. I saw the problems, too. A speed of life that left me always feeling I was barely keeping afloat, should be doing more, making more of myself. An odd lack of communication despite the easy abundance of it, and a distance between neighbors and family. And, on the other hand, I come here, and I'm even more aware of our rampant classism and prejudice, which they also still struggle with in the modern world.

So much to think about, and it's been difficult settling into my skin here. Difficult to act as if I'm content with my lot, happy to be a Victorian woman again. I'm finding the rhythm, though. Finding my confidence, too. As I browse the library, I'm well aware that the books should be off limits to staff. Yet I'm Edmund's governess with an excuse for perusing the library. August is not his brother and would not begrudge his staff a borrowed book or two.

When August walks in, I'm curled up in a chair reading. At his entrance, I merely set the book aside and straighten in my seat without haste or fear of blunder.

"Good evening, sir," I say, and my voice sounds normal, but he gives a start and blinks at me, and I realize that perhaps I'm inhabiting my old skin a little too comfortably, my manner not quite governess-appropriate.

I rise. "Do you have a few moments? I wish to discuss a confidence your son shared with me."

He tenses, and the look that slides my way is guarded. It has been only a few days, and Edmund is already sharing confidences? August throws

off any discomfort with a roll of his shoulders, and then his voice takes on a distinctly clipped tone.

"If it is a matter of safety, Miss Smith, then yes, it is appropriate to share it. But if it is a small confidence he expects to be kept secret perhaps you should do so. My son's trust is not a thing to be trifled with."

"Agreed," I say. "But he has given me permission to share it."

He relaxes, settles into a chair and motions for me to do the same. I take the one I'd been using.

"As you are aware," I say, "I had an incident that led to... Well, I heard stories of hauntings."

"Bloody hell." August thumps back in his chair. "Is that what this is about? Edmund has heard the servants talking, and he's frightened." His head snaps up. "You were not encouraging that, I hope."

"I was not," I say, my voice brittle. "I *would* not, sir. I have no idea what is happening in this house, but *that* isn't the behavior of a ghost."

I say it with far more conviction than I feel. Then I wait for him to realize I have said something very different from *There is no such thing as ghosts.*

August only nods, his gaze moving to the window, distraction settling in.

I try again. "I have known people who see ghosts, and they've never had one do anything like what happened last night."

Another nod, even more distracted, as if I'm just repeating myself now.

I continue, "Naturally, Edmund has heard the stories. He is not frightened, though. In his experience, ghosts do not have malicious intentions."

Now his gaze swings to me. "What did you say?"

There's a look on his face I know well, a darkening that warns of a sparked temper. I pull back. I have indeed blundered this evening. I'd promised Edmund I would approach this gradually, feeling out his father's thoughts on the subject of ghosts. Instead, I gave two feeble attempts to ascertain those thoughts, and then, when I received no response, I plowed forward.

My son's trust is not a thing to be trifled with.

Yet I've done exactly that. As much as I reassured Edmund I would proceed with care, in my gut, I thought there was little need. August had

readily accepted my sister's Second Sight. Embraced it, even, fascinated by the possibilities and pestering her with questions until she would run mock-shrieking from the room.

That man believed in ghosts. That man would not blink at his son seeing them, especially not when he knew the Sight ran in Edmund's maternal family.

Yet now I see the flash in his eyes, and I shrink back, an inner voice screaming I've made a mistake, that his attitude has changed.

"Did you just say my son sees *ghosts?*"

I choose each word with the care of picking my way through shark-infested waters. "I have known people who do, which I did not divulge to him. He saw something in the forest, and when I pressed him—concerned it could be an interloper—he confessed that he occasionally sees figures that he believes to be ghosts."

"Why would he not tell me this?"

I inwardly breathe a sigh of relief while keeping outwardly stoic. "Is it possible he feared he might not be believed? That, like many, you might doubt the existence of ghosts?"

August sputters. "Of course not. The Sight runs in his moth— My sister-in-law has it."

"And he knows that?"

August settles back into his seat. "Well, no, but I don't understand why my son did not trust me with this, yet trusted you, a new governess."

"Your son's secret was discovered before me. By someone who convinced him to keep it from others."

That spark again, temper rising. "Who? If one of the staff counseled my son to silence, or worse, doubted whether he was seeing—"

"No," I cut in. "No one currently on staff was involved."

"A governess then. One of those blasted girls vastly overstepped her bounds."

My voice ices. "One of those *blasted girls* worried for Edmund. She believed him but feared you would not. She counseled him incorrectly

out of kindness. She did not know you, and so she feared your reaction. I do not know you, either, yet I was emboldened by your open-mindedness regarding his reading problems, and all his reports paint you as a loving and devoted father. Being undoubtedly older than that *blasted girl*, I took a chance she dared not."

My tone is not at all correct for a governess speaking to her employer, yet August is too preoccupied to notice. He's busy realizing that his son sees ghosts, and my defense of this unnamed governess barely skims the surface of his consciousness.

He wants to know more about Edmund's experiences, and I tell him what I can. I leave out one particular part: his son's suspicion that the ghost may be his mother's. I do not want to hear August's thoughts on that.

I remind myself that all will be cleared up soon. *Very* soon, because just as I began to fret about the speed of Bronwyn's potential intervention, another possibility landed on my lap. One that fills me with far greater excitement, no disrespect to the new Lady Thorne.

"You mentioned your sister-in-law," I say. "I presume you are referring to his mother's sister."

August flinches, just a little, at the word *mother*, and I bite my tongue against tartness.

"She should speak to him," I say, "as soon as possible. Is she in London?"

He does not answer. His gaze returns to the window.

"Sir," I say. "Is your sister-in-law—?"

"I do not know. We communicate very little these days."

"*What?*"

His head spins my way, and I hurry on to cover my shock with blather, but I barely hear my own words. Whatever I'm saying, it does not erase the horror and, yes, outrage on my face. I push to my feet and make a show of fussing with the fire, saying all this talk of ghosts has given me quite the chill.

What gives me quite the chill is his words. He communicates little with Miranda? With Portia, too? That will not be their choice. Not in a million years.

I've spent four years waiting to get home to my husband and son, but they are not the only people I grieved for. I missed my sisters with an ache only slightly eased by the knowledge that they were capable young women, already embarking on their own lives. They had an income and each other and August. That is where I'd laid the largest heap of my relief. They had August. He loved them as a brother and would be there for them. And now...?

We communicate very little these days.

I cannot begin to fathom this. I cling to one last desperate hope to absolve him of guilt.

"Is your sister-in-law abroad?" I ask.

Silence that speaks so much.

"I presume that is a no," I say, pushing to my feet and slamming the poker back with more force than I intend. "I realize I am overstepping, sir, but with your wife gone, female relations would be important to your son. If your wife has sisters—"

"You are indeed overstepping, Miss Smith."

I lift my gaze to lock with his, but he's already turned back to the window. "My sisters-in-law play a role in my son's life. It has been difficult for all of us. They disagree with my assessment of the cause of their sister's absence."

I snort, and he turns sharply, but I'm back at the fire, crouched as if to warm myself though my anger could light the very logs ablaze.

"I believe his aunt should speak to him," I say. "That is *my* assessment of this as his governess. You may disagree..."

"I'm not certain I dare. In fact, I'm quite certain I do not."

I glance over to see him, half-shadowed in the firelight, a tiny but unmistakable smile on his lips.

He turns back to the window. "I shall write to her. I believe she is in London. I will ask her to come forthwith. You may even post the letter yourself if that helps assuage your concerns."

My heart trips so fast I have to duck my chin in a nod and pray I don't glow with joy. He expects me to demur, perhaps even apologize for my

presumption. I will not. I'll only nod and hope he actually does give me that letter so I might see the address and send one of my own.

Miranda will come. My Miranda. My *sister.* She will get that letter and fly here as fast as she can, and I can explain it all to her and this nightmare will finally end.

SIXTEEN

N MY ROOM, I write letter after letter to Miranda. None of them are quite right, and I inwardly joke that I'm simply intimidated writing to my literary sister, fretting over word choice and punctuation. The truth is that this terrifies me almost as much as telling August.

My husband and son are not the only ones I abandoned, however unwillingly. It doesn't matter if Portia was twenty-five when I vanished and Miranda twenty-two, both adults embarking on their own lives, accustomed to doing so since my marriage. It still felt like abandonment, and if even August hasn't been there for them…

Pain and confusion and anger surge.

My sisters, August? Truly. Did they remind you too much of me? Look too much like me? Sound too much like me? Their very expressions and gestures echoing those of the woman who left you?

Emotionally, I understand the estrangement. Rationally, I cannot fathom it. When August felt that abandoned child's urge to shun my sisters, surely, his mind would have rebelled against it, horrified by the thought of keeping Edmund—their only tie to me—from them.

What have you done, August?

And can I ever forgive you for it?

That last, I fear, will not be an issue. I am beginning to suspect he will neither need nor want my forgiveness. If he shunned my sisters, whom he'd loved like his own, then that speaks to a pain that will not dissipate on learning the truth.

It should dissipate, shouldn't it?

You were mistaken, dear August. I never left you. I spent four years trying frantically to return.

Logically, I should be forgiven. Yet it is becoming increasingly clear that logic has little to do with guiding my husband's actions. In the world of business, yes. In the world of his heart? No, and I'm a fool if I ever thought otherwise. He married me, didn't he? As illogical a choice as any man has made.

I can still hear his brothers after he'd announced the news and I'd retired with the other ladies.

Are you mad, August? A baker? A doctor's daughter? She's practically penniless. Certainly pretty. Is that what's turned your head? She is a beautiful girl, but she has nothing else to offer. And she's four-and-twenty. An aging dowryless spinster who is in trade.

I force those memories to let the "aging spinster" part nudge more pleasant thoughts. Are my sisters wed? They were old enough when I left. Past old enough, many would argue, but despite the historical fiction I read in the twenty-first century, we were not all expected to wed by eighteen. While August's brothers blustered, by twenty-four, I was the equivalent of a thirty-year-old in the modern world. Getting older but certainly not beyond my wedding-cake expiry date.

Upon my marriage to August, he had settled both my sisters with dowries. While he'd been inclined to be generous, even lavish, I'd counseled for modest dowries. My sisters did not require bribes to find husbands, and the larger the dowry, the more likely they'd find fortune-hunters instead.

When I left, Portia had been engaged to a lovely young man with a solid name and a future as a solicitor. Did they wed? I hope so. He had

truly been lovely, the perfect match for my brilliant, earnest sister. Then there was Miranda. Ah, Miranda, I hate to say that I hope you did not wed the young fellow you were courting. I'd been far less pleased with that match. Miranda, who saw more than mere ghosts, who saw entire worlds beyond our own and feverishly chronicled the stories of her imagination. Miranda, who'd been on the verge of publishing her first novel when I disappeared. Miranda, whose taste in men was questionable at best.

I finally give up on writing the perfect letter and settle for an adequate one. Two letters, to be precise. Anyone who has younger siblings knows the perils of treating them as a unit. They are separate people deserving unique letters, even if the core of the missive remains consistent. Both letters will need to go to Miranda though I now wonder whether I should have suggested August also mail his other sister-in-law.

Which would require "Clara Smith" knowing he has another sister-in-law.

I ought to find a way to broach the subject before the letter is posted. As he claims not to quite know where to find Miranda—which I'm certain is a falsehood—it would make sense to also send a letter to any other relative. Such as another sister, perhaps?

There are many holes in my plan, but I paper over them all. I *have* a plan with multiple prongs that will ensure I can reveal myself in the next few days. Bronwyn Thorne will come or Miranda will or even Portia, who might not be able to help Edmund but would surely fly here upon learning I'm alive.

Strategy in place, I crawl into bed and am soon asleep.

Go, a voice whispers into my dreams. *Go while you can. Go before it is too late.*

I toss and turn in sleep, that voice like a gnat at my ear, annoying but nothing more. Even in my subconscious, I have declared myself set upon

a course, and I am going nowhere. Yet the voice keeps whispering until "Begone!" trumpets in my ear, and I bolt awake, shivering so hard my teeth chatter, covered in goosebumps, my bed slick with sweat.

Even in my waking confusion, this does not seem right. I was not dreaming anything frightening. The voice did not scare me. My heart is not racing. So why am I so cold my teeth chatter?

Because I've lost my blankets. Earlier, I'd cajoled Violet into providing two extras to go with my threadbare coverlet. In the modern world, I saw many a Victorian drama depicting sleepers snug in their beds with a roaring fire, and I'd laughed heartily at the notion. Even in wealthy families where there is an abundance of wood and coal, keeping the fire going all night would be a frivolous luxury. It is lit in the morning, leaving sleepers in a drafty room where the window is always open to allow "miasmas" to escape—miasmas being the alleged cause of disease.

To compensate for the cold room, bedclothes are thick and warm, as are blankets...unless you're the governess stashed in an icy room with the most miserly of coverings. Also, if you're a governess who has grown accustomed to the modern habit of sleeping unclothed. I'm wearing a nightgown for modesty, but I'd borrowed one of Bronwyn's Victorian ones, and let's just say she clearly shared modern sensibilities. It is the sort one would wear here in July, not October.

All that is to explain why I woke shivering. I'd kicked off my blankets, and I just need to pull them up again. I reach down to find that my blankets are not at the foot of my mattress. Nor are they on the floor. As I blink in the moonlight, I see a heap clear across the room.

That makes no sense. I could hardly hurl them there in my sleep. Could I have forgotten to put them on last night?

No, the fire had been quite out when I finally went to bed, and I'd snuggled beneath my new blankets smelling of sweet lavender.

I must have moved them there in my sleep. While it isn't something I do habitually, I had walked in my sleep a few times both after my parents'

deaths and after I crossed into the modern world. Stress-induced somnambulism as they would say in the twenty-first century.

Even as I rise to retrieve the blankets, my brain whispers that this explanation does not make sense. I'm half-consumed by those thoughts when my hand touches down on the bed, propelling me from it. It is wet. Cold and wet.

That's what I'd woken to, hadn't I? Not just the freezing chill but a dampness I'd initially chalked up to night sweats. Except I wouldn't be sweating in the cold, and I hadn't been frightened by any dream. Also? My bed isn't just damp. It's *soaked*, as if with ice water.

It isn't ice water, though. Not the modern sort, from a tap with cubes. There's a stink to this water, the smell of rotting vegetation. Pond water. Cold pond water.

Like the pond where August's sister died. The pond where Margaret may have met her own untimely end. I lower my face to the sheets, double-checking the smell.

That's when something touches my foot.

I leap up and fumble with the lantern. It won't light, and my heart hammers as I try again and again.

A cloud passes over the moon, plunging the room into darkness. Something whispers past me, ice cold, and I let out a shriek. Gripping the lantern in both hands, I move to the window. It's wide open, the bitter night air whipping in.

I close it and huddle there against the gray of the cloudy night as I lift the lantern. The wick is gone. I turn the knob to raise it, but there's no wick at all.

I back against the window, surveying the room. It is empty. Empty and still now that the window is shut. Yet I stay there, pressed against the cold glass.

There's a candle in the wardrobe, five paces away. I saw it when I was putting away my clothing. A candle there and matches over the fireplace. I mentally map out the route.

Really? You're in an empty bedroom, not a forest beset by wolves.

Am I sure it's empty?

Where would someone hide? Under the bed? You can see it's clear. In the wardrobe? Your five-year-old son would barely fit in there.

That isn't what I mean, and I know it. I keep remembering that whisper, that cold air sliding over me.

Yes, the whispers that you dreamed. The cold air when the window was wide open.

As I take a step toward the wardrobe, something moves outside my window. I barely catch the motion, and I spin to look out. I'm gazing down on a circular drive and gardens, and it is empty.

Cold fingers creep over the back of my neck.

Stop that. You're just spooking yourself.

I rub my neck and peer out the window. A bolt of orange near the gardens has me yelping...until I see it's only Surrey pouncing on a mouse. I swear the cat sees me and glowers up before trotting off with her midnight snack.

I take a deep breath and turn and—

Nothing. Nothing catches my eye, nothing whispers, nothing reaches icy fingers to touch me. In three long steps, I'm at the wardrobe. I yank open the door with a little more force than necessary, my gaze skating across the shadowy room. It remains still and silent, but I keep one eye on my surroundings as I feel around the wardrobe shelf. I know I saw a candle here, on a heap of discarded clothing—extras from governesses past.

My fingers touch the clothing, running over thin wool until they find wax. I grip the candle and pull it out, the shift coming along and—

Something thuds to the floor, and I jump, squeaking, hands raised.

Is that a karate chop? Really? Two self-defense classes, and you're going to karate-chop a ghost?

I quickly lower my hands and scan the room. It remains empty and silent. When my gaze dips to the floor, I see a book and a woolen shift. The book must have been wrapped in it. By now, the clouds have shifted

from the moon, and I can see clearly enough to set the candle aside. I lift the book. It's a journal. I'm cracking it open when the knob on my bedroom door jiggles.

I'm about to call a "hello?" when I remember the situation. Yes, two minutes ago, I was pressed against the window, heart hammering, gaze tripping over the room looking for a ghost. Now my doorknob turns, and I almost call a hearty welcome.

Well, not exactly "hearty." It is the middle of the night. Still, I almost speak as if there's a person at my door. There could be. In fact, there probably is. My yelps and shrieks may have woken someone deeper in the house. Yet that is not an enquiring rap. Someone turned the handle. No, jiggled it—not even a true turning.

I creep to the door to see the key in the lock, still engaged. I'd locked it last night so I could relax without my wig and makeup and "figure enhancers." It is still locked.

Which means no one was in my room. No one whispered in my ear. No one stole my blankets. No one soaked my bed. No living person anyway.

The knob rattles again.

Three long strides, and I'm snatching up the fireplace poker. Gripping it in both hands, I creep to the door and press my ear against it. Silence.

I turn the key as carefully as I can. When it still gives a hard click, I tense, listening for the sound of running footsteps. Nothing comes, and I turn the knob and ease it open.

The hall is empty. I step out, fire poker in hand. A moment's consideration, and then my gaze flies to the nursery door down the hall, suddenly afraid that something woke Edmund and he'd come cautiously looking for me, looking for reassurance.

His door is shut. I tiptoe to it and put my ear to the door. Nothing. It is silent inside and, from the sliver around the door, it is dark. I touch the knob. As Edmund's mother, I long to open it and creep in and make sure he is all right as I did when he was a baby, waking in the night and feeling

compelled to spend five minutes hovering over his bassinet, watching his chest rise and fall in sleep.

As Edmund's governess, though, I cannot enter his sleeping chamber without cause, and I have no cause. I'm stepping back from the door when a whisper slides down the hall. I wheel, poker raised. Another whisper, and I can't tell whether it's a voice or fabric brushing the walls, but it comes from around the corner.

I slip down there, step by careful step. When I reach the corner, I adjust my grip on the poker, my palms slick with sweat. I strain to listen but hear nothing. Two shallow breaths, and then I swing out just as someone darts around the next corner, leaving me nothing more than the flip of a skirt.

I don't bother to be silent now. I race down the hall and reach the top of the steps to again catch only the blur of a skirt disappearing around another corner. I jog down the stairs and along the corridor, chasing nothing. There is no blur of motion ahead. No patter of footsteps. I slow to listen and hear nothing, but still, I pursue, running through the front rooms until—

Something moves beyond the massive front parlor windows. I freeze and turn to see what is undeniably a person outside, slipping through shadows, barely more than a shadow herself as she flees. A female figure. Long light hair. Pale blue dress. That's all I can make out from here, and I tear my gaze away to run to the nearest door. I fumble with the lock, and then I'm out. Down the step and onto the drive, stones cutting into my bare feet and then grass, cold and wet with autumnal dew. I keep running, but the figure is long gone. I don't care. I saw where she went. Heading toward the forest.

I'm running across the wet grass when...

I'm not certain what I hear. The click of a door that should be too far for my ears to detect? Perhaps I hear nothing at all. Perhaps I merely sense something that has me turning to see light blazing in an upper room. Light blazing and a figure on the balcony. The unmistakable figure of August, staring out at me.

I wheel, words jamming in my throat as I see him there, in his night-shirt, gripping the stone parapet wall. I see him, and it doesn't matter how many times I've seen him since I've returned, my heart seizes with grief and longing and pain.

This is what I missed out on for four years of my life. This is what I might never have again. My husband, not the distant and distracted ver-sion I get as Clara Smith, but the man I saw every morning, hair tousling over his forehead, face smooth and young and sweetly innocent.

How many times did I see him like this after we'd wed, when we'd come to Courtenay Hall, and he'd appear there to watch me return from my ride? I'd see him, and my insides would light up with firecracker bursts of joy and pleasure and desire, and I'd tell my horse to hurry, please hurry. Take me home. Take me back to August.

That was Rosalind Courtenay, young bride. I am not that girl—or woman—and so the words stopper in my throat. I swallow them back and instead lift a hand in greeting, ready to call out an apology.

So sorry to wake you, sir. Why yes, I am running about the yard in my shift, brandishing a fire poker, but I have an excellent explanation. Or I will, once I think of one.

As I begin to call to him, the clouds shift again, casting him into focus, and I see his expression and the words again die in my throat.

The way he is looking at me… Well, yes, I'm scandalously attired in my shift and bare feet, but the look he's giving is a very different sort of shock. The same shock one might give upon seeing a ghost.

Does he think me a ghost? In my white shift, I'm sure I look like one. I glance down and see myself, my too-thin body in this oversized shift, big enough to accommodate my figure-altering disguise…which I am not wearing.

I am not in any disguise. No makeup, no shape-changing garb and no wig. It's me, standing on the lawn in my shift, looking up at my husband, fifty feet away on a balcony, clutching the edge as if he might fall.

Run to him.

Run right now. Run to stand beneath his balcony, Juliet to his Romeo.

I am back, August. It is me, and I have come back to you.

His lips part, and even if I'm too far to hear his words, it still reaches my ear.

Rosalind.

I take one step, and he staggers back, and any expression on his face vanishes, the wall slamming down as he backs away.

I see his face, and fear rushes through me. Ice-cold fear. Wild, gibbering fear. I will run to him, and he will slam the door as surely as he's closed off that expression. I will run to him and tell him everything, and he will not see his wife returned—he will see a traitor who tried to trick him, who only stepped forward when she was caught.

I have bungled this. Bungled it so badly, and yet even in this wild moment of despair, I don't see what else I could have done. I needed information, and I needed assistance and support.

I did not run directly to him from Thorne Manor because I feared he might be wed, and I needed to know the situation in advance.

I arrived as his governess by mistake, Fate taking a hand to place me on this board while cackling with delight at her fine trick. You want to go home, Rosalind? Here, let me take you home, where you must either play governess to your son or tell the truth and risk Mrs. Landon calling for a straitjacket.

I played along, waiting for August's return, thinking I could then tell him all, only to realize he hated me and would believe I had abandoned him unless I had proof of my story.

I set that proof in motion—with Bronwyn Thorne—and planned to bring my sister to intercede sooner. Intercede and protect me from prison or a lunatic's cell.

And here I stand, exposed and revealed, my husband recoiling from the sight of me.

August keeps backing away until he is in the house. The door shuts with a firm slap. He saw me—saw his wife on the lawn, the wife he has

not seen in four years, the wife he swore he loved with all his heart—and he went back into the house and shut the door.

Begone, Rosalind. Please, please, begone.

My chest seizes, a sob half-torn from me. Another light turns on, this in the staff quarters. I pause for a split second. And then I run back to the house.

SEVENTEEN

AM IN MY room, waiting to be summoned. Waiting for someone to come and tell me Mr. August wishes to speak to me. Or wishes me gone.

I made it back to my room undetected. Someone had been awake downstairs but had not left their room yet, and I'd escaped to mine. From my quarters, I cannot hear what is happening in the rest of the house, and I dare not sneak out to investigate. I do, however, leave my door open and pull the rickety chair over to sit beside it with my candle.

When they come, I will be ready.

They do not come.

I catch distant sounds, but none that indicate alarm, nor that the master of the house is up and calling for staff. There would be a flurry of activity for that—the nighttime appearance of an angry or agitated master of the house.

Nothing happens, though, and I can only draw one conclusion. August has decided he imagined me. He did not recognize me as Clara, the governess. If he did, he'd have ordered me brought to him or turned out of the house. He woke, drawn to the balcony, where he thought he saw

his long-departed wife on the lawn. And he promptly decided he had not. He was imagining me or, better yet, still asleep.

So he went back to bed.

He saw me, fifty feet away…and went back to bed.

I want to flee. Grab what I can and run, and I can pretend that is the best course of action, but really, I just want to run. Run and hide and sob until I can sob no more.

I squelch that urge, but I must seriously consider leaving. I do not want August "discovering" me. That will seem as if I tried to trick him. I want to tell him the truth with an explanation, one that requires me stepping from the shadows of my own accord. I cannot take the chance that he yanks me from them. I dare not wish for a reconciliation—tonight proved yet again that was a foolish fancy—but I must reunite with my son, and to do that, I need the moral high ground. I will lose it if August uncovers my "plot" to wriggle back into my son's life under false pretenses.

I have made such a mess of this. I can cut myself some slack with the reminder that I didn't see another way. That I thought I'd considered all options carefully and logically, and if I did not, it was a failure of imagination or a lack of recognition that emotion would play a role. The point is that I did not rush in headlong. I considered my options, as carefully as I always do, and I made mistakes.

Had I foreseen myself sitting here, in this position, terrified of being uncovered, I'd have said to Hugh at the train station, "I am Rosalind Courtenay," and worked with whatever came of that. Of course, that's easy to say now. I'd have sung a very different tune if I'd done so and was now in an asylum, begging for someone, anyone, to listen to me.

A plan then.

I will not flee in the night. I won't do that to Edmund. He just revealed his deepest secret, one he'd been warned might not be believed. If I disappear in the night, he will blame himself. He is too bright and too sensitive—too much his father's son in every way. I will never undo such damage to our relationship.

I will go, though. I must, before this gets worse. I will see Edmund at breakfast and tell him I must leave for a day. I'll tell him I'm going to fetch someone he can speak to about his ghosts. Then I will leave a note and go, invoking Mrs. Landon's wrath and August's disgust, but I hardly need worry about retaining my job after that. Edmund is all that matters. Speak to Edmund.

My bed is still drenched, and I'm not venturing out for new sheets. I'll hang the sheet out the window to dry in hopes I won't need to tell Violet. If I do, and she looks askance at my wet sheet, well, I won't need to worry about that for long.

Talk to Edmund. Leave my note. Slip away. Return with Miranda and, if I'm truly fortunate, Bronwyn Thorne as well. Return as Rosalind Courtenay, and whether August accepts me or not, he cannot take my name from me. Nor can he take my son. That is all that matters in the end.

⁓↶↷⁓

I T IS morning, and I am not gone. I cannot go. Not yet, and I inwardly rage at that. Rage at myself because I cannot tell whether I'm making a rational decision or an emotional one.

I wake to a house in disarray. The master has left. Cook and Mrs. Landon might grumble that August returns without suitable warning, but that only means when he travels for business, he returns as soon as he can to be with Edmund. Leaving is an entirely different matter. In that, August is as punctual as any newly hired clerk. Barring any emergency, the staff know exactly when he will depart, and he does not go one moment sooner.

This is not an emergency. This is…

"Hugh says the master is in a state, miss," Violet whispers as she brings my breakfast tray. "I ought not to spread tales, but I thought you should know. In case young Edmund is alarmed."

"Do you know what happened?" I ask. "So I may come up with a story for Edmund, halfway to the truth. That is always best."

"I don't know anything, miss. Hugh only says Mr. August was in the stable at dawn, asking for his horse to be made ready. Hugh and the stable boy were the only ones there, and Hugh's only been head groom since his father passed last spring. He's young for the position, and he hasn't any experience with such a thing."

With such a thing. Part of me wants to laugh. August wishes to leave early, and it throws the staff into such tumult one would think he'd shown up in a leather jacket and jeans and started crooning "Blue Moon" to the horses. But while I can rail against classism and the restrictions on staff, the upper class is not free to do as they wish, either. A master who disrupts the efficiency of his household risks panicking the staff *and* drawing the ire of the housekeeper.

Hugh's confusion, then, is understandable. According to Violet, August had not eaten breakfast—which Cook would already be awake preparing—and had not even dressed properly, which would upset Price, the butler who also served as his valet. His fire hadn't even been laid, and the poor housemaid who served the master's chambers would be in a tizzy, worried sick that she'd be reprimanded for failing to realize he'd woken early.

Hugh had sent the stable boy to fetch tea and a cold breakfast—and inform Cook—but August rode out before it could arrive.

"And he said nothing about the reason for the departure?" I ask.

You know the reason for the departure, Rosalind.

I silence the voice and keep my face neutral as I say, "Business perhaps? He has great responsibilities since his brother passed, and I heard he also has his own business interests with a friend."

"Lord Thorne, yes, but it wasn't business, miss. No telegraph came. Mr. Price said he heard the master up in the night. His room was lit, and he was pacing about, but he told Mr. Price he was fine and did not wish to be disturbed. Then he rode out in a state this morning, not even shaven." She pauses. "He did tell Hugh he'll return by dinner. You can tell the young master that. If Mr. August promised it, he will be here."

And that is all I have. August saw me in the yard, spent the rest of the night awake and pacing, and rode off this morning. I have no idea what that means beyond this one thing: that I cannot leave, too. I must stay for Edmund's sake. I'll go tonight, though. I'll speak to Edmund later about my departure and slip off as soon as August returns.

For now, I must act as if nothing has happened. Reassure Edmund. Tell him that his father had to leave—before he could say good morning—but he will be back for dinner.

THE MORNING passes without further incident. My sheet was dry enough that I did not mention last night's disturbance to Violet. With August gone, a possible haunting is the last thing on my mind.

Sorry, specter, but I have more important things to attend to. Please return to terrify me properly at another time.

I put the haunting from my mind. I must, or I'll spend the morning picking it apart, weighing the likelihood it is a ghostly opponent versus a living one. It is my opponent either way. That seems beyond question.

Ghost or human, they have been frightening away governesses long before I arrived, and it is almost ironic that I'm being scared off for that role in Edmund's life rather than for the real—and much more serious—one I occupy as his mother.

Edmund accepts the news about his father with equanimity. He's disappointed, but they hadn't planned to do anything together until that evening. Edmund had lessons, and August had paperwork.

Edmund does not ask where his father went or why. He is a boy of his time and class, and however attentive August is, Edmund will not expect an accounting of his father's time, unlike a modern child his age, who might watch the clock for a parent's return from work.

It is a blustery day, threatening an ill-favored afternoon, gray clouds already rolling in. We decide then to walk immediately after breakfast,

despite Mrs. Landon's grumblings that it was not healthy to take exercise so soon after dining. Yes, there were many, many things about Victorian health care that I'm just going to need to ignore, lest I scandalize people with proclamations like "illness is caused by germs not miasmas" or "you cannot catch cold from cold weather" or, worst of all, "young ladies can exert themselves without fear of dislodging their reproductive organs."

In the modern world, I'd spent hours reading medical blogs and listening to podcasts, fascinated by the advances there. I can laugh now, but even my father, who was advanced enough not to believe the uterus wandered, held many incorrect beliefs, understandable given the limited knowledge of science at the time.

So we must bundle up against the cold morning, or if Edmund sniffles later, I shall be blamed. Once out, we shed the more confining garments, and walk and run and play games in the forest.

Am I hoping Edmund might see his ghost again? Yes. I want a fuller description to see whether she matches the figure I chased last night. Yet he sees nothing, and when the rain begins drizzling down, we return to the house for hot tea and the last of the cookies.

Lessons come next. Then lunch and more lessons. It is nearing midafternoon when I'm summoned to speak to Mrs. Landon. Alone.

"I'll watch the young master, miss," Violet says when I express concern. "One of the barn cats had kittens last night, and Hugh was hoping he could show them."

"An excellent idea," I say. "Thank you. I will not be overlong, I hope. If you finish with that, bring him inside, please, and wait with him in the library."

She agrees, and I go to speak to Mrs. Landon.

⁓⁓⁓

AM I terrified of what Mrs. Landon wants with me? Of course I am. In my experience, housekeepers are formidable creatures. The only exception is

William Thorne's, but William is always the exception. Never one to follow convention, his housekeeper is not only kind but also married with
children, which is common enough in the modern world…but not in this
one. I would never say that marriage and children soften a woman, but for
the Victorian housekeeper, unless she is a widow, she will be middle-aged
with nothing except the all-consuming task of running someone else's
household. Little wonder they are intimidating women.

Last night makes me even more concerned that the timing of this
meeting bodes ill. Perhaps August did realize the woman on the lawn was
me, both as Rosalind and Clara. Perhaps he's fled to let his housekeeper
fire me. Or perhaps Violet reported an odd smell to my bedsheets, and I've
been summoned to make an accounting for it.

Or maybe, just maybe, Mrs. Landon is simply being a world-class pain-
in-the-ass, summoning me to prove that she can, whenever she likes. Yes,
that is the truth of the matter. There is no urgent reason she needs to speak
to me midafternoon, when I am tasked with watching my charge. She just
decided that this was a fine time to take me aside for a thirty-minute chat.
I'd have appreciated that if it really was a chat, a friendly conversation
between an older professional woman and a younger one, ensuring my
transition into the household is smooth for all.

Instead, she expresses her displeasure with my "newfangled" teaching methods and warns that the only reason I'll be permitted to continue
is that Mr. August approves. Which, one would think—as the boy's father
and our employer—should be the only opinion that mattered. She wants
me to know that she's watching me in every possible way. She isn't convinced that I'm suitable either as a governess or as a member of her staff.
She berates me for being distant and aloof with the staff while also berat-
ing me for spending too much time talking to them, treating them as my
equals and forgetting my loftier position.

In modern terms, she called me in to give me shit and make a power
play. Governesses and housekeepers do indeed inhabit a loftier position,
one that might be called equal. Mrs. Landon is reminding me that we are

 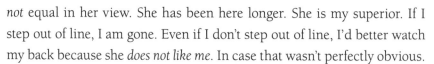

not equal in her view. She has been here longer. She is my superior. If I step out of line, I am gone. Even if I don't step out of line, I'd better watch my back because she *does not like me*. In case that wasn't perfectly obvious.

After our talk, she invites me to take tea with her, which should be a friendly gesture. It would be from anyone else. Here it is yet another power play. *I dare you to refuse.* I get the message, but I still try, with a reminder that I'm supposed to be watching Edmund and he will be ready for his tea soon.

"Violet has him, does she not? Violet and Hugh?" Mrs. Landon's gray eyes pierce mine. "I trust them. Don't you?"

"I do not know them well enough to say, other than that I find them both lovely young people, and I am certain they would not be in your employ if they could not be trusted."

"They can. Hugh grew up here, and Violet came with the highest personal recommendations."

"Then I will take tea though I cannot linger. I do have two more lessons before dinner and the return of Mr. Courtenay." I smile. "I know Edmund will wish to be done his work before then."

Mrs. Landon sniffs. "The boy is far too attached to his father, and his father to him. It would do him good to have lessons in the evening."

"Perhaps, but his father does not wish him to work after dinner, and I must do as he wishes."

Mrs. Landon calls for tea, and it has only just arrived when Violet runs in, panting, her hair in disarray.

"Violet!" Mrs. Landon says, pushing to her feet. "We do not run through the house like children. What kind of example does that set for young Edmund?"

"It-it is the lad—the young master," she pants. "He-he is gone."

EIGHTEEN

DMUND WAS IN the stable, watching the kittens, seemingly engrossed in them, and so Violet stepped aside to speak with Hugh. Speak with him? Or steal a few private moments with him? I have my suspicions about the nature of their relationship. I would never say anything in front of Mrs. Landon, or no matter how good an employee Violet is, she might find herself without a position. Groom and maid liaisons were common, expected even, so long as they led to marriage and not a nine-month stay in the country. Also, if the grooms are romancing the maids, there is less likelihood the master of the house will seduce the young women. Still, I suspect Mrs. Landon runs a tighter ship than that.

What they were doing is not important. The point is that Edmund is missing, which is more cause for panic from Violet than the housekeeper. As I learned on my first evening here, Edmund often runs off. I suspect even that phrase—running off—puts too severe a face on his actions. It is his home. If he tires of his current activity and wishes to wander and explore and play, that should be his prerogative. It would be, if he weren't five years old.

As Edmund's mother, I should be in a panic. But, while my stomach twists and I'm certainly out of my chair in a flash, I inwardly side more with

Mrs. Landon, who declares, "That boy!" and chastises Violet for her panic, saying, "He is fine. We simply need to find him before his father returns."

Even Violet, I suspect, is panicking mostly because the young master disappeared on her watch. She will be reprimanded for this, and I'm not certain whether I can help her there. Nor, to be honest, whether I should. While I sympathize, Edmund *was* in her care, and this will be a lesson in what that responsibility truly means.

"You don't need to go out, miss," Violet says, tripping along at my heels as I stride toward the door. "Hugh and the grooms are searching."

"And so shall I."

"But it is—"

A howl of wind whips away her words as I yank open the door. It is so dark out that I cannot help checking my pocket watch to assure myself it is merely four in the afternoon. The storm that threatened earlier is rolling in, and a gust of wind nearly whips the door from my hand.

I step out. The sky is steel gray, and the wind is ferocious, but it has not yet started to rain. When thunder rumbles, it takes at least ten seconds for lightning to crack. I run outside, Violet following, as she continues trying to dissuade me.

My son is out here as a storm is approaching. I will not be dissuaded.

I tell her I'm fine. I know the property. I know where he likes to go. I will search for him. I will find him. I don't say the last—that is pure hubris. I feel it, though, if only in grim determination.

I will find my son.

Before his father returns.

That second part may be even more important than the first. Yes, Edmund is only five, but I've seen him out here. He stays well away from the pond and lake. He knows these fields and forests as well as I do. He is as mature about his escapades as a child twice his age, perhaps more. Even if he can swim like a fish—according to Hugh—he will not set foot near the water because of his father's fears. As I've said, he is a sensitive child, in all the best ways, understanding others' emotions and respecting them.

August, though? It does not matter if he taught his son to swim as soon as he could toddle. It does not matter if he knows, in his heart, that our son stays well away from water when he's unchaperoned. August's fears will consume him here. He will panic.

And he will blame me.

I can tell myself that matters not. I am blameless. I could not overrule Mrs. Landon's demands. She knew Edmund was with Violet and approved of it. If anyone is at fault, it is she for misjudging. Yet I am the one responsible for Edmund, and so I will be blamed.

I head up to the Grecian folly first. He is not there. Then it is into the forest, toward the tower ruins. That is when the rain begins, and it does not begin with a drizzle or a sprinkle. From the first drops, it is a downpour, and I run into the forest, hoping for shelter, to find little. I'm drenched within three heartbeats.

Well, there's one good thing about being drenched. You can stop trying to stay dry.

I roll my shoulders and remind myself that I'll be in front of a blazing fire soon enough, drinking hot tea. In my Victorian world, we do know how to get warm and cozy. You need to in this North Yorkshire climate.

The downpour will undoubtedly drive Edmund back to the house. Yet I continue on to the tower ruins and hunt for him there as the ice-cold rain pounds against me, the forest so dark I wish I'd brought a flashlight. Which would be so much more helpful in a world that had flashlights. Lanterns and candles do little in a storm.

I call for Edmund, shouting to be heard over the rain. Then I loop toward his other favorite spot in the forest—a thicket he likes to hide in. When I don't find him there, I make my way back toward the house, calling and squinting against the rain as I go.

I'm halfway across the lawn when Violet comes running to meet me. I pick up my pace to a jog.

"He's back?" I say.

"No, miss, he's not." Her rain-streaked face is pure torment. "And now Mr. August is here, and I had to tell him, and he ran straight off without a word, and no one can find *him*."

"He's gone to the pond," I say, raising my voice to be heard.

"You saw him?"

I shake my head, wig nearly sliding off. I put my hands to it as if brushing drenched hair from my face. "His sister died there. It is where he will go."

She looks dubious, but I'm already turning to run back into the rain. That is where I'll find August. I know I will. I know, too, that my "ruse" ends here. It must. I will find him at the pond, and I will need to convince him his son is not in there, and I cannot do that as Clara Smith. I'm not even certain I can do it as Rosalind Courtenay. I only hope that perhaps the shock of my revelation will distract him enough to come and look properly in places where we might actually find our son.

The pond is past the gardens along the west side of the front lawn. As I run, I wonder why in God's name it has not been emptied. It served a purpose once as a drainage pond, but even at the time I was here with August, it was no longer used for that or for pleasure boating. There'd been none of the latter since his sister's death thirty-five years ago.

Even then, I'd asked why they did not drain it as it served no purpose and only worried August for a time when his children would be older. The answer, unfortunately, had been simple then and undoubtedly had not changed. The earl would not hear of it being drained. Not August's father and not his older brother once his father passed. Drainage would be an unnecessary expense.

August had offered to pay for the procedure himself. His father and brother refused. Which proved it had nothing to do with the expense and everything to do with refusing to "coddle" the baby of the family. And by "coddle," they meant "pay the slightest bit of attention to his emotional health."

No matter. I will resolve this.

I run through the gardens, sloshing through puddles and miraculously slipping on neither cobblestones nor mud. My boots are soaked through, squashing with each step and probably ruined beyond repair. When they do slide, my ankle twists, and I pause to yank off the blasted things.

I'm throwing them aside when I hear a cry. Had I still been running, I'd never have noticed it. I'm not sure how I did even without the sloshing of my footfalls. The rain seems to drown out all sound. Except that one. Except the cry of a child.

"Edmund!" I shout. "Edmund!"

I cup my hands behind my ears, as if that will help me hear. And perhaps it does because a soft "Here!" pierces the rain and wind.

"Keep calling!" I shout.

He does. My darling, perfect boy does exactly as he's told, calling as loudly as he can, a "Here! I'm here!" every few seconds as I home in on the sound of his voice.

I find him lying on the stone path between two raised beds. Seeing him, I let out a cry of my own and fly to his side.

"My boot," he says, words coming in a tumble. "When the winds came, I knew I had to get to the house, so I ran, but I slipped, and my boot is stuck, and I know I ought to remove it, but I cannot reach."

I see the problem easily enough. His undone lace caught, and in falling, he trapped and twisted his foot. Twisted it badly, I realize, as he bites his lip when I touch his boot. It's twisted behind him, and he was unable to get it off from that angle, and it was too painful to turn. So he'd been kneeling on the path, and his face is puffy enough that I know not all the dampness on his face is rain.

I want to hug him. Just hug him and hold him as tight as I can and tell him he's been brave, so brave out here in the storm. First, though, I bend and free his bootlace. Then I touch his ankle, checking it before I whisper against his ear.

"May I lift you, Edmund? I don't think your ankle is broken, but it will hurt to stand."

"I can do it," he says, gritting his teeth as he begins to push up.

I lay one hand under his elbow. "You don't have to. May I lift you? Please? I don't want you hurting your ankle further."

It's the last that convinces him, and he collapses against me, and I lift him then, the small body that I have not held in four years. I lift him as easily as I did back then, folding his body against mine as I sit back on the raised bed, and I'm glad then of the rain, washing away the tears that pour hot down my face as I hold him and rock him and tell him all is fine.

That is when I remember August.

I reach out to wipe a wet curl from Edmund's face, and if that touch is too familiar, he doesn't realize it, only looks up into my eyes and manages a weak smile.

"I will be fine," he says. "There is no need to worry."

I give him a little hug and whisper in his ear, "Your father is looking for you. I think he will have gone to the pond. May I take you back to the house first?"

His eyes widen as he shakes his head. "If he is at the pond, we must go to him. He'll be worried."

"He will be," I say. "May I carry you?"

"I don't think you're big enough for that. I'm awfully heavy."

I smile. "Not so heavy. I'm stronger than I look, and it is not far."

He nods, and I scoop him up and make my way along the path toward the pond.

NINETEEN

HERE IS NO one at the pond. I curse at that, not because I don't see August, but because I see no one—none of his staff have come to look for him. Did I not say that this is where he'd be? Where are they looking for him? Are they looking at all?

No. They are looking for Edmund as they should be. Their master is a grown man of nearly forty.

A grown man, yes. But, in this moment, he is his son's age again, remembering that his beloved sister's body was pulled from the pond.

All that matters not because he isn't here. I've brought Edmund, and damn it, August is not even here. Perhaps he never was. I've admitted he is not the man I thought he was, so why am I so adamant—

A gasp. A gasp that I should not hear any more than I heard my son's cry. Yet I do. Over the rain and the wind, I hear a sound in the pond.

Hear it, but see nothing, can see nothing, with the rain driving down, the sky pitch dark, the pond's surface roiling with the wind, as storm-swept as the lake.

It does not matter. I heard that gasp as surely as I heard Edmund's cry. Clutching Edmund to my breast, I run to the pond's shore, and I slide on

the mud just as something breaks the surface. A blond head in the middle of the pond. It rises and then disappears again, diving like a seal.

"Papa!" Edmund cries.

"Yes," I whisper against his ear. "That is your papa."

Your mad, mad, impossible papa.

"Call to him," I say. "As loud as you can."

"You, too," he says. Then he shouts Papa, and I do the same, echoing him, knowing it is the one word that might stop August's wild search.

I watch him surface again, less than twenty feet out now, and it doesn't matter that I can barely see my hand in front of my eyes. I see him. I see August, hair plastered to his face, his expression pure terror for our son as he dives, madly, ridiculously dives in the one place Edmund will never be. I see his fear and his love for our son and the wild panic of the abandoned boy August was, and I love him. I love him, and I can tell myself I will be fine if we cannot work this out. I even tell myself I might not want to try working it out after how he has behaved about my disappearance, how he has cut my sisters from his life.

Lies.

The most damning lies I've ever told.

I will not be fine. I *must* try to work this out. I will pray it can be worked out. If it cannot, then I will have lost something for which I will never stop grieving. I will be fine, in the end, but only in the way I would eventually be fine if something happened to him. I would survive, nothing more.

When August surfaces, he is nearly fifty feet away. We have only a moment before he dives back under.

"Together," I whisper in Edmund's ear. "Now!"

We shout "Papa!" together, and August's head stays up, his gaze swinging to us. We both wave frantically, and Edmund calls, "I am all right, Papa!"

For a moment, August only paddles there, staring at us. Then he begins to swim. He swims as fast as he can, long and powerful strokes, and yet that must not be fast enough because he dives, as if that will get

him to Edmund faster. Or as if he must dive, or he'll keep stopping to check, to be sure it's his son on the shore.

He is a mere dozen feet when he dives into the inky, wind-swept water, and I hold my own breath, waiting for him to surface.

"Right there," I say, pointing to the water as we move to the edge. "Your father shall pop up right there. The silly, silly man."

Edmund giggles, and I set him on the ground, where he can sit, telling him to be ready. Any second now, his father will break the surface.

Any second now.

Those seconds tick past.

"Miss Clara?" Edmund says as I kneel beside him.

I count off five more seconds.

"Miss Clara?" Edmund's voice rises.

I'm already on my feet, already moving to the water's edge, looking into its black depths, nothing visible beneath the surface. I count three more seconds. And then I dive.

The pond is no natural thing, with reedy shallow edges. It was dug from the earth and lined with retaining walls. Even at the edge, it is ten feet deep, which makes it such a hazard for children and wandering guests alike. In the modern world, this monstrosity is gone. Filled in and replaced with a shadow of its former self, a shallow duck pond.

That is not the water I dive into. This is deep and cold, and it stinks. The smell from my drenched bed fills my nose even as I hold my breath.

I don't care about the smell. Or the cold. Or the depth. Right now, all that matters is the darkness. The complete and utter blackness of the waters. I swim blind with strokes that could take me inches from August without ever seeing him.

When I feel a tug at my head, I remember my wig. I almost ignore it, but when it dislodges, my hand strikes it, and I grab it and shove it into my bodice.

I propel myself up and look about wildly, orienting myself as fast as I can. There is Edmund, standing on the shore, braced on his good leg. He

is five feet away and off to my left. I swim quickly to draw parallel to him, where I know August aimed. Then I go under again.

I dive to the bottom, and I kick and sweep my hands. I swim until my lungs scream. Then I swim until my brain screams, telling me I can't help August if I drown myself.

I surface. Find Edmund. Reorient myself. Go back down. Swim, swim, swim, arms as wide as they'll go, legs wide, too, as they kick. And then my foot brushes something.

I twist myself around and go back, frantically feeling about, heart pounding.

You felt him. You just felt him. He's right there. How can you not—

Silken tendrils wave through my fingers. I clench my fist, and I have hair. I know I do. My hand wraps in August's hair only to be wrenched away as he struggles frantically.

Struggles frantically. He is alive. Alive and caught.

I dive down deeper. I find his shoulder and then his torso, and I keep going, feeling my way blindly, fingers plucking at his clothing, terrified I'll lose him in this utter blackness. It would only take a moment. He's struggling, and he only needs to pull from my fingers, and I will be searching again, precious seconds ticking past as he drowns.

I find his leg, stretched behind him and then...

Fate. Fate, you are a fickle, fickle wench with the cruelest sense of humor. Only minutes ago, I found my son with his shoelace caught and ankle twisted, and I'd thought, *Oh, that's not too bad.* Not fatally danger-ous, at least. So this is Fate's reply. My husband is trapped in almost the same way, his foot caught in the weeds growing at the bottom of the pond. Like our son, he cannot free himself—he's trying, but he cannot get to his foot, twisting and writhing to reach it. Unlike our son, he will not lie here, facing merely a terrifying night alone in the storm. He will drown.

Freeing him is not as simple as tugging off his boot, as I did with Edmund. I cannot get his boot free, my numb fingers fumbling even to find the laces. Then I reach them, and I cannot hold him, and he has stopped struggling. Dear God, he has stopped struggling.

Because you are here. Someone is here to rescue *him*.

I wish I could believe that. I know better. August would fight as long as he could fight. He would never relax and trust someone to set him free. If he has stopped struggling—

I claw at the weeds. I grab them and I pull, but it's like pulling wire, and the icy water goes warm, and I know that is blood. Blood from my fingers. I don't care. I need to breathe. My lungs are on fire and if I don't surface soon…

I don't care.

I rend at the weeds and wrench and—

One strand comes free. I grab another and rip it with my nails. It frees and the third… The third is where Fate tires of this very amusing game. The third and final strand comes unmoored from the pond floor. The strand whips through my fingers as August's foot slides away. I grab for it, clawing at the water until I find it.

My fingers clamp around August's ankle, and it floats there. Just floats.

Move, damn it. Move, August. Kick, however weakly. Just kick.

His foot does not move. I grip it as tight as I can, and I begin to swim. I surface to Edmund's shout of "Papa!" and I blindly flail toward it, half-swimming as I tow August by the foot, not daring take even a moment to find his head instead. The shore is there. Right there.

And then I'm there, too…at the end of a pond that does not end in a gradual slope. I'm clinging to the edge, holding August's foot, and I panic. Complete and utter panic. How will I get out without losing him? There's no one here except Edmund. Why is there no one else here? Where *are* they? My husband is unconscious, drowned, and I'm mooring his body by the foot, and I'm trapped here at the edge of the bloody pond and—

Breathe. Just breathe.

Two breaths and then, "Edmund? I need you to do a very difficult thing."

"Papa." That's all he says, all he can say. He's staring saucer-eyed at the trouser leg clenched in my fingers.

 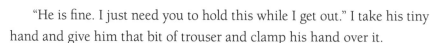

"He is fine. I just need you to hold this while I get out." I take his tiny hand and give him that bit of trouser and clamp his hand over it.

"Hold tightly for one moment."

As soon as he grips it, I scramble out of the water, keenly aware that I could be doing the worst possible thing for my son. If he loses his grip, if the storm-tossed waves pull August from him, he will never forget this moment. The moment he lost his father.

I'm out and twisting, and I have August's boot in hand. It starts to slip, and a half-stifled scream escapes me as I imagine his foot coming free from the boot, his body sliding out into the black pond…and dragging our son with him.

I grab his trouser leg instead, one and then the other, and I pull. I pull with all my might, and Edmund does too, and it seems to take forever—*forever*—to drag August from the water. As soon as he is on the shore, I scramble to his chest as he lies facedown on the grass.

He isn't breathing.

I knew that. I just could not think of it until now. I drag him farther from the edge and then ask Edmund to help as I flip August over.

I know how to perform CPR only in the most academic way. Two years ago, I'd been passing a public pool in York and seen a notice for CPR classes. It showed a child who'd been pulled from a pool, his mother resuscitating him. One look at that picture, and I'd been on the phone, signing up for the class.

I will go home, and I will teach August how to do this.

That's what I'd thought. All I'd thought, moving as if in a trance as I dialed that number. Here was something I could give August when I saw him again, because I *would* see him again. I would teach him this skill, and it would help alleviate his fear. He would know how to save our son if Edmund fell into the water.

When I took the class, they were very clear on one thing. CPR was not a substitute for professional help. Call 999 before you start because that is what may save your child.

I cannot call 999. And I can barely remember that bloody course. Or so I think until I have August on his back, and I'm checking his airway, and everything comes back, as if I'm crouched beside that pool working on the CPR dummy.

Check for breathing.

Perform thirty chest compressions.

Clear the airway.

Give two breaths.

Repeat.

Sitting at his father's side, Edmund is silent. Utterly silent as he stares at August's face. He glances my way once or twice as I perform CPR, and there is no curiosity in it, only conviction. Whatever I'm doing, it will save his father. Otherwise, I would not be doing it, would I?

I am an adult, and I am doing something to help his father, and therefore it must be the right thing. The magical grown-up thing.

Thirty compressions. Two breaths. Repeat. Thirty compressions. Two breaths. Repeat. Thirty—

August coughs. One half cough, and then sputtering, and with Edmund's help, I turn August over as he retches pond water onto the ground. More coughing, deep retches that seem ready to break him in two.

Finally, he goes still, on all fours, staring down at the grass. Then, slowly, he lifts his head and sees his son there. A sob, one sob that might be August, might be Edmund, might be both together, and August reaches for our son, who collapses into his arms.

TWENTY

E ARE IN the house. I left August and Edmund on the pond bank as I ran for help. I was almost to the house before I remembered to yank on my wig. In the darkness of the storm, Edmund hadn't noticed my short blond hair.

Everyone came, all except Violet, who'd been sent for the doctor. From that moment, I'm on the periphery. The outsider looking in, anxiously hovering as Hugh carries Edmund and the other men help August back to the house.

It is only there, once everyone is inside, that I'm needed again. I'm Edmund's governess. Thank the heavens I am his governess because it means I can take charge of my son once Hugh sets him in his bed.

The maids get the fire blazing, and I call for more blankets and hot milky tea and broth, and I warm Edmund and comfort him. Whenever he asks after his father, I send the stable boy to run to August's quarters for an update, and that is partly pure selfishness. I cannot be with August, and I so desperately want to be. I want them both here, in this bed, where I can warm them and feed them and watch over them. But here I'm only the governess, and so my duty is Edmund, and I will be grateful for that.

The doctor arrives within the hour. August insists he check Edmund first. Our son is fine. Chilled and frightened, but with only a slightly twisted ankle. As for August…

August is unwell. According to the doctor, that is clearly the result of swimming in a bitterly cold pond in October. In the modern world, we'd say hypothermia, but that isn't quite what he's talking about. I swam in the same lake, and my teeth have only just stopped chattering, but if I experienced hypothermia, it was mild. What the doctor means is that Victorian concept of temperature changes causing illness. Even in the twenty-first century, I'd had people insist they "caught a cold" by being out in the rain. We'd call that an old wives' tale, but in Victorian Yorkshire, it is accepted fact.

August is unwell. That's all I know. He's running a fever, and the doctor wants him to stay in bed for a few days. I do not know why he would be sick—I can only guess that he'd already caught a virus, or that he'd swallowed something in the pond water, or simply that his stress level in the last twenty-four hours lowered his immunity and triggered a latent illness. Yes, I may be a doctor's daughter, but I'm no physician myself. August is unwell but not drowned, and that is all that matters.

Edmund sleeps fitfully. When he jolts awake, I ease onto the bed to comfort him, and he ends up on my lap before I know it, cuddled there as he did when he was a baby, arms and legs pulled in. He drifts off, and then I'm free to whisper everything I want to whisper, how much I love him, how sorry I am that I left, that I never would have if I had the choice, how he is even more perfect than I could have imagined, how I will never leave him again.

An hour passes, and thankfully no one peeks in, so I'm able to stay where I am, holding Edmund as he sleeps. Then he rouses, and I try to slide away—knowing I should—but he clutches me sleepily, and I stay where I am as he lies there, only his breathing telling me he is awake.

"She was there," he says finally, his voice so soft I wonder whether I've heard it at all.

"Hmm?"

"The ghost. She was there. At the pond."

For a split second, I am plunged back into those dark waters, ice cold running through me.

"The ghost was at the pond?" I say as neutrally as possible. "When your father—when your father went under the water?"

His sharp chin nods against me. "When you were trying to save him. I saw her across the way, walking back and forth. She was talking. It was hard to see her, in the rain, but her mouth was moving."

"She was talking to you?"

He shakes his head. "To you and Papa, I think. She didn't seem to see me. I only noticed her a couple of times. I was busy watching you and Papa, but when I would look over, she was there, watching you, too."

"I see," I say because I don't know what else to say.

He snuggles into my arms, and I kiss the top of his head, light enough that he won't feel it. His heartbeat slows, and I think he's drifted off, and then he murmurs, "I think I know who she is now."

"Hmm?"

"The ghost. When I saw her, watching you and Papa, she looked worried. Frightened. I think…" He swallows, the movement rippling down my arm. "I think Margaret was correct. It is my mama."

I stiffen.

"It is my mama, watching over us," he says in the tiniest of voices. "I know she is supposed to be dead, but I hoped…" Another swallow. "I hoped she was not. I hoped she…she could not come to us. That something— someone—kept her away, but she would come back, but then the ghost… The ghost is her. I know it is."

Enough.

This is the end, and I do not care what comes after this. I do not care if I make the most horrible mistake in these next moments, a mistake I will regret for the rest of my days. Only a monster could stay silent now.

"Your mother is not dead," I whisper against his soft hair. "Your mother is here, Edmund. Holding you. Finally holding you again."

I barely breathe then as I wait for his reaction. For him to tense. For his head to shoot up. For him to blurt a question. Instead, he just keeps breathing, slow and even breathing.

"Edmund?" I whisper.

No response, and tears fill my eyes. Tears of grief and of laughter, all at once. I have done it. Unburdened myself to my son. Taken a leap of incredible faith and told him the truth. And he is asleep.

He unburdened *himself*. Told me his deepest hope and deepest fear, the latter seeming confirmed tonight, and then he promptly fell asleep.

"No more," I whisper against his hair. "No more of this nonsense. You will not spend another waking moment thinking your mother is dead, Edmund."

A floorboard creaks. I jump to see a figure in the entrance, still clutching the door. He holds a candle in his free hand, and the light of it casts his face into shadow, but the blond hair is unmistakable.

"Aug—" I stop myself as the flickering light illuminates enough of his face for me to see his expression.

He's staring at me. My hand almost flies to my head, thinking I've taken off my wig. Then I realize he isn't staring at me. He's staring at us. At me holding his child, as if I was the boy's own mother.

It isn't outrage on his face. Or even shock. It's… It's as if he's seeing a ghost.

The ghost of me, holding our son.

"H-he was distraught," I say. "He needed comfort."

He breaks, as if from a trance, and I realize I've used my "Clara" voice. Is this what I'm doing? Keeping my secret longer?

No.

No, it is not.

He steps into the room, waving off my explanation. Then he stands there, candle in hand as the door closes behind him.

"I…" He begins. Then he straightens. "I owe you everything, Miss Smith."

"You—"

"You saved my son. And you saved me. I do not know how I can ever repay you but…" The candlelight wavers, and I realize he's swaying. I see his eyes then, clearer in the moonlight. They burn fever bright.

I scramble from under Edmund, sliding our son onto the bed.

"No," August says, his voice thick. "Stay with him. Please. He… He has not had…such comfort…in a very long time."

"Au—"

"I did not wish to disturb him. I only came to…to thank you. For saving us. For finding him. And for me…for…"

I hurry over as he sways, but he backs up, alarm in his fevered eyes. "I am fine, Miss Smith."

"You are not fine, August, and I am not Miss—"

His eyes roll back, and he collapses to the floor.

TWENTY-ONE

UGUST COLLAPSES, AND Violet rushes in, followed by Mrs. Landon, and they discover me crouched over the unconscious form of their master. Naturally, Mrs. Landon accuses me of doing something to him, as if a woman my size could knock out a man like August.

Fortunately, Violet listens when I say he fainted and needs the doctor. Soon the doctor is there, and I'm banished to my room. Literally banished. Mrs. Landon has forbidden me to leave my quarters, as if she still harbors some certainty that I'm responsible for August's condition. I will humor her for now, at least while Violet scampers back and forth, updating me on August's condition.

It is the sudden fever that has felled him. The doctor still maintains August contracted an ailment in his icy swim, and there's little I can do about that except trust that he will treat the fever as best he can. According to Violet, August has woken and was temporarily delirious, calling for his dead wife. That almost sends me running pell-mell down the hall, shedding my disguise as I go. I restrain myself, though. Even were I to be at August's side in his current condition, he would not know me.

I do ask Violet to convey a request to the doctor. Tell him that I am the daughter of a physician and well-schooled in the art of nursing, which

is only a slight exaggeration. Tell him I would like to help at night while Edmund sleeps and does not need me.

"I'll do that, ma'am," Violet says. "I don't know what's gotten into Mrs. Landon, but I know you had nothing to do with this. You saved his life."

"Thank you, Violet."

When she runs off, I'm alone again. I'm wishing I'd brought a novel from the library when I remember that I do have a book in my room. The one I'd found while searching for the candle. The one that had been wrapped in a woolen shift in the wardrobe.

It is truly a testament to my mental state that nearly a full day passed between finding a hidden diary and cracking open the cover. Any other time, I'd have devoured the entire thing by now. But right after finding it, I'd heard my doorknob turning, chased a ghost into the yard, been spotted by August, and from there, the day was nothing but chaos.

Even now, when I think of the journal, I hesitate, not from the indelicacy of reading another's diary—if they wanted it kept private, they should have taken it—but because, in my current state, even the prospect of such a delicious thing hardly tempts me. If I did have a novel, I'd probably have spent the next hour reading without processing a single word.

With some reluctance, I take the diary and lower myself back onto my narrow bed. I open the book to the first page, expecting the usual name and date. The first few pages have been torn out. That piques my interest until I begin reading.

I've said I'm not a writer. I've never even penned a diary. If I did, though, I'd hope it would be more interesting than this. More legible, too. It's written in a cramped hand with no entry dates and no paragraph breaks. It's page after page of the most tedious mundanities.

Last evening, we went to dine with the curate, whose housekeeper served stewed eels. After dinner, we played charades, and it was such fun!

I quickly begin to skim and skip, only idly interested in what connection the writer seems to have to Courtenay Hall. After a few pages of tedium, I come across more ripped-out sheets, and slow down. Whatever could she be tearing out? There isn't so much as a cutting observation or a sarcastic remark.

I pass the ripped pages to hit a line that stops me dead.

There is something wrong with this house. Wrong with this house and with this child.

I back up before the torn sheets and read more carefully. There I see what I missed in my skimming.

I have obtained my first post as a governess! Mama is so pleased, which makes me laugh. Most mothers would not be at all delighted to see their well-born daughters go into service, but Mama has high hopes for this particular position. It is with the son of an earl! Third son, to be sure, but still. He is widowed and has a young son, and the Emerson sisters say he is deliciously handsome. I know Mama is hoping I'll catch his eye, but I have no such plans. My heart is taken. For me, this is only a lucrative position that will allow M and me to wed when he returns from his sojourn at sea. Only one more year! Surely I can mind a small boy for that long.

I suspected the diary belonged to a former governess. With that paragraph, any doubts are erased. When she speaks of something being wrong with the house, she means Courtenay Hall. And when she says something is wrong with the boy, she means Edmund. My son.

The pages between those two paragraphs are missing. Her arrival at Courtenay Hall. Her introduction to life here. Why tear them out? As I skim the next pages, I think I know—she seems to be avoiding names. It is all "the

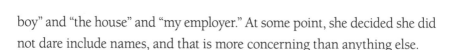
boy" and "the house" and "my employer." At some point, she decided she did not dare include names, and that is more concerning than anything else.

She's ripped out any identifying pages, including those at the front of the volume. What scared her so much she thought she had to disguise identities and hide her book? And why did she leave without taking it?

"Miss?"

I jump at the voice, and I realize I hadn't locked the door. Fortunately, I'm still in my full disguise. I look up to see Violet peeking in.

"The doctor wishes to speak to you."

I tell her I'll be a moment, and then I tuck the journal under my mattress before hurrying after her.

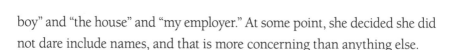

I FEARED what the doctor might want with me, what accusations Mrs. Landon might have made, but I needn't have worried. I arrive to find the doctor packing up his bag. He's bleary eyed and slurs his words slightly, and he apologizes for that, saying he was called to a difficult birth in the wee hours the morning before.

The questions are perfunctory. What sort of nursing have I done? What do I know about treating fevers? Have I had any experience with delirium?

The doctor—Dr. Cunningham—clearly just wants to get to his bed as quickly as possible. In his defense, this is the nineteenth century, when most women have some experience with nursing. It is considered part of the womanly arts, and one didn't hire in a nurse unless absolutely necessary. There were always women around with experience in that role who were expected to simply add nursing a sick loved one to their daily list of chores.

I never had any interest in medicine myself. My sister Portia inherited my father's passion. I do know how to care for fever, though, and once assured on that point, Dr. Cunningham leaves August in my care and promises to tell the staff that I will be August's primary caregiver during his illness, which is truly more than I'd hoped.

Once the doctor is gone, I hurry to my husband's bedside. Despite Dr. Cunningham's exhaustion, the man did his job well. August is sleeping soundly. His sheets are fresh and dry, any sweat-soaked ones clearly having already been changed. When I touch his forehead, it is worryingly hot, but he is at peace.

I steal these selfish moments for myself. Yes, my poor husband is in dire straits, suffering from a serious fever, but these are our first moments alone when I'm in no danger of him snapping at me or striding from the room. I sit on the edge of the bed, and I pat a cold cloth to his fevered brow, and I brush sweaty locks from his forehead, and I stare at him. I take these moments to be with him, half nursing and half just being there, watching him, remembering him in that pond, desperate to find our son.

I will fix this. In whatever way I can, I will fix it.

I know not to linger on the bedside. While the house seems asleep, I cannot risk anyone walking in to see me staring lovingly down at my employer. Once I'm sure he's resting soundly, I move to a chair by the bedside. Of course, that only means that I'm now staring lovingly at him from farther away.

I rise and scour his chambers for a book. I know there will be one here someplace. I'm only hoping it'll be fiction. I'm not in the mood for a treatise on tariff reform. Okay, I'm never in the mood for that, but particularly not tonight.

When I find what I'm looking for, I have to chuckle. It's hidden in a drawer under a stack of exactly the sort of pamphlets I feared. The way he's secreted it away, you'd think it was something salacious. It's an adventure novel in the vein of Robert Louis Stevenson, but the sort that won't endure to the twenty-first century. And, while the cover shows a dashing pirate aboard his ship, knowing my husband's taste in literature, there will be at least as many scenes where the dashing pirate is aboard a lovely lady.

A quick glance at the door, then I bend to kiss August's cheek before retreating to the chair, where I pull up my feet under me and dive into the adventures of…

Oh, well that's interesting. The "dashing pirate" is actually a woman in disguise. Let's just hope the gender-switch doesn't mean a lack of "boarding" scenes. I smile and settle in to read.

I NEEDN'T have feared. While the novel's primary character is a woman, she finds plenty of men willing to be boarded. It's also a wonderful tale of adventure, full of sword fights and double crosses and narrow escapes. When my vision begins to blur from my colored contacts being in far too long, I pop them into their case so I can keep reading.

I lose myself in the book, and when August gasps, I jump, the novel leaping from my hands and slapping onto the floor. He gasps again, his face red as he struggles for breath, and I fly to him. I grab the cloth and crawl onto his bed, where he thrashes.

"August?" I say as I take his shoulder and press the cloth to his forehead. His temperature is lower than it was before, but he's fighting to breathe, and I can't see why. I'm tipping his head back and leaning over his face when he gives a huge gasp, as if surfacing from the water to gulp air.

I exhale slowly. He was having a nightmare about being back in the pond.

"Edmund," he whispers, his eyes still closed.

"Edmund is fine," I say. "He was never in the pond. He only hurt his ankle. He's fine, and you're fine."

After a few deep breaths, his breathing seems to return to normal. Then it hitches, and I lean over him again, and his eyes snap open, and he stares up at me.

I don't know whether he can see me. His eyes are wide, and he seems to be still in the dream. I brush a sweat-soaked curl from his forehead and smile down at him.

"It's all right," I say. "You're safe. Edmund's fine, and you're—"

"Rosalind." The word comes out on such a croak that I'm not sure I've heard right. Then he says it again, and as he does, his fingers reach to touch my cheek.

That's when I see my spectacles on the side table, alongside the case that holds my colored contacts.

"Rosalind," he whispers. "Tell me you are not a ghost again. Please tell me you are not."

My mouth opens, and nothing comes out, and I realize I'm afraid. No, I'm terrified. In my mind, I see him standing in the library, face contorted as he tells me that his wife abandoned him. I see his blazing hate, and I'm terrified of revealing myself.

A thousand excuses fly up. This is not the time. It is not safe. It is not wise.

"Rosalind," he whispers. "Tell me I am not imagining it. Tell me you are not a ghost. I see you everywhere, and you are always just out of reach. I tell myself it cannot be you because, if it is, then you are well and truly gone and I shall never get you back. Please. Say something. Do not be a spirit come to torment me."

I pull off my wig. Pull it off and take his face between my hands and say, "It's me, August. I've come back to you."

The moment the words are out, I curse them. Come back to him? Is that not confirming his worst fear? That I abandoned him and our son. I open my mouth to say more as quickly as I can.

August pulls me to him in a crushing kiss, and before I know it, I'm in the bed with him, fever giving him sudden strength. He pulls me to him, and he kisses me.

His kiss swallows me whole, body pressed to mine, fingers digging into my back, my hips, as if he can draw me closer still. My own arms are around his neck, and my fingers in his hair. I wrap myself around him as if he is my anchor to this world, as if letting go even for a second will send me toppling through time.

I barely notice the first cough, but when it comes again, I remember he is sick, and I break the kiss. He dives to recover it, but another cough

stops him. Then he is gasping and shivering convulsively, and I'm scrambling out of his grasp to grab the damp cloth again. I pull up the cover and wipe his brow as he shivers. When I press a glass of water to his lips, he croaks, "Not really what I wanted," and I have to laugh. I laugh as tears stream down my face.

He sips the water and then catches my wrist, and when I look down at him, he says, "Rosalind."

"I didn't leave you," I blurt. "I never would have left you."

"But you're back," he croaks. "Just tell me you are back."

"I am. I'm back, and I will not leave again. I shall tell you everything and—"

He begins to shake, and I realize this is not the time to unburden myself. He isn't asking for explanations. That will come. For now, he needs care. When I turn to wet the cloth, he catches my arm again. This time, he tugs me into bed with him.

"Cold," he says. "So cold."

I slide under the covers and press myself against him, and his lips quirk, just a little.

"Knew that'd work," he says, and I laugh, and he pulls me against him, still shivering and then drifts back to sleep.

TWENTY-TWO

WAKE TO AUGUST'S hands on me. All over me. I'm pressed against him, and he's caressing me and pulling me to him. I snuggle closer, but when he starts to pull me on top of him, I slide back down to his side.

"This will have to wait," I say. "As much as I hate to say it, you are in no condition for that."

He presses his hips against me, his erection pushing into my stomach. "I believe I am in perfect condition for that."

I sputter a laugh, and again my tears well because this is August. My August. Exactly as I remember him, such a far cry from the man in the library.

This is my husband, the best of the man I love, and I'm both joyous and terrified again. Terrified because I know he is fevered and not in his right mind, and that is letting me catch a glimpse of his true self, one that might evaporate when the fever passes and he remembers his anger.

I cannot worry about that. What am I to do? Deny myself these moments in case they are all I get? If these are crumbs of a cake I shall never get to eat, I don't care—I'll devour them anyway.

"No," I say firmly. "I will not have you dissolve into a fever fit again. There will be time for that later. First, we need to talk."

"Edmund," he says. "How is Edmund? Violet saw him heading for the pond."

I assure him Edmund is fine. Then I say, "But we must speak about what happened. Where I went."

"I do not care," he says, pulling my lips to his. "You are here, and that is all that matters."

He kisses me, and there is a quiet desperation in that kiss that cracks my heart in two.

Do not tell me.

That's what he's saying.

Do not tell me what happened, because I am afraid it will not be enough. I fear your explanation, and so I do not want it.

"You're back," he says as he kisses me. "You're back, and you're staying, yes? That is enough."

Oh, God, the way he says it. The truly heartbreaking way. All my anger at him dissolves as he pleads for me not to say anything more, not to ruin it. He may rail against the faithless wife who abandoned him, yet that is a front. Inside is the abandoned child who cares only that I'm back.

"August." I take his face in my hands. "I am going to explain. I did not abandon you. I never would. *Never.*"

He nods, but his gaze shifts, and his Adam's apple bobs.

"Do you remember William Thorne's girl? The one you said was from the future."

That has his gaze snapping back to mine.

I continue, "You will find this hard to believe, but she truly was."

"From the future?"

"Y-yes. You know her as—"

"Bronwyn. His wife. But how did you know where she's from?"

I stare at him a moment before a laugh burbles up inside me. He knows about Bronwyn's time traveling. That will make this so much easier. Please tell me it will make it easier.

"There is a spot in Thorne Manor," I say, and then I tell my story. It spills out, as muddled a narrative as there ever was, but he seems to follow it, nodding as I go.

I tell him about my wild ride to Thorne Manor to retrieve my ring. About the cat in the box. About ending up in twenty-first-century Thorne Manor and getting stuck there, the weeks of trying to get back before I made a life for myself, always returning to try again and again.

"Until it worked," I whisper, his arms around me. "After I saw Bronwyn and William in York, I came back, and it worked and then..."

I swallow. "And that, apparently was just the beginning of my adventure, because I found myself on a train—"

A rasping sound cuts me off. A sound suspiciously like a snore.

I lift my head to look into his face and find he has fallen fast asleep, claimed by the fever weakness.

"Well," I murmur. "That is not quite how I imagined it going." Then I sputter a laugh, and as I do, I realize I have laughed more in this past hour than I have in years. I hug him tight, and kiss his forehead and then lie in his arms until morning comes.

WHEN THE first light of dawn seeps through the heavy drapes, I crawl from August's bed as carefully and quickly as I can. He's sound asleep, having not stirred in the last hour. I check, of course, to be sure he's all right. Still fevered but sleeping soundly, which is what he needs most.

I put my wig back on and return my contacts and spectacles. I don't know what the next step will be for us, only that I fear when the fever breaks, August will have forgotten everything and we'll need to start anew, from a very different place.

No matter. I've seen past his anger, and I understand what lies there. That doesn't mean I am not still hurt by him telling himself—and how many others?—that I abandoned him. We'll deal with that. The important

part is he wants me back. We will mend this. It just won't be as easy as having him wake in his right mind and pull me into his arms again.

So I must remain Clara Smith for a while longer, as much as it chafes. I've barely settled into my chair when footsteps gallop along the hall and the door flies open, Edmund racing in.

"Papa!" he shouts, and in a few hobbling bounds, he is across the room and launching himself into August's bed.

"Papa?" he says, when August does not respond.

I hurry over. "He is fine, Edmund, but exhausted with fever. We'd best let him sleep as long as he can."

Edmund's disappointment mirrors my own. I might say August needs sleep, but I cannot help hoping his eyes will snap open, and he'll grin, and we will, in a heartbeat, be a family again.

A lovely fantasy, but I can also imagine the nightmare version of it, where August wakes to see me beside him, realizes who I am and sends me packing, terrifying our bewildered son in the process.

I settle for a middle ground and hand Edmund the cloth. "Why don't you gently wash his face. The cool will soothe him, and if he is ready to wake, he shall."

Edmund does as I suggest, but August is not ready to wake.

I reassure Edmund that his father is fine, and that he woke briefly last night, and his first words were asking after his son.

"How is your ankle?" I ask.

"It is better, miss. It hurts, but I can walk on it."

"I saw that. Well, your father's fever should break today. When it does, he'll need as much liquid as possible. Fever dehydrates. That will be our job today. Getting your father to drink. Water, broth, tea, whatever we can get into him. Do you think you can do that?"

Edmund nods solemnly.

"Then our first stop shall be to Cook, to ask for broth, because while tea and water will hydrate, he also needs salt. Do you know why?"

Edmund shakes his head.

"What happens when you eat something salty?" I ask.

His eyes round. "Oh! I get thirsty. Salt will make Papa want to drink, which will help with the de-de—"

"Dehydration. It's a funny word, and we'll write it out. What salt also does is make our bodies hold on to water. Have you ever tasted sweat?"

He makes a face. "Only when it gets on my lips. Oh. Yes. It's salty, isn't it?"

"Correct, and so when your father sweats with the fever, he's losing salt and water. We need to replace both. That will be our first science lesson of the day. There will be more as I teach you a few things about nursing."

"You will do no such thing." Mrs. Landon walks in with Violet trailing after her, tray in hand. "Nursing is women's work."

I could argue that everyone should know the basics, but I only say, demurely, "Medicine, I meant. In caring for his father, Edmund shall learn medicine, which is a valuable science."

She sniffs. "Not for an earl's nephew. Did I not say we'll have no more of your strange teachings, Miss Smith?"

"But I like her strange teachings," Edmund pipes up. "They're fun."

Behind the housekeeper, Violet winks at him.

"An education is not supposed to be *fun*," Mrs. Landon says. "What happens to the boy when he's sent off to school? When he refuses to take his lessons because they are not fun?"

"Papa says I will never be sent off to school unless I wish to be, which I do not."

Mrs. Landon's face darkens. "We'll see about that." She turns to me. "Please escort the young master to his quarters for his breakfast. Then take him outside for his morning's exercise followed by his daily lessons. Which will *not* involve nursing."

"But the doctor put me in charge of Mr. August."

"She's right, ma'am," Violet peeps up. "Dr. Cunningham said—"

"Dr. Cunningham is not in charge of this *household*. I am. Violet? You will stay with Mr. August. If he wakes, you may call Bridget to fetch

Master Edmund so that he may see his father. If evening arrangements are required, we shall make them at that time."

I press my lips together against argument. At least she is promising to call for Edmund when August wakes, and that is really what matters.

I murmur something like thanks to Mrs. Landon, and then I escort Edmund from the room.

AUGUST DOES not wake before lunch. I swing between worry and paranoia. Has he regressed? Is the fever growing worse? Or is he waking and Mrs. Landon is telling Violet *not* to send for us after all?

I'm delighted that our son has inherited August's empathetic nature. Yes, it is not considered a "masculine" trait—and one of my greatest disappointments in the twenty-first century was discovering that has not changed nearly enough. To me, empathy is one of August's greatest strengths. Right now, though, it means that Edmund picks up on my mood easily, and even if he does not yet have the language to express what he's sensing, he still senses it and is troubled. So I must push aside my fears to focus on distracting both of us.

We walk, and then we embark on lessons, but clearly, neither of us is in the mood for study, so after lunch, we are outside again. I've tucked the unnamed governess's journal into a schoolbook, promising Edmund that I'm bringing a book for my own study and not his. We hike to the ruined tower, and I play with him for a while before he finds amusement constructing a barricade of fallen tree branches. I leave him to it and pull out the journal.

I flip back to where I'd left off, at the lines that first caught my eye earlier.

There is something wrong with this house. Wrong with this house and with this child. When I first heard that my predecessors sent

him outside on his own, I was appalled. No wonder they did not last if they could not even spare time to walk and play with their charge! Yet I find myself doing exactly the same. This morning, I told myself I would not. It was a lovely day, and I would walk with him. And here I am, writing in my journal instead while he plays in the side yard.

The child is odd. There is no other way to put it. He is far too well mannered and well spoken for a child of his age, and yet he cannot read. I have begun to think he is only feigning idiocy, because he is clearly no idiot. Yet when I challenged him on it, he insisted the words do not stay fixed on the page. What does that even mean? I told him that is nonsense, and he began to cry, and his father came running, and I was nearly sent packing!

I must stop there and let my blood cool. Something wrong with my son because he seems intelligent yet cannot read? Dyslexia may be a modern diagnosis, but it is hardly a new condition. Any governess worth the name should understand that children learn in different ways.

I take deep breaths to calm down, and I remind myself that this is a very young and very new governess. Then I continue reading.

That is only part of the problem with the boy, and it is far from the worst of it. The trouble is… Oh, I scarcely know how to say this! I have always hidden my diary, but now I shall be extra certain of it because what I claim here could see me sent to Bedlam.

The boy speaks to ghosts.

There, I have said it. One might notice my wording there. I said he speaks to them, not that he thinks he does, and that is the confession that would surely have me locked up in an asylum. This house is haunted, and the young master is at the center of it.

The diary goes on from there, detailing exactly the sorts of experiences I've had. The governess has seen Edmund speaking to people who are not there. He is cagey and furtive when out of doors and quite happy to be let loose without a governess's care. She herself has been the subject of night-hauntings similar to my own: whispered voices and opened windows and scraping upon the glass. She has also seen a figure in the halls at night. A young light-haired woman.

> It is the boy's mother! I know it is! That was my first guess because I have been told she was fair-haired and slight of stature. Then I confessed to one of the maids with whom I have become quite friendly, and she told me the ghost is the boy's mother. Everyone knows it! They all know she haunts the house, and she drives off the governesses, and yet no one does a thing about it. The maid says they are forbidden to warn new governesses. Well, I was having none of that, so I confronted the housekeeper, and she locked me in my room!

That stops me. I glance up to be sure Edmund is fine. He's fussing with a stick that he can't quite shove into the ground, and I rise to help him before I resume reading.

> She would not dare do that if the master was home, but when he is away, she does as she pleases, knowing even the boy dares not tattle on her. I spent the entire day locked in my room while the grooms tended to the boy. Then the housekeeper came in and asked whether I was "past that nonsense." I said I was.
>
> Now I am in my room again, of my own volition, scribbling in this diary because I do not know what else to do. Last night was the worst yet! I woke seeing a figure in my room, and it was not the pretty woman in blue. Or it was, I think, but in her ghastly death clothes! Her face was bloated and torn, as if... I dare not even imagine. She was nightmare come to life. Then she spoke!

She told me to stay away from her boy. To leave now while I still could. I ran for the door, but I tripped. There was a bloody sheet on the floor! A sheet soaked in blood, and I tripped over it and raced to the door, and it was locked! Locked!

I pounded on it. Pounded and pounded, and no one came. When the maid brought my tea in the morning, she found me asleep by the door. She told me I must have been walking in my sleep because the door was not locked and no one heard anything that night. She lies! I thought she was my friend, and now she lies to save herself!

I do not know what is going on in this nightmare of a home, but I blame the boy. His mother's ghost haunts this place, and he—wicked child that he is—can see her and speak to her, and he must tell her nasty things about his governesses to make her scare us away. Well, I am not staying! I need to figure out how to sneak out and then—

The entry stops midsentence, only to resume on the next line in a hasty postscript.

Someone's at the door. I'll answer it, and then I'll return!

The diary ends there. I flip through empty pages, shivering with dread. Nothing.

I check on Edmund, who is still at play. Then I take deep breaths to calm myself.

Something happened to this girl, and I might be furious with her for blaming poor Edmund, but her fear is palpable. While there may be ghosts here, her haunting was human-made and obviously designed to make her flee. Except she never got the chance, did she?

What happened to the governess? That will be far easier to investigate as Rosalind Courtenay, which I should be able to do soon enough.

Unless August forgets last night. Unless I reveal myself and he casts me out—

Enough of that. I'm borrowing fear from the future. Either way, I will discover what happened to this governess. The name at the top of the list is obviously Mrs. Landon. Locking the poor girl in her room because she confessed to a haunting? At least I hadn't met that fate. If I had, I'd have crawled out the window, found a way down from the third floor and marched in the front door as Rosalind, and I doubt that would have gone well for either of us.

A member of the staff haunted this poor girl, and while Mrs. Landon is a likely suspect, there is another.

Whoever did the haunting played the role of, well, me. Dead me, returned from my watery grave. Could Mrs. Landon pull that off? It depends on how terrified the girl was and how monstrous my dead body appeared. Mrs. Landon is four inches taller than me and quite robust in build. While it is possible, I fear another suspect is more likely.

The unnamed governess befriended a maid. That maid was the one who told the story of the dead Rosalind, who insisted the ghost was her and "everyone" knew it. The same maid who turned Judas on that last day, claiming the door had not been locked and no one heard a thing.

As I ponder this possibility, I watch my son playing. He's barely limping after yesterday's ordeal. I shudder to think what might have happened, and how I would have been blamed for not watching him, despite the fact that I was not the one in charge of him at that moment.

And who was in charge of him?

As calmly as I can, I say, "Yesterday, before your father jumped into the pond, you were with Hugh and Violet. And then—"

"The ghost called me away," he blurts before I can ask the question.

"What?" I take my tone down a notch. "What do you mean, Edmund?"

He swallows. "I was playing with Surrey in the barn. Violet and Hugh were in the next room. They were..." His cheeks flush. "They are very good friends."

"Ah." I smile to show him it is all right. "Were they kissing?"

He nods.

"And then?"

"Then I thought Violet called me from outside. She seemed to be look-ing for me, and so I hurried out, and it was just starting to rain. I thought I saw her running for the house, and so I followed, but when I got closer, it wasn't her. It was the ghost in the blue dress."

"You followed?"

He flushes and nods. "I know I ought to have gone back to the stable, but I thought if the ghost called me, it meant she needed me, so I followed, and then I tripped."

I bend and set a stone on the ground and then a larger one. "If this is the stable and this is the house," I say, "and over here is where you fell…" I set a pebble down.

He nods. "Yes."

"Where was the ghost the last time you saw her?"

He sets another pebble down. "She was here, near the hedge maze, and she must have disappeared behind it."

I follow the trajectory from the stable to where Edmund fell to where the "ghost" had vanished. To where she had been leading him.

To the pond.

The woman in blue had been leading Edmund toward the pond when he fell.

And who had sent August running toward the pond? Who had said she'd seen Edmund running in that direction?

A maid. One who is, like me, "light of hair and small of stature."

The same maid Edmund thought he heard call his name when he ran out from the stable. The same maid he'd compared the ghost to, saying she was of a similar height and build.

Violet.

TWENTY-THREE

BUNDLE EDMUND OFF to the house. As we near it, I see Hugh and Charlie—another groom—in the yard and ask them to please watch him momentarily. They joke about appreciating the break and promise him another swordplay lesson. I head into the house and straight up to August's room. The door is shut. I ease it open to see Violet bending over a meal tray. When I clear my throat, she jumps back as if scalded.

"Oh, miss!" she says, hand to her heart. "You gave me such a fright."

"What are you doing with the master's lunch tray?"

"Taking it back to Mrs. Landon." She hefts it up. "I'll bring Mr. August his tea. He ate only a little of this, but at least he did eat."

"He woke, and you did not send for Edmund?"

She stammers excuses, saying August woke only briefly, and he was incoherent, and she decided Edmund shouldn't witness that. Also, we were out, weren't we? Yes, that's it. She is quite certain she saw us walking toward the woods, and so she couldn't call us in.

"Mr. August is still poorly, miss. He barely got any breakfast down and less lunch."

"Breakfast? He's been awake twice then?"

"Only briefly. *Very* briefly. We didn't have time to summon you."

"Which is it, Violet? You didn't have time? Or Edmund shouldn't see him like that? Or we weren't in the house?"

Her eyes flash, a show of spirit I haven't seen until now.

How much haven't I seen until now, Violet?

I'm stepping toward her when August whispers, "Rosalind."

I turn sharply to see him twisting under the covers, his face contorted as if in pain. I hurry to him and sit on the side of the bed. I lay my hand on August's forehead. It's only slightly warm, but he's sound asleep, moaning under his breath.

"You said he is unwell," I say to Violet. "His fever seems to have broken."

"I know, but he complains of stomach pain."

Alarm zings through me. "Has the doctor been summoned?"

"He came by this morning. He says that the master must have swallowed something in the pond. He gave him something to help him rest."

I curse under my breath. That's the reason August is so deeply asleep. A sedative. It is entirely the wrong course of action. If August is ill from swallowing the water, he should be encouraged to vomit it up, and he can hardly do that while sleeping.

"Did Dr. Cunningham say anything else?" I ask.

"Only that you ought to be nursing him, but Mrs. Landon said—"

"Mrs. Landon is wrong. I will look after Mr. August now."

"Shall I tend to Master Edmund?"

"No." The word comes sharply. "Hugh has him. Ask Hugh to bring him inside for tea, and afterward, to escort him up here to see his father."

Violet scampers off, leaving the tray behind, despite having been so eager to whisk it away earlier.

I suspect Violet is behind the hauntings. What I lack is her motivation. I don't know her well enough for that. Perhaps she has her eye on the governess position. That would be a life changer for a girl like Violet. I doubt she has the education for it, but she may not realize how much

teaching is involved, or she may think that with Edmund's difficulties, it will not be required. She seems fond of him.

Yet she led him toward the pond?

My chest seizes at the thought. I tell myself she meant him no harm. She probably intended to "find" Edmund wandering near the pond, and I'd have caught the blame. Perhaps now that August and Edmund have been injured, she will stop this foolishness.

My gaze moves back to the tray and lingers there, though I don't know why.

"Rosalind," August mutters, thrashing his head on the pillow.

I creep to the door and shut it. Then I hurry back to the bed and sit beside him with his hand in mine.

"I'm here, August," I whisper as I bend to kiss his cheek. "I am right here, and I am not leaving."

That calms him, and he lapses into sleep again. I try to return to my bedside chair, but when I do, he croaks my name and thrashes until I'm beside him, holding his hand. I prop my back against a pillow and sit there, listening for footsteps.

He sleeps soundly for no more than twenty minutes. Then a gasp, and his eyes fly open. He looks first at our clasped hands. Then up at my face.

"Miss Smith?" he says, jerking away and backing from me. "What the devil are you doing in my bed?"

My hopes crash around me as his face twists in outrage, devoid of recognition.

Then in a blink, he grins. "I could not resist. You should see your face, Rosie."

I stare at him. Then my hand flies to his forehead. He tugs it away. "I am not fevered nor delirious. I see you, and I cannot fathom how on earth I did not before. It must be the wig. That is the most dreadful wig." He squints. "Also the most dreadful spectacles. And whatever did you do to your eyes?"

I've fallen asleep. I must have. I drifted off, and now I'm dreaming that when August awakes, he will be *my* August. He will remember last night, and we shall move forward from there.

He frowns. "Rosie? Are you all right?"

"I-I'm dreaming, aren't I? I must be dreaming. I-I-I—"

The rest is swallowed by a sob that rocks my entire body. August reaches for me, and I fall into his arms. He holds me, cradling me and kissing my head between tugging off the wig and murmuring, "That's better," and kissing my head again as I hiccup a laugh.

I pull back and remove my spectacles and then the contacts, and when I look at him again, he's smiling.

"There's my Rosalind," he says, and I fall into his arms again.

I hug him tight, and then I back away. "How much do you remember of my story last night?"

"All of it, I think, though I seem to have forgotten how you ended up as our son's governess."

"Because you fell asleep during that part."

"Ah." His face goes somber, almost sheepish, that little boy again, uncertain as he says, "I… I should not ask you to repeat any of the story, but I was fevered and…"

"And you need to be sure you heard correctly." To be sure he did not imagine that I have a valid reason for disappearing.

I tell him about the wild ride to Thorne Manor that night four years ago, finding the cat and falling through time.

"Pandora, I believe her name is," I say. "Fittingly."

I'm smiling when I say it, but his gaze is down, his aspect troubled.

"August?"

"You left because of me."

I tense. "No, I left—"

"To fetch your wedding band in the middle of the night. Because you feared I would think you'd removed it for a tryst with William, even though I'd seen you helping Mrs. Shaw with her bread."

My cheeks heat. "I overreacted. I understand that now."

"No," he says slowly. "That is far from the reason I seem upset. I am horrified because I must acknowledge that you did *not* overreact. That if you said you left your ring at Thorne Manor, I'd have escorted you back to ensure it was indeed where you said it was. That is unconscionable."

"As unconscionable as thinking I had abandoned you?"

I don't mean to say that. I mean to be gentle until he is well enough for that conversation. Yet the words slip out, and his face fills with such shame that my breath catches.

"I... I..." he manages.

He sits up suddenly. His eyes widen, face contorting. I reach for him, but he twists away, turning instead over the side of the bed and vomiting.

At first, I think it is the realization of what he has done. His stomach is already upset, and so he vomits with the stress. Yet he doesn't simply throw up. He is wracked by heaves, his whole body convulsing with them, and I leap from the bed, shouting for help. I throw open the door and shout.

When Violet arrives, I'm holding the chamber pot before August, but nothing comes from him. His stomach has emptied, and he is heaving and retching, the sound agonizing.

"Miss?" Violet says carefully.

"Get the doctor," I say. "Now!"

She only stares, and I snarl the words, and I think she is staring in shock, half at her poor master's condition and half at my very un-Clara tone. Then I see something on the pillow. My wig, with the spectacles on the table.

"M-miss?" she says.

"I will explain," I say quickly. "For now, fetch the doctor. *Please.*"

To her credit, she turns and runs. August falls back into the bed, moaning and writhing.

"Rosalind," he rasps.

"I am here," I say as I set down the bowl with a clatter.

I grab the cloth and then climb up to sit beside him, mopping his brow as he moans. His eyes close, and his breathing comes quick, his temperature rising fast.

"Rosalind," he says again.

"Right here," I say. "I'm right here."

"What is the meaning of *this?*" a voice says from the door.

I look over to see Mrs. Landon with the butler—Price—who stands behind her, his mouth in a grim line.

"I can explain later," I say. "For now—"

"You will explain *now.*"

"He's sick," I say. "He suddenly started vomiting—"

"That is not what I mean, and you know it."

I take a deep breath as I continue to mop August's sweating face. "My name is Rosalind Courtenay."

She stares at me. Then her face purples with rage. She turns to Price.

"Get Miss *Smith* out of here," she snaps. "Take her to her room, and lock her in."

"What? No! I'm Rosalind—"

Price grabs me and pulls me from the bed. I twist to my husband.

"August," I say. "Tell them. Please."

But he cannot. He has lost consciousness, his face slack as Price drags me from the room.

TWENTY-FOUR

DO NOT GO easily. I beg Price to bring Hugh. He will remember me from before I disappeared. I beg Price to ask me anything only Rosalind Courtenay would know. He ignores me. He is new to his position, an elevated valet who has not yet found his authority as butler. Finally, as he pushes me into my room, all I can do is beg him not to tell Edmund, to make up some excuse for why his governess is not there.

This is why I do not scream and shout. It is why I do not fight as hard as I could. I do not want to bring my son running. I do not want this to be his first view of his mother, being dragged away screaming by the family butler.

In the end, it is not as if I'm being dragged to the asylum, August unaware that his son's governess was anyone but a mousy madwoman. August knows who I am. I am frightened for him—terrified by that sudden attack of vomiting—but I'm a physician's daughter, and I know it must be something he swallowed in the pond. A mild toxin that his body needs to rid itself of, and since the doctor did the entirely wrong thing by giving him a sedative, his body had no choice but to violently expel the substance as soon as it could.

The sedative and the vomiting have left him exhausted. He will sleep, and then he will wake and ask for me, and it won't matter what anyone says—he will find me. He knows it was me beyond any doubt. I must hold on to that certainty and wait this out.

An hour passes before the door opens. I scramble to my feet. Mrs. Landon walks in, her face unreadable.

"Is he all right?" I say. "Is August—"

"Mr. August to you." She spits the words, and that mask cracks as she advances on me. "No, he is not all right, Miss Smith. You have poisoned him."

"Wh-what?"

"You heard what I said. You were the only one in with him last night, and now he is poisoned."

I shake my head. "He swallowed water, that is all. Still and foul water. The doctor's sedative kept him from vomiting it up, and now that he has—"

"The doctor says the master has been poisoned."

"Then it was not me. He was fine last night. Fevered but otherwise well. I barely got a half glass of water into him."

"You poisoned him. Poisoned his body *and* poisoned his mind, pretending to be his poor dead wife."

"I am his wife." I throw up my arms. "Do I look dead to you?"

"Let me guess. You were knocked on the head and lost your memory. Forgot who you were for four years and then remembered and snuck back by playing governess?"

"I—" I pull myself up straight, remembering who I am. "I do not need to explain to you, Mrs. Landon. My husband shall do so when he is able. I will say only that, yes, a calamity befell me, and as for how I ended up here—"

"Do not give me your excuses, Miss Smith. I know exactly what you're about. You bear some resemblance to the master's dead wife, and so you disguised it to sneak here and ingratiate yourself with his household and

his son. Then, when he is fevered and cannot think straight, you unveil yourself. Right before you poison him."

"Why would I *poison* him?"

"Let us not hide behind simpering masks, Miss Smith. August Courtenay is a wealthy man from an excellent family. What happens to you if he dies of this poison? Preferably after he wakes just long enough to name you his wife?"

"You—you think I want his *money?*"

"Or perhaps he survives, and you manage to convince him you truly are Rosalind. It wouldn't be difficult. It has been four years, and he is still a man haunted by his loss. He's banished every portrait of her. He wakes at night, thinking he sees her on the lawn."

She shakes her head sharply, throwing off what seems like true pain on August's behalf. Then she murmurs, "I knew it was you behind the haunting."

"How? I only arrived a few days ago. According to Violet, this has been going on for years."

Mrs. Landon sniffs. "According to a silly girl, listening to other very silly girls. The only haunting is in Mr. August's grief-stricken mind. The governesses hear him on the parapet, calling to her, and their imaginations run away with them, and soon they're packing their bags and leaving us."

"Is that what happened to the other governess you locked in here?"

She frowns.

"I found her diary," I continue. "She thought she saw me—Rosalind—and when she told you, you locked her in here."

Mrs. Landon's face screws up. "Whatever are you—?" She shakes her head sharply again. "You are trying to confuse me. Making up stories, as if that will save you. I've worked for the Courtenays all of my life. I was a maid here when Mr. August was a boy. When his brother Everett left, I went to work for him. After the old housekeeper retired, Mr. Everett gave me this position, where I tend to Mr. August and the boy."

"The boy you think is spoiled? The boy you think is weak?"

Her eyes flash. "If I am concerned for Master Edmund, it is because I care for him. For him and his father, and I will not let them fall prey to one such as yourself, Miss Smith."

"Fine," I say. "You don't think I'm Rosalind? Bring Hugh here. He knew me. Or wait for my sisters to arrive."

She rocks back on her heels. "Sisters? That's why you mailed Miss Miranda. I saw the letter, and I thought you must be up to no good, so I put it aside."

"You opened my mail?"

"No, I did not. I feared I was being overly suspicious. Perhaps you were mailing for advice about the boy. I will read the letter now and see what machinations you had intended, and I'll be calling for the constable in the morning. Until then, you can wait right here, Miss Smith."

I glare at her, but again, for Edmund's sake, I do not scream or fight. I can wait this out. At worst, I can find a way to unlock the door or crawl from the window. So I settle for a glare, and then I turn away.

The door shuts, and I relax. Then I hear a footboard creak, and I wheel to see Mrs. Landon still there, something white in her hand. She lunges and presses the handkerchief to my mouth and nose, and I inhale a sharp and acrid scent. For a moment, I'm too startled to fight. By the time I come to my senses, it is too late. I lash out and slip, and as I fall, the world fades to black.

The last thing I hear is Mrs. Landon's voice at my ear. "I will not let you destroy this family, Miss Smith. I will *not*."

TWENTY-FIVE

WAKE TO THE hiss of a gaslight lamp and the feel of my hard bed beneath me. I clearly drifted off and dreamed Mrs. Landon confronted and gassed me. As the thought flits through my brain, it teases a memory. Was there not another time today that I believed I'd accidentally drifted off to sleep?

Yes. When August only pretended to think I was still Clara Smith. When he'd teased me about that and then admitted he remembered everything. Seeing my perfect reunion unfold, I can be forgiven for thinking it a dream. Yet now I've dreamed of Mrs. Landon gassing me. What if *both* are the product of sleep? What if Violet never came to fetch me after August's near drowning and everything that has happened since has been my imagination?

I bolt upright and gulp air. Then I stop. The air has a taste to it. The terrible taste of dirt and dank and rot.

The stench of mildew wafts up from my bed, and I blink down to see black mold on the sheet. With a yelp, I leap up, and my feet land on icy stone. I wheel. There's a single gaslight lamp, but it does no more than cast a sickly glow over the room.

The room...which is not my room.

I don't know what room it is. I see only darkness, as if the very walls themselves are woven shadow.

My toes scrunch against the floor. I'm wearing my stockings, having taken off my shoes when I returned to my room. Through the sheer fabric, I feel damp and cold stone. Squinting down, I see only darkness swallowing my feet. I bend and gingerly lower my hand until I touch water-slicked rock. With a shudder, I yank my hand up to see dirt on my fingers.

I glance at the oil lamp. The few feet between me and it seems like a mile, and I shiver, pulling my dress tight around me. Then I start toward it, my toes curling in revulsion each time they touch down and again when they rise, dirt clinging to the bottoms of my feet.

I grit my teeth and make my way to that lamp. As I near it, I see what it rests on: a primitive table, little more than rough-hewn wood nailed into a table-like form. I lift the lamp, but it does little to cut through the darkness.

I hold it at arm's length, and that lets me see the bed. It's narrow, like mine, but it is clearly not mine. It's as rough-hewn as the table, and the sheets are speckled with mold.

I pivot, arm outstretched, light arcing around the room until I can make out a wall. I move toward it, and soon I can see stone. Stone walls covered in black mold and moss. They're sweating, dirty water beading up.

I shiver convulsively now and steel myself to move closer to the wall and then to follow it until I reach a small iron door. I squint, searching for a knob. There is none. No knob. No hinges. Just a solid metal door.

I lift my hand and rap on the metal. The iron muffles the sound, and it is as if I barely tapped. I hit hard and succeed only in skinning my knuckles.

"Hello?" I call. Then louder. "Hello!"

My words echo back to me, trapped within this place as much as my knocking. My teeth chatter, and I allow myself to shiver until the count of three. Then I take a deep breath—ignoring the stale stink of the air—and I continue my circle of the room.

It does not take long. The place is no bigger than my bedroom. Four walls. One impenetrable door. A table. A bed. That is all.

Where am I?

Underground, that is for certain, given the smell, and the weeping stone and the mold.

Under Courtenay Hall?

I have been in the basement storerooms. They are dark and ill-lit, but not like this.

As I think that, though, a memory flutters past from our first summer at Courtenay Hall. As newlyweds, we'd spent a good part of our days enjoying one another's company in the most intimate fashion. Even as I think that, I snort a laugh, the sound echoing through the stone room. That is a very pretty way of phrasing it, but the truth is that August and I had never needed the excuse of being newly wed. Whatever issues we might have had later, our sex life was not affected.

One would think that such a massive estate would afford plenty of privacy. Again, this is another thing that I preferred in the modern age. Close my apartment door, and I shut out the world. Here, while August might be considered master of the house in his brother's absence, he's more like the boss in one of his family factories.

The estate runs smoothly under the watchful eye of the housekeeper and butler, yet there was a constant hubbub of activity surrounding us, and at any moment, someone might need August's attention. We couldn't cuddle in a sitting room without a maid walking in. We couldn't even be assured of privacy in our bedroom, particularly during the day, when a closed door and muffled noises meant a tentative knock and an "Is everything all right, sir?"

That summer, we discovered every spot on the estate where we could be assured of an hour's privacy: the stables, the hedge maze, the boathouse, the follies—particularly the Grecian temple. Even, on one particularly sweltering day, the icehouse.

The memory that rises now is of us finding a relatively welcoming spot in the basement, atop a bed of discarded sacks. Afterward, as we'd

been sneaking out, I'd spotted a heavy door, quite unlike the others. I'd opened it to see a dark staircase leading into blackness.

The subbasement, August had said, tugging the door closed.

It looks deliciously dark, I said. *Is it spooky? Filled with spiders and rats?*

Definitely.

I grinned. *Secret tunnels and terrible dungeons?*

No, he said, sharply enough to startle me. Then he made a face and pulled me to him. *That came out wrong. It is just that I have not been down there in many years, and I…* A shadow crossed his face. *I would prefer not to experience it again. It is a dreadful place.*

I nodded, and he leaned in to kiss me and then whispered, *If you are looking for secret spaces, there is an old poachers' shack at the forest's edge, complete with a tunnel that may not have completely caved in yet. Will that do?*

It will, I said with a smile, and we left the basement, that door firmly closed behind us.

I am in the subbasement.

I almost exhale with relief. I am still in Courtenay Hall. Mrs. Landon has stashed me here until she can fetch the constable. I will spend a very uncomfortable few hours, but then this will be resolved.

Isn't that what you said earlier?

I shake off the doubt. There is no need for panic. Mrs. Landon said she would call the constable in the morning. August knows I'm back, and he will fix this.

But he's sick. What if—?

No, enough of that. Mrs. Landon had come to see me last evening. That means it is, at earliest, the wee hours of the morning and may even be well past dawn. Either the constable shall come and hear my story, or August shall wake and demand to see me.

I must only be patient. I will not panic. I will not.

I AM panicking. It has been hours. I can scarcely guess how many. I am attempting to tell time by the lamp. I've used a broken bit of stone to mark the oil level on the glass. I know that lamps burn approximately one ounce an hour. There'd been a time, after our parents died, when that information had been critical, allowing me to ration oil so Miranda and Portia might read on winter's evenings.

I would estimate this lamp holds no more than a cup of oil. That is sixteen hours of light. With the burn rate, I could more accurately assess how long I'd been in here, presuming the lamp had been close to full. I'd been asleep for around eight hours when I first woke, meaning I'd expected the constable to arrive at any moment.

Now the lamp is nearly empty.

Hours ago, realizing how fast the oil was disappearing, I adjusted the flame to make it smaller and conserve the fuel. It gives off such a faint light now that I can scarcely see my own hands.

I have been in here nearly sixteen hours.

I must have miscalculated the rate of burn. That is what I want to think, but my empty stomach tells me I have not miscalculated. I'm light-headed, and my throat aches with thirst. I'd been too preoccupied yesterday to eat since breakfast. There's no chamber pot in here, but I haven't needed one. I'm weak and dehydrated, and no one is coming.

No one is coming.

How can that be?

Because August is sick. Very sick. Poisoned by someone in this house.

Someone? No, I know who poisoned him. Even when I suspected Violet of the fake hauntings and of leading Edmund toward the pond, I'd ascribed the most innocent of motives to her. A naive girl hoping to better herself by proving she could be the governess Edmund needs. She'd gone about it the wrong way, but as a woman of ambition myself, I know what it is like to be young and foolish and desperate to make one's way in a man's world.

I underestimated Violet. That was my downfall here. I'd seen her hovering over August's meal tray and thought it odd, especially when she left

without taking it. Perhaps the moment Mrs. Landon said "poison," I ought to have remembered that. Yet I'd been too shocked. This wasn't some fictional crime unfolding on a movie screen, where my mind can race ahead to solve the mystery. This was my husband being poisoned by a member of his own staff.

It was not until I woke here that I remembered Violet's guilty jump when I caught her hovering over that tray.

Violet poisoned August. I can only pray she had no motive more sinister than making him ill.

He is very ill. I know that. It explains why he has not set upon Mrs. Landon and demanded answers regarding my whereabouts. However, that does not explain why the constable hasn't come for me. It does not explain why *no one* has come for me.

Perhaps Mrs. Landon is mad. That is the conclusion that keeps whispering in my ear. Locking me in here is, of course, madness, but again, I had ascribed the most innocent of motives to her. She is fanatically loyal to the Courtenays, and she thought I was trying to kill August. She doesn't believe I am Rosalind. She sees only a threat and has locked me in the subbasement until she can summon a constable.

Locked me here for sixteen hours with nothing to eat or drink.

I will not let you destroy this family, Miss Smith. I will not.

She did not call the constable. That was what she said to make me relax and turn away. I did, and she pretended to leave, and then she attacked.

She's left me here to die.

I rise to walk to the door one more time. To pound on it one more time, as if that has done any good the last dozen iterations, my blows making as much noise as a fist hitting a mattress. As I push myself from the bed, my knees buckle, and I grab the bed frame while dizziness rocks me. I squeeze my eyes shut, and when I open them, I catch a flash of movement in the dim lighting.

My first thought is, *Rat!* My second is, *Rat! Maybe there is a hole!*

It is no rat. It is a figure flickering in the gas-lamp light. A figure so faint I cannot make out more than the blue of a dress.

A blue dress.

The hair on my neck prickles as I stare at the faint figure of a woman in blue.

I blink hard. It is the light-headedness. It must be. While I do believe Edmund sees ghosts, I've already determined that the one I saw—the one in blue—was Violet.

I squeeze my eyes shut and lower myself to the bed, and when I look again, she is still there, just the barest outline of a form, the dark wall showing through her as if she were a modern hologram.

When the figure moves, I shrink back, but she's only lifting her arm. Pointing to something. No, touching something. Her fingertips rest on the small table. With her other hand, she beckons me closer.

I squint, trying to make her out better. Blue dress. Pale hair. Small of stature.

This is not Violet. It is the ghost Violet is pretending to be. The ghost Edmund has seen. He told Margaret about it, and either he also told Violet or the governess did. Now I'm seeing Edmund's ghost, hazy and faint, as if I have just enough of the Sight to see this much.

"Who are you?"

Even as the words leave my mouth, I think I'd laugh if I had the strength. Such cliché ghost-encounter dialogue. Next, I'll be asking what she wants.

Still, I must ask. I must say something. She doesn't answer, though. She only points at that small table. I walk to it. As I do, she remains in place, yet no matter how close I get, her figure comes no clearer. Light hair. Blue dress. If she were not slightly taller than me, her hair more light brown than blond, I might think I was seeing a fetch.

I can make out faint features. A stronger nose than I possess. A rounded chin rather than my sharp one. Brown eyes. Yes, not a fetch come to call me unto death. Just a girl in a dress.

A girl. While I can't make out enough to determine age, I get the impression of youth. She's looking at me, and then her gaze moves to the

table. I follow her arm to where her fingertips rest on the top. When she moves, I give a start, but she's only bending. She points under the table. I crouch, and the room seems to tilt, dizziness threatening to engulf me again. I manage to get down on my knees and peer under the table.

It truly is as roughly constructed as I thought. There's a wooden skirt around the tabletop, and that hides what she was indicating. White paper stuck up in the joint between the tabletop and skirting. I tug it out and then turn to her, saying, "Is this what you wanted me to find?" but she is gone.

I rise carefully, bracing myself on the flimsy table. The ghost has vanished, and I am left with a sheet of paper, densely written on both sides, the ink faded with time.

I move back to the bed and position the lamp to shine on the paper as much as possible. Then I begin to read.

TWENTY-SIX

HE WRITING IS tiny but the penmanship exquisite, and I can make it out even with the fading of the ink. It is not the same writer as the journal. I already knew that. As for who she is, I think I know, but I put that aside to focus on the letter.

I have been in this room for three months now and only just managed to convince Tilly to bring me paper and pen. I'd have hoped for more than one sheet, but I will make do with what I have. I need to put this in writing, if only to prove myself not mad when this nightmare finally ends.

Where to begin? At the beginning, I suppose.

My name is Charlotte Courtenay, daughter of the Earl of Courtenay. I am sixteen years old. A girl my age ought to be expected to make foolish and romantic mistakes, but there is one she is not allowed to make, and I have made it. I fell in love. Or I thought it was love, but looking back, I see foolish naiveté. I will not name the man, only say he is twice my age, with a title twice my father's, and I am a very silly girl who believed him when he said he loved me and would marry me. Swept away in love and

passion, I allowed him to do the things that a girl ought not to allow, and it got me into that place feared above all others with my belly growing until I could hide it no longer.

Other parents would send their daughters into the country. My mother is long gone, and my father decided I needed to be punished as well as hidden. My only solace is books, which my father makes Tilly burn after I've read them in case I try to send a message to the world. I could laugh at that. Who would I send it to? Harrison probably hasn't noticed I'm gone. Everett would lock me in here himself if he could. The only one who will be mourning my disappearance is August, and he is too young to read any missive from me, much less come to my aid.

Tilly tells me August is fine. He has been told I've gone away to our aunt's, and he misses me terribly, but he is well. I do not believe her. August is as friendless in this horrible house as I am. It is just the two of us against them all, and I have tried my best to be both sister and mother for him, but now...

Dear Lord, I hardly dare give voice to my fears. I did not foresee a day when I wouldn't be there for him, not until he is grown and gone with friends and family of his own making. Now that he is alone in this house, I wonder whether I have done the wrong thing, whether it would have been better to have prepared him to be alone in this world.

My tears fall on the letter, and I wipe them away.

"No, Charlotte," I say. "Whatever fears August has, they were not of your making. You made him as good and as kind a man as one could be, growing up in such a household. I would never have wished him to be harder, no matter how much easier that might have made his life."

A flicker of blue across the room has my head shooting up.

"That *is* you, isn't it, Charlotte?" I say. "You cannot speak to me, but you can hear me. I *hope* you can hear me."

No answer. No more flashes of blue, either. I return to the letter.

I cannot think of August at this moment. Whatever damage has been done, I shall undo it once I am free of this wretched place. Father thinks he shall put my child in a foundling home. He shall not. I have a plan. I will go along with whatever he decides, play the biddable and cowed daughter, and then I shall take August and run for my aunt's. She is my mother's sister and has long offered to take me in. I have refused only for August's sake. A daughter means little to him, yet he would never have released his hold on a son. So I will take him. Take August. Take this babe in my belly. Flee to our aunt's before I can give birth.

Is that the plan of a child? The same foolish girl who believed a handsome man's lies? Perhaps, but I am not a fool. I have not spent three months in this hole sobbing into my pillow. I have plotted my escape. Oh, so many plots, all of them fruitless. Now, though, I have the one that will work because it does not rely on anyone except myself. I have stolen a spoon and used it to chip away at the mortar on one stone beside the door. I have dislodged the stone entirely now, and when I reach through, I can unlatch the door from the outside. Someday, I will tell this story to my child, and he or she shall be amazed that their old mum was once so clever. Ha!

I am biding my time. The baby is still a month away by Dr. C's reckoning. I shall use that time to make absolutely certain I can flee in safety. It is fall now. Summer has ended, and Harrison has returned to school. Tilly says Father and Emmett have business on the coast, and after that, they shall take August to London for the winter. That is my window of chance. That week when my father and brothers are away, and August is here alone. I need only wait until Tilly tells me Father is gone.

I will hide this note where they shall not discover it. I write it only in the event that I am caught and Father tries to claim I am mad, talking of being locked in the darkest cellars of Courtenay Hall. This letter shall prove I do not lie. With any luck, I shall never need it.

The letter ends there. I clasp it between shaking fingers as I process the contents. I want to believe this is proof that Charlotte Courtenay is still alive. She'd escaped this room, and being unable to take August with her, she'd fled and gone into hiding with her child. That is the romantic interpretation. It is not the truth.

"You didn't make it out, did you, Charlotte?" I say to the empty room. "You did not survive your escape."

A hint of blue flickers against the darkness. The lamp sputters, and I quickly lower the flame, conserving what little remains. The ghostly figure appears for a moment, only to fade as fast as the light.

"I'm not strong enough to see you," I murmur. "It takes all your energy to appear to me."

Another flutter, as if in assent. Then in a sudden surge, she stands before me as if she is flesh and blood, and when I see her, there is no doubt to her identity.

"Charlotte," I say, as my eyes fill. "I'm sorry. Whatever happened to you, I am so sorry."

Her lips move, but no sound comes out. A flash of annoyance crosses her face, and it is so familiar that I cannot help smiling through my tears. Both August and Edmund make the same expression when they are frustrated by a thing they cannot do.

"The fault is mine," I say. "My sister will be able to hear you, and I will bring her so that you may say all you need to say."

She nods and then points toward the door, and I smile again.

"Right," I say. "That was the purpose of having me read the letter, wasn't it? Sharing your story, yes, but also telling me how to escape so that I might share it beyond these detestable walls."

I rise as I tuck her letter deep in my bodice. "Save your strength, Charlotte. I may need your help to find my way out of here."

She nods and disappears, and I pick up the lamp. It flickers once and then sputters out, leaving me in blackness.

I sigh. "Well, that is par for the course, I believe. Let us see whether I can manage this in the dark."

TWENTY-SEVEN

ID CHARLOTTE EVER escape this room? I do not know. The stone is in place, but that means little. Perhaps she returned it to its place so she could escape again if she were thrown back in here. Or perhaps someone else returned it after she left. All I know is that the stone has not been mortared in again.

Removing it takes effort. Charlotte pried it out before I was born, and whatever dirt has collected has acted as a glue. I also lack her handy spoon. I have only the oil lamp, and since it no longer works, I decide to use it for another purpose.

In the darkness, I remove the knob that raises the wick and use the shaft to pry out the rock. By the time it moves, my fingers ache, and blood trickles from skinned knuckles. When there is finally movement, I do not bother tugging the stone out quietly as Charlotte would have. I brace myself, raise both palms and shove so hard one of my wrists snaps back, pain slamming down my arm. My reward is the most satisfying thud as the stone falls to the floor.

Reaching through the hole, I twist to push in up to my shoulder, but it isn't necessary. Charlotte chose her stone well, and I easily reach the latch.

That's all it is. No lock. Just a latch that rises and lowers. I pull it up, and there is another satisfying sound: the clunk of the latch falling free. With one push, the hinges creak, and the door swings open.

For a moment, I stand in the opening, breathing and shaking with exertion. I blink, but there's nothing to see except darkness.

Of course there are no lights in the corridor. That would make this far too easy.

I take a deep breath, and I step out. Slick cold stone underfoot makes me shiver anew.

I'm free. I will be fine.

Am I sure I'm free? I can't even see whether I'm in a corridor or another room with another locked door. Or a locked hallway exit, and that is why Charlotte never made it to safety.

I square my shoulders and step forward just a few scant feet before my hands hit another wall. Definitely a corridor. Now choose a direction and follow it.

I pick left and walk step by careful step, hands searching all around me so I don't bash into a wall. After ten steps, I nearly do exactly that.

Wrong direction.

I turn around and head back. A chittering comes from somewhere up ahead.

Rats. Naturally, there must be rats.

I adjust my skirts and keep going.

When the chittering comes again, I pause. That is not a rat. It's a rattling, scraping sound, as if someone is trying to open a door.

Mrs. Landon? Do I have time to dash back into my room and slam the rock into place?

I don't even have time to *decide* before the door cracks open. A curse rings out, and a lantern swings up, my husband's face reflected in the glow.

August stands at the end of the hall. He wears his nightshirt, legs and feet bare, someone behind him saying, "Sir, please. You should not be out of bed."

I glimpse Hugh over August's shoulder. The young man goes still, his eyes widening, and then he dips his chin and retreats, and it is only my husband and me, staring at each other.

"Please tell me I did not cleverly escape my captivity only to discover I was mere moments from being rescued," I say.

When August speaks, his voice is a croak, but a sparkle lights his tired eyes. "Would you have rather been rescued, Rosie? You have never struck me as the type."

I purse my lips. "No, you are quite correct. This is the best of all possible outcomes. I managed to free myself, *and* you appeared—in your nightshirt—to rescue me." I waggle my brows. "It is a very sexy nightshirt."

A bubble of laughter, and in five steps, he is to me and scooping me up in the tightest of hugs, whirling me around the hall. I entwine my fingers behind his neck and kiss him as I have not dared to kiss him yet, a kiss with no fear for the future lingering behind it. A true reunion kiss, which ends with us against the wall, and his hands hiking up my dress. He stops himself and shakes his head.

"And that is not at all the proper way to show my wife how much I have missed her. Let us get upstairs to a bed."

I reach down to tug up his nightshirt as I wrap my legs around him. "I have not eaten nor drunk in a full day, and I suspect you are in little better shape. I fear if we wait for a bed, we shall both collapse into it, snoring." I wrap my arms around his neck. "There is all the time in the world for proper lovemaking after this. Right now..." I press into him. "I do not care to wait."

A groan as his mouth comes down to mine, and he gives me what I want.

⁓ঞ⁓

I'M NOT quite certain how we do make it upstairs after that. I only know that we managed to not collapse in a heap of intertwined bodies for the poor staff to find. On our way upstairs, I spot faces peeking from

doorways, but August sends them scattering with a glance. When he sees Hugh again, he says, "Bring us food and drink directly from the pantry, and see that it is not poisoned this time."

We make it to August's quarters—*our* quarters—and collapse into bed. Then I sit upright.

"Mrs. Landon," I say.

"We cannot find her. She has apparently been missing since last evening around the time you were last seen. I presume she is responsible for your confinement."

"She locked me in a cellar room to await the constable. She did not believe I am me."

He growls deep in his throat. "Whatever madness seized the woman, it shall be dealt with when she is found. I am only sorry it took this long for me to come searching. I was unconscious until nearly noon. I woke looking for you, and then Edmund came and—"

"Edmund!" I say. "Where is he?"

"Sleeping, thankfully. I did not tell him about you, but he could tell I was distraught. First, I am ill, and then, I am in a state. He was already exhausted, and as soon as I calmed him, he went straight to sleep. He is in there."

He points at the adjoining sitting room. I leap up—or try to, stumbling in my weakness. August climbs from bed to help me, and we make our way to the adjoining door. I open it to see Edmund asleep on the settee, Surrey watching us, her glower warning us not to disturb him.

"We will tell him as soon as he wakes," August says, kissing my cheek as his arms wrap around me.

"I-I'm not even sure *how* to tell him."

August's arms tighten, and his chin rests on my shoulder. "It will not matter how. He'll scarcely hear the words. What will matter is that his mother is home."

I break then. I don't even feel it coming. One moment, I'm watching my son, my husband's arms around me, and four years of grief rush back, and I sob, the pain like a knife to my gut.

August picks me up and closes the door. I protest that he is weakened from the sickness and ought to put me down.

"You are as light as our son," he says. "We will need to fatten you up. Entire dinners of cream, I believe. You may need to share with Surrey, though. She is quite a beast when it comes to cream."

I smile through my tears and let him lower me into bed. When he crawls in beside me, I try to speak but end up sobbing again instead, my arms around him, face against his chest. He holds me and whispers that he is here, he will always be here, that he is so sorry for what I have lost.

That is when I truly do break down. Those words. He is sorry for what I have lost. I have not articulated it, and yet he knows. He understands I am sobbing in relief and in grief, too, overwhelmed by these years that have passed without me.

"You are such a good father," I say when I am able to speak. "I have watched you with Edmund, and you are everything I could have wanted for him."

"A good father, perhaps," he says, "but not a good husband."

My voice catches. I open my mouth, and his finger to my lips stops my words.

"That is not a plea for you to tell me otherwise, Rosie. In my terror of losing you, I saw threats everywhere, and I did not see what was right before me—a wife who gave me no reason to fear. Instead, when you disappeared, I took it as proof I had been right, even when others told me I was mad for thinking such a thing. I *was* mad, in my way. I lost my mind. I could not bear to think you had died, and the only other possibility was that you had left us. If you left, you could come back. If you died—"

He shakes his head sharply as his own eyes glisten. "That is no excuse."

"It is an explanation," I say softly. "One I had already realized, even if it did not justify what you did." I take a deep breath. Part of me wants to brush this under the rug. I cannot, though. I must speak now, or I never will.

"Our son was stolen from me, and I was stolen from him," I say. "It is a horrible thing for any child as you well know. But you made it worse.

You kept my memory from him. I know you said only good things, but you raised him in a world without me. No portraits. No talk. You erased me, August."

The horror in his face makes me want to pull back the words, tell him I don't mean them. But I do. This is what he must understand. He hurt me, and I am still here. It is not an unforgivable trespass. It is simply one that must be acknowledged.

"I-I-I did not think..." he begins.

"No," I say firmly. "You did not. You were in pain, and you erased me to ease it. These are things we must work on, August. I am here. I want to be here forever, as your lover, your partner, your wife. You need to let me do that. Let me in all the way. You need to say, 'I am afraid of losing you,' not 'You are going to leave me.' I raced to Thorne Manor to save my marriage, and I had done nothing to damage it. I was in a constant state of worry, endlessly trying to soothe your fears, feeling as if I must be doing something to arouse them."

"You did not."

I look up into his eyes, meeting his gaze. "Yes, I did not. The problem is yours, and we must treat it as yours. I cannot allow your fear to infect me, and I absolutely will not allow it to infect our son."

He nods, his face a beautiful ruin of regret and pain. I let him have that moment, and then I crawl into his arms and whisper, "Tell me we can do this, August. I do not know if I can survive losing you ever again. Please tell me we can do it."

"We can do it." His arms crush tight around me. "I *will* do it."

TWENTY-EIGHT

OOD AND DRINK arrive after that. August brings them in and closes the door with a warning that we are not to be disturbed before morning.

On hearing a female voice respond, I scramble up.

"Who was that?" I say.

He brings the tray to the bed. "Mrs. Beechworth herself. If they have news of Mrs. Landon, they will tell us."

"I mean Violet. She…"

I trail off, realizing that to even enter into that conversation requires talking about the ghost, and the fact that I know who that ghost is, what happened to his sister. He must be told. Just not now. Not yet.

"Is Violet around?" I ask as innocently as I can.

"No," he says slowly, gaze locking on mine. "She had a sudden emergency at home and left before I woke. That was not an emergency, was it? You believe she was in league with Mrs. Landon."

"No, I… I…" I must get at least part of this out, or I endanger him and our son. "I believe she is the one who poisoned you."

"What?" Tea sloshes over the cup as he pours. "Violet?"

"It is a theory, one I must still prove. Until then, I only ask that she be kept away from both you and Edmund."

His eyes widen in alarm. "You believe she would harm Edmund?"

"No, I..." I take a deep breath as I meet his gaze. "It is a very long story, August, and not one to share now. You have been ill. I would like for you to recover before we discuss this. All I ask is that Violet be kept away."

"I think we need to discuss this immediately, Rosalind," he says. "You're shaking."

I clench my fists as I realize he is correct. My throat is so dry I can barely draw breath. When I shift on the bedspread, the note tucked in my bodice seems to crackle as loud as gunfire.

"Rosie?" he says, moving to me, hand on my leg. "Whatever it is, I am strong enough to hear it. I have you back. I am strong enough for anything."

When I look up at him, tears make his face swim before me. My lips quiver.

I take Charlotte's letter from my bodice. "I found this in that room. Hidden under a table. I would have spared you this. But yes, you need to know. I think... I think she would have wanted you to know."

He unfolds the letter. Then he begins to read. As his gaze tracks the words, slow paralysis claims his face until even his eyes are unreadable. He finishes, sets it down and stares, just stares into nothing.

When I can take it no longer, I manage a choked, "I am so sorry, August." His arms open, and I fall into them. We hold each other tight through a long silence before he says, "Thank you."

I pull back. "For what?"

He lifts the letter. "Closure." His voice cracks, and he clears his throat. "There are still questions, but at least now I know it did not happen as my father said."

He turns to me. "He told me she'd gone to my aunt's. Then she returned, and before she even came to see me, she went out for a boat ride and drowned. I never knew how to cope with that. I wanted to say it could not be true, that she'd have come to see me first. Then I feared I overstated my place in her life and that she truly did forget me on her return."

"You did not overstate your place in her life. You could not."

He nods. "I see that now. I spent my life trying to love my father in spite of all he did to me. I spent my life trying to win his approval. Now I am glad I never did, and I only wish he were alive so I could confront him with this." He pauses. "Or perhaps I should not wish that, because if he were, you might have a murderer for a husband."

He takes a deep breath. "I ought not to say that."

I crawl over to him. "You may absolutely say that to me, August. Your father was a monster, and it is a miracle you survived that. Not only *survived* but grew into the man you are. You have Charlotte to thank for that."

"And you," he says, his voice husky. "I have you, too, Rosalind. Charlotte started me on my way. Meeting you—*winning* you—returned me to that path, and I think that is why I struggled so much with the fear of losing you. I could not believe I had won you." He looks at the letter. "My father's voice still rang in my ears, telling me I was too soft, too empty headed, good for nothing but flitting about balls like a pretty girl."

I hug him. I do not tell him that isn't true. He knows it, and he is not asking for reassurance.

"He locked me in there once," he says against my ear. "In what might be the same room where you and Charlotte—" He clears his throat as it closes. "It was only for a night. I would not stop crying for her, and he locked me in there, and now I realize he'd been locking me in the very room where she might have—"

I cut him off with a kiss. Then I pull back. "We do not know what happened to Charlotte, but we will get the whole story soon enough. Her ghost showed me where the letter was, August. I must have just enough of my family's Sight to let her appear to me, however briefly. We will ask Miranda to come, and we will learn the whole truth."

He's silent for a moment. Then he says, "So it is Charlotte who haunts this place. Charlotte who Edmund sees. Charlotte who even I have seen, outside my window." He looks at me. "The other night, it was obviously you, but I have seen a ghost on other occasions. A light-haired woman in a blue dress."

"While I do think Edmund has seen Charlotte, I believe you were seeing Violet impersonating the ghost that Edmund sees, which Violet mistook for me."

His brows knit. As I explain, his face gathers in anger.

"She led Edmund toward the pond?" he says. "Then she sent *me* there?"

I lift my hands. "It's a theory."

"It's a theory based on indisputable fact," he says. "She was with Edmund that day while Mrs. Landon was keeping you busy. That suggests they were in league together. Also, yes, Violet did know Margaret. Violet arrived shortly before Margaret left, but they became fast friends in that time."

"How long has Violet worked here?"

"Two years. I was very upset with Mrs. Landon for hiring her. I'd told her that I did not want any young maids in the house. Not with Everett around."

I nod. His brother is known to prey on pretty and vulnerable maids.

"There'd been an incident shortly before that," August says. "Bronwyn caught Everett with a maid who'd been brought in because Mrs. Landon took pity on her family. The girl is now in London working for us. Then I returned to find Violet here. I was furious."

"What was Mrs. Landon's excuse?"

"Nothing. She just told me that Violet deserved a chance. She hinted that my family owed it to her and that she could guarantee Everett would not touch her."

I go quiet, biting back the obvious solution to that mystery.

"Yes," August says, as if I've voiced my thoughts aloud. "My fear, naturally, was that the poor girl was Everett's own daughter. I confronted her with that. If it were the case, I would have insisted Everett do right by her, which requires far more than giving the child a maid's position in her own family home."

"What did Mrs. Landon say?"

"Only that I was mistaken. She would not discuss the matter further, and since it is not my house, I had no say in the matter. I now believe she brought the girl in for this scheme. That the haunting was not Violet's idea.

It was Mrs. Landon's. While Margaret and Violet became close, Margaret was friendly with Mrs. Landon first, from our visits in the previous year. We know Edmund told Margaret about the ghost. What if Margaret then told Mrs. Landon, who hired Violet because she matched the physical description of the ghost as told by Edmund?"

"Because Violet looks, not like me, but like Charlotte." I glance at August. "She does, doesn't she?"

"That is why I suspected her of being Everett's child."

When I resume eating without comment, August says, "Rosie? You're thinking something?"

"I realize this is an indelicate question, addressing a memory you will not wish revisited, but you have said that you were there when they found Charlotte in the pond."

He flinches and then comes back with a firm, "I was."

"Was it possible to tell, in hindsight, whether she was pregnant?"

He pauses. Then he pales. "I had not thought of that. She was found shortly after drowning, and so there was no chance of mistaking a pregnancy for water bloat. She must have already given birth." He looks sharply at me. "Violet? But she is scarcely sixteen. I cannot imagine any sort of disguise that would make a thirty-five-year-old look *that* young."

"Not Charlotte's daughter. Her granddaughter."

"Granddaughter?" He sputters. "How...?" He trails off as if doing the math and realizing it is entirely possible for a thirty-five-year-old to have a daughter Violet's age.

"We cannot think on that now," I say. "Set it aside until we can find and confront Mrs. Landon." I push the tray toward him. "Eat. We need food and drink and sleep. Also, a bath. I am in desperate need of a bath."

I DO not get my bath. Nor anything else I might have hoped for after we are fed and cleaned up. I finish my meal, and then August takes the tray

away, and I watch him go. I comment about how much nicer the view would be without that ridiculous nightshirt. The next thing I know, I'm waking in bed, entwined with August, who is no longer wearing the night-shirt, and I apparently fell asleep before I ever got to see him remove it.

Now he's soundly asleep, snoring softly, and I'm wide awake. I kiss his lips. Even kiss his chest, my kisses going ever lower in hopes that will wake him. When it does not, I briefly consider continuing my voyage to its desti-nation, but he is so soundly asleep that I must admit I ought to let him sleep.

I crawl from bed to discover I've been equally disrobed, which makes me wonder whether August attempted his own gentle waking efforts, and I'd snored right through them. I smile and look around for something to wear before I check on our son. I open the wardrobe, and I'm planning to take out one of August's shirts when I spot something hanging at the very back. I pull out a simple ivory dress that makes my chest tighten. It is the one I'd worn when August proposed to me. I'd accidentally left it behind, and on our next visit, we'd put it into the wardrobe, joking that it belonged at Courtenay Hall.

As I run my fingers down the fabric, my eyes fill with tears. Happy tears this time. Not sorrow for the memories I missed, but excitement for the ones still to come.

I tug on the dress without undergarments, which feels hilariously ris-qué after just a few days back in this world. It will be decorous enough to visit my son, though.

I ease open the door and go inside. Edmund sleeps as soundly as his father. I sit on the floor beside him, and stroke his hair and kiss his cheek. I do not try to wake him. August should be here for that moment. I just want to spend a little more time with him now that I know the end of my ruse is near. In a few short hours, I will be Rosalind Courtenay again, reunited with my family, the culmination of every dream I've had in the past four years.

I lay my head down beside my son's, and I close my eyes and imagine all the wonderful things we will do together. When I open my eyes, I give

a start, seeing August in his nightshirt, watching me from the other end of the settee.

I blink rapidly as I lift my head. "Did I fall asleep?" I whisper.

August nods.

"You ought to have woken me," I say.

He doesn't answer. He slides from the settee to the floor and tugs me to him. Then his fingers touch the collar of my dress.

"I thought I was seeing things," he says hoarsely. "I must surely be dreaming, to wake and find you sleeping beside our son, wearing this dress."

"You kept it."

Pain crosses his face. "I kept everything, Rosalind. I may have pretended otherwise, but I locked away everything you left. Some pieces, though, I could not bear to hide, and I only tucked them out of sight. Memories for me alone."

As I crawl onto August's lap, Edmund makes a noise in sleep, and I press my fingers to my lips and motion to the door. August scoops me up before I can protest. He takes me from the sitting room and shuts the door behind us. Then he turns to the left, through another door into the bath.

"I believe you mentioned wanting this?" he says, and I see the tub is filled with steaming water.

"However did you manage that?" I say.

He smiles. "You may have been sleeping for quite some time. I remembered you had requested a bath, and I prepared one for you."

In the modern world, it would be a fairly simple—if still very considerate—thing to draw me a bath. Not so here, where hot water requires both heating and hauling.

"Thank you," I say.

I shift to climb from his arms, and he sets me down on my feet but keeps hold of me, one hand on each side of my waist.

"I presume you will require help with your bath, Mrs. Courtenay?" he says. "You have suffered a great ordeal."

I can't help grinning. "I absolutely require help, Mr. Courtenay. My ordeal has left me quite weakened."

"Then please do not exert yourself. Save your energy, which you will require later."

"Shortly?" I say, waggling my brows.

He waves a finger at me. "None of that. I have a task to complete, and you shall not interrupt me."

"Is that a challenge? Please tell me it is a challenge."

He chuckles. "It would be the easiest challenge you have ever faced, my lady, and so I beg of you, do not attempt it."

"Beg?"

"Stop…"

"When you say *beg*, do you mean do not make you beg? Or that I should not beg. I could beg if you'd like. I could beg very prettily."

There's a growl in his voice as he says, "I seem to recall you do so *very* prettily."

"I could do so even better now. It has been nearly four years, and that brief interlude in the basement, while decent enough, was not quite what I would call adequately satisfying." I look up at him. "Would you like to know what I call adequately satisfying?"

"*After* your bath, yes. I would like to know in great detail, which I shall take as direction. However, while it may have been nearly four years for you, I am not quite so starved, having been visited on many nightly occasions by a certain fair-haired nymph in my dreams."

"Nymph? How shocking."

"Even more shocking, she greatly resembled my wife. Looked like her, sounded like her, even smelled like her."

"Did she"—I whisper a word in his ear—"like her?"

His eyes widen. "Mrs. Courtenay, wherever did you hear such language. And the answer is, yes, she did so exactly like her."

"Tell me more."

He shakes his head, choking on a laugh. "You are determined not to have this bath that I so lovingly drew for you, aren't you?"

I sigh and reach around for the buttons on my dress. "Fine. We shall do this your way, but you had better make it worth my while."

Another sputtered laugh. "I will take *that* as a challenge." He taps away my hands. "Enough of that. This is my job, remember?"

His hands slide up my back to the row of tiny buttons, and one by one, he flicks them open. Then he peels the dress forward off my shoulders and lets it slide to the floor. Then he stares at my naked form.

"Mrs. Courtenay," he says. "You seem to have quite forgotten your undergarments."

"They were in far too disreputable a state after my confinement. Which may be an excuse. I must warn you that I have become quite accustomed to twenty-first-century underthings."

"Dare I ask what those might be?"

I look down at myself. "Well, that depends. First, there is the brassiere, with two pieces of fabric to cover the breasts. Then there are the panties, which would be like bloomers if you cut off the leg pieces."

"That sounds dreadfully uncomfortable. Is the brassiere absolutely necessary?"

I smile. "It is not, at least not when lounging about. I am rather fond of the pretty ones, though, with lace and ribbons. As for the panties, the smaller, the better. There is one type, called a *thong*, which is just the smallest scrap of fabric for the front and then a strip around back that nestles between the buttocks. It is far more comfortable than one would imagine, and I daresay it looks rather fetching."

"I suspect *fetching* is not quite the word," he says, his voice hoarse. "Would it be impolite to impose on Lady Thorne to purchase these items and return them for you? For your comfort, of course?"

"That's very thoughtful of you. Also, while we are at it, there are the cutest little nightgowns that barely cover—"

He cuts me off with a kiss. "I think we'd best postpone this discussion for later. Rest assured, I am quite certain we can find whatever funds are required to fully outfit you in whatever you desire."

"We can choose from the catalogs," I say. "I'll ask Lady Thorne to bring one."

"Ca...catalogs?"

"With models wearing the goods. So we may see how they look, which is important. Yes, I'll ask for catalogs that we may peruse together." I peer at him. "Your illness seems to be returning, Mr. Courtenay. Your eyes seem fever bright, and you appear to be"—I glance down at his crotch—"in some discomfort."

He scoops me up and plunks me into the water.

"I take it you do not want to shop the catalogs together?" I say. "If you would rather shop them alone—"

"Stop."

"You could shop them alone, and I could watch you shop them alone. Your face is getting red now, Mr. Courtenay. Are you certain you are all right?"

"I am quite all right. I just seem to have forgotten what a minx my wife can be."

"Is that a problem?"

He kisses me. "It is normally the opposite of a problem. Except when I am trying to complete the task of bathing her. Yes to the catalog. Yes to viewing them in whatever manner you like, Rosie. Just stop talking about it. Please. I am determined to get through this as hard as you are making that."

My gaze drops again to his crotch. "Very hard, it seems."

"Exceedingly so."

"You aren't wearing any undergarments yourself, are you?" I say, more closely examining the area in question now that it is at eye level.

"Rosie..."

"Yes, yes, I need a bath." I slide down, hands going over my head as I drop under the water. I give myself a shake there and then fly up again. "Is that sufficient?"

His gaze travels down my body.

"Do I look clean enough to you, Mr. Courtenay? Please, conduct a careful examination."

I rise until my body floats above the surface and wriggle for him.

"Do you need more time?" I say. "Closer examination?"

"Closer examination, I believe," he says, his voice hoarse.

I wiggle onto my knees and lean over, taking the hem of his night-shirt. "This appears to be impeding closer examination. May I remove it?"

"You may."

He lifts his hands, and I pull it off. Then I take a moment to fully appreciate the sight of him before I clasp his hands and pull him into the tub.

TWENTY-NINE

HEN WE WAKE again, it is morning. The door to the sitting room is still closed, and there is no sound of Edmund stirring within, so we take advantage of the opportunity for an intimate waking up.

"I do believe, Mr. Courtenay, that you are trying for a second child already," I say as we finally rise to dress.

"I did not instigate *that* session."

"So you *don't* want to try for another child so quickly?"

He gives a low laugh and scoops me up. "I said nothing of the sort, Mrs. Courtenay. We may begin whenever you wish. Immediately seems like a fine plan."

A rap at the door has me struggling to get down as fast as I can.

"One moment," August calls.

It takes a little longer than a moment for me to tug on my undergarments from the day before and then my engagement dress. It takes August even longer to get to the point he considers decent, which means looking as if he's about to go into a royal breakfast. The man does love his clothing, and I love him for it. Yet another thing I'm glad his father and brothers never managed to drive out of him. We should all have the things which bring us joy, and no one should be able to shame us for them.

When he does pull open the door, his flawless attire is lost on Bridget, who is far too busy gaping at me sitting on the edge of the bed.

"Yes, that is my Rosalind," August says. "I will introduce her properly to the staff later. Right now, we require breakfast. A tray for three, please. We'll be dining with Edmund. Oh, and bring him a pot of honey for his bread." He glances at me. "He's very fond of honey. I try to regulate his consumption, but this seems a special occasion." Back to Bridget. "Also, please unearth a bottle of champagne from the cellar. Yes, it is far too early for alcohol, but I am in the mood to celebrate."

Her mouth opens to answer, but he's still speaking. "Has there been any sign of Mrs. Landon?"

"No, sir, but—"

"Violet?"

Bridget frowns. "She went to her family, sir."

"Yes, I know, but if she returns, I wish to be told immediately. Until then, my greatest desire is to be left alone. The staff will have questions, and I will answer them before lunch. First, I will be dining with my wife and son in our quarters, undisturbed."

"Yes, sir, but Master Edmund is not abed, sir. He's off riding with Hugh and Charlie."

"What?" August spins toward the closed sitting-room door.

"He slipped out an hour ago," Bridget continues. "He came to find Miss Smith but, er..."

"Oh, no," I whisper. "Please tell me he did not see his governess in bed with his father."

August snorts a stifled laugh, and Bridget's face turns scarlet.

"N-no, sir," she says to August. "He did not seem to realize his father wasn't alone in, er, his, um..."

"Bed, Bridget," August says. "The word is *bed*, and it is not a foul one. Also, when my wife speaks to you, please address her directly. She is mistress of this house as I am master when my brother is not at home."

He says it gently, but Bridget's cheeks still pink. She glances slightly to the side of me, as if my sitting on August's bed is far too suggestive.

"I am pleased to make your acquaintance, ma'am," she says. "As to your question, no, Master Ed—er, your son did not see you with your husband. In truth, I did not know what to say when he asked about you—er, Miss Smith. Hugh said we ought to say nothing until we were certain you had spoken to him."

"Hugh is correct, thank you."

"We told him that you, um, that Miss Smith was sleeping in the governess's quarters after an ordeal and should not be disturbed. That is when Hugh offered the horse ride as a distraction."

I glance at August. "I was under the impression Edmund did not like horses."

August sighs. "He takes after his father in that, I fear. My sister helped me overcome my fears, and so we are helping Edmund and have every hope he will turn into as fine an equestrian as his mother. Or, barring that, an adequate one like his father."

"Adequate?" a voice calls from down the corridor. "I do believe that oversells your skill, August."

I leap from the bed. "William?"

"Y-yes," Bridget says quickly. "I'm sorry, sir, but you have guests. I had not gotten to that part. It is Lord and Lady Thorne. I asked them to wait in the parlor."

"She did," says Bronwyn's voice, a moment before the woman herself appears in the doorway. "We quite ignored her, and it is entirely William's fault."

William appears then with little Amelia on his hip. As he walks in, he covers the toddler's eyes. "Shield your gaze, Ami. It is an unmade bed."

Bridget withdraws as quickly as she can. William strides in and looks from the bed to me to August. Then he turns to Bronwyn.

"I fear we have arrived too late," he says. "We have missed the chance to play our proper role in this romantic drama." He looks at August. "You couldn't have waited for us?"

"Waited for you to do what?" August says.

"Swoop in and save the day, obviously. Have you never read a romantic novel, sir? Your poor wife was trapped in another time, and you were being an absolute ass about her disappearance."

"Ass?"

"Absolute ass. So the poor lady returns and very clearly, being an ass—"

"You just like saying that, don't you?" August mutters.

"I do," William says. "And I would suggest you get used to hearing it. Being an ass, clearly you will question her return. Or, perhaps more accurately, you will question the explanation she gives for her absence. Time travel? A likely story. And so, Bronwyn and I return home to find a letter entreating us to come to poor Rosalind's aid so that she may reveal herself to her utter ass of a husband."

"*Utter* ass?"

"It's a slight step down from absolute. Stop interrupting, or you will lose the points you've gained. We fairly fly to Courtenay Hall, where surely we shall find poor Rosalind in dire straits, having been prematurely unmasked, beseeching her infuriating husband to believe her story. Instead, we find…" He waves at the bed. "We are too late. You have skipped the misunderstanding part of the story and already reunited."

"Does the fact that I believed Rosalind straightaway alleviate my ass-ery?"

William purses his lips. "I'm not certain. The fact that you seem to have easily reunited, skipping the misunderstanding stage of the drama, would seem to indicate that you never truly believed she had abandoned you after all. You just claimed she did to be—dare I say it—an ass?"

Bronwyn walks to me. "This matter doesn't seem likely to be settled soon. I say we leave them to it. A proper introduction is in order." She puts out her hand. "Bronwyn Thorne. I believe we have met."

I open my arms and say, "May I?"

"Of course, if you can get around this."

She gestures to her pregnant stomach, and I laugh and embrace her as tightly as I dare. Then I whisper, "Thank you. If not for you, I would still be there."

"Well, then we have Fate to thank for bringing me to your bakery. I only wish I'd trusted my intuition faster. I recognized you from your portrait, but I needed William to be sure. If I had introduced myself, we'd have avoided all this."

I shake my head. "I saw you and William together, and I could have stepped forward then. I did not because I was afraid. The thought that I might be stranded in your time—passing messages to August and Edmund—was too much. I needed to know whether something had changed and I could finally return."

"Eh-eh!" a tiny voice says, and we all turn to see Amelia bouncing in her father's arms.

"She is saying she has been patiently listening to our nonsense long enough," William says. "We have been in Edmund's house for an hour now and have yet to see the prince-ling himself."

"Soon, Ami," Bronwyn says, taking their daughter. "Edmund is off riding his pony."

"Eh-eh!" Amelia says even louder, bouncing hard enough that Bronwyn needs to readjust her grip.

"Now you've done it," William says. "The magic word. P-O-N-Y."

I smile. "Someone takes after her daddy, does she? I saw the photo in your office. She looked very at home on horseback."

"She is," Bronwyn says. "Do not even ask how many hours we spend holding her on her pony and leading her around the stable. I said a rocking horse would be quite sufficient, but no, her daddy bought her a pony before she drew her first breath."

"Lucky girl," I say. "I didn't get mine until I was seven, and then I had to share with my sisters."

Amelia stares at me.

"Yes, isn't that shocking?" William says. "Poor Aunt Rosalind was very hard done by."

"I think she's staring because she has no idea who this strange 'Aunt Rosalind' lady is," I say.

"This is Edmund's mommy," Bronwyn says. "She had to go away for a while, but she's back now. Can you wave hello, Amelia?"

The toddler continues to stare.

"She inherited her father's manners, I'm afraid," Bronwyn says.

"Here," William says. "Try this. Ami? This is the woman who baked those jam tarts for you? Remember the jam-jams? She made them." He points at me. "Jam-jam lady."

Amelia squeals and reaches for me. "Ja-ja! Ja-ja!"

"In that, she takes after her mother," Bronwyn says. "We will find you jam-jams later. Right now, perhaps you can steal a bit of Edmund's breakfast." She looks at William. "Just easy on the honey, okay?"

"Modern mothers," he says, rolling his eyes. "Back in our day—which is right now—we gave our babies everything. Including opium. Children of the future are terribly deprived."

As I laugh, he walks over and pats my back. "It is good to see you, Rosalind. I haven't said that yet, but it is."

"You may give her a proper hug," August says. "I promise not to be an ass about it ever again."

I hug him then, letting my face press into his jacket and feeling the strong warmth of his arms. As I back away, I wipe at my eyes.

"Ja-ja!" Amelia says, pointing at me.

"Yes, jam-jam lady has something in her eye, but I think it is happiness," William says.

"I'm going to be jam-jam lady forever, aren't I?" I say, wiping away tears.

"Until you bake her your famous scones," William says. "Then you will be sco-sco lady, and also her mother's *dearest* friend."

Bronwyn rolls her eyes. Then she motions to ask whether she may sit beside me on the bed. We both lower ourselves, and she sets Amelia down between us.

"I do not even know what to do now," William says. "We came for a rescue, and there is no rescue required. It is like showing up to a party, only to find that you have missed it."

"In your case, you'd consider that a blessing," August says. "I do commiserate with you, though. Just last night, I arrived mere moments too late to free Rosie from the subterranean prison our evil housekeeper had locked her in. She freed herself." He throws up his hands. "Women."

Bronwyn blinks at him and then turns to me. "Please tell me that is a private joke."

"No," I say. "I really was locked in the subbasement by the housekeeper. We've been having a bit of an adventure, however inadvertent."

I start to tell the story, but their blank looks insist I back up to the beginning, which I do, reversing to the tale of how I became Edmund's governess.

"Wait," William interjects. "While I am horrified, August, that you hired a governess sight unseen and paid her a quarter's wages in advance, the real question is…" He waves at me. "Your wife disguised herself as a governess, lived in your house, and you never recognized her?"

"It was a very good disguise," I say. "Also, in his defense, he scarcely looked at me. Seems he's had some trouble with governesses."

I bat my eyelashes, and Bronwyn and William laugh. Then I continue my story as breakfast arrives, and we dive in. By the time I'm done, so is the food.

"Well, that is quite the tale," Bronwyn says. "You are correct about the ghost. I've seen her myself. I also thought she might be you, but a photograph clarified the matter. I presumed she was a maid. I never thought…"

Her gaze moves to August. "I am sorry, August. That sounded flippant. I only meant that I can confirm she is here and that I hope Rosalind's sister can communicate with her. Charlotte did not seem distraught when I glimpsed her—she helped me with something—but she was unable to communicate."

"We will summon Miranda," I say. "I'd tried to, but Mrs. Landon blocked it."

"Mrs. Landon," William says. "Heretofore known as Mrs. Danvers."

I choke on a laugh as August frowns.

"It is from a novel that has not yet been published," I say. "An apt analogy, and your reading habits surprise me as always, William. While yours do not." I turn to my husband. "Cross-dressing lady pirates, hmm?"

His face reddens. "It is actually a very well-written book."

"Agreed, and I look forward to finishing it. For now, I believe it is time to go find our son. I have not yet been properly introduced."

Bronwyn's brown eyes widen. "Oh, my God. I am so sorry. Yes, you were saying that as we arrived, and we did not mean to hold you back." She rises and scoops up Amelia. "Go. Meet your son properly. I cannot—" Her voice cracks as she looks down at her daughter. "I cannot begin to imagine what it has been like for you."

"I believe you *can* begin to," I say with a gentle smile. "But I may be stalling on a proper reunion myself. It is not going to be easy to explain."

"It shall be very easy," August says as he comes to take my hand. "His mother was kept from us, and she desperately wanted to get back to him." He meets my eyes, and when he says, "Desperately," again there is no doubt that he understands exactly how terrible this separation has been.

I hug him. "Desperately wanted to get back to both of you. To my family." I pull away. "But now I am here, and I am delaying the inevitable. Amelia? Would you walk us outside with your parents, please? Then we shall find Edmund and bring him to you."

We head out, the four of us chattering away like old friends. Another apt analogy. I may not know Bronwyn well, but I cannot wait to get to know her better. Amelia even lets me take her on my hip, and I promise her that we'll bake jam-jams together—she and her mother, Edmund and I.

We open the side door, and I'm nearly thrown flying by Charlie, the groom who'd been with Edmund and Hugh.

"Charlie?" August says, catching the young man by the arm as Charlie's chest heaves as if he has been running. "What is it?"

"The young master, sir. We stopped for a picnic, and he saw a ghost in the woods, and he…he ran after her. He is gone."

THIRTY

ILLIAM TAKES AMELIA and runs to find someone to watch her. By the time he catches up, we are racing up the hill toward the Grecian temple. As we near it, we see the horses—two geldings and a pony—tied to a column.

"We were picnicking inside," Charlie says as we run. "Then Master Edmund let out a cry. He ran off, and Hugh said he saw a woman in the forest. The woman in blue. The ghost of…" His gaze swings to me, and he audibly swallows. "I—I am sorry, ma'am. We have thought it was you."

"It is not." I struggle to speak as we run uphill. "But you said 'he' saw a woman. You mean Edmund?"

"Presumably, that is what set the boy off, but I mean Hugh. He saw her, and he ran after Edmund, and he told me to wait here for them. I did for a few moments. Then everything went quiet. At first, I heard them running and Hugh shouting, and then I did not, and I hurried into the forest but could find no sign of them and thought it best to alert Mr. August."

"You did the right thing," I assure him as we slow near the horses. "Can you tell us where they went?"

He jogs to a path into the woods. Then August tells him to go back to the house and let us know if either Edmund or Hugh returns.

Once he is out of earshot, I whisper, "Hugh."

August nods grimly as we continue jogging into the forest. "I do not think Edmund happened to catch a glimpse of Charlotte's ghost this morning. He saw the imposter. It is convenient that Hugh saw her and Charlie did not. Also that he told Charlie to stay back."

"You think Hugh…?" Bronwyn says. "*Oh*. Hugh, then, and not Violet? Or Hugh *and* Violet?"

"They are a couple," I say. "I ought to have thought of that. But Hugh…"

"I have known him since he was a boy," August says. "It is not easy working for my brother, but Hugh's father was such an excellent groom that I did everything in my power to keep him, and Hugh seemed to be following in his footsteps. No one has an unkind word to say about the boy, and Edmund adores him."

As we move quickly along the path, August squeezes my shoulder. I'm trying not to think about Hugh. Trying even more not to think about what he may have done with our son.

I'm in the lead, barreling down the path, blind to everything as I listen for the sound of my son, for any sound at all. But the forest is silent. Eerily silent, and when my foot strikes something on the path, I nearly fly over it.

August catches me and yanks me back, and I see what I have nearly tripped over. An arm stretched over the path from a body lying in the undergrowth.

"Hugh!" I say.

August tries to hold me back, but I drop beside the young man's still form. Blood drips from the back of his head. My fingers fly to his throat.

"He has a pulse and breath," I say. "He is alive."

William kneels on Hugh's opposite side. He has more medical experience than any of us, even if it is more veterinary than human. He tries to rouse Hugh and then checks his vital signs.

"He is deeply unconscious," he says. "Possibly even sedated. As this seems to prove he did not kidnap Edmund, I'm going to suggest you allow me to ride one of the geldings back to the house and have the staff call for the doctor while you search for Edmund. I will return and join you as quickly as I can."

We agree, and he is off, and after one final guilty check to be sure Hugh's vitals are strong, we abandon the young man to resume our search for Edmund.

VIOLET AND Mrs. Landon have our son. Of that, we are certain. We combed the forest, and we took a boat on the pond, after which we posted a groom there so August does not spend the day feeling the agonizing pull of that body of water.

Hugh has not awakened. The doctor has been sent for, and Bronwyn stands guard with Amelia in his room. If he stirs, she will fetch us immediately.

August has sent for a neighbor's hunting dogs to follow Edmund's trail. We are now in the house, scouring it in case we have spent all day on the estate grounds only to discover our son is being held under our very noses.

Naturally, the subbasement is our first stop. Thus far, I've managed to banish thoughts of my captivity there. I tell myself it did not last long, and I was never in as dire of straits as poor Charlotte. Yet as we head back down there, my body and mind rise up in rebellion.

The mind is an unfathomable thing. A treacherous thing, holding on to trauma long after the event has passed. August only needs to swing open that subbasement door for the smell to overwhelm me and set me back on my heels.

William is behind me, and he catches me and steadies me. August turns sharply, and my body reacts again, certain that I will see the storms

of jealousy on his face as another man—even his best friend—touches me. Instead, it is only alarm, as if I've fainted dead away.

August takes me with a nod of gratitude for William, and here I see the change these years have wrought in my husband. He told himself I had abandoned him, not because he believed I found another but because he believed he'd driven me away with his jealousy. I have returned to find a man who does not even need to stifle a flare of jealousy.

I returned to him. I fought every obstacle to return to him. I am his as I have always been, and to doubt that is to doom us.

"I am recovered, thank you both," I say. "I believe I tripped on a nail." I look down at the floor, willing a popped nail to appear.

August gives me a hard look. Then he leans to my ear. "After my father put me in here, I haven't ventured down there until last night, and I am ashamed to say I faltered even then. You do not need an excuse for trepidation, Rosie."

I nod and say nothing.

"Why don't you go upstairs and sit with Bronwyn and Amelia?" William says.

Now I'm the one turning a hard look on him.

William sighs. "It was worth a try. While I very much doubt your son is down here, I understand that you must go yourself. Shall we continue then?"

We take our lanterns down the stairs, the yellow glow flickering against the darkness. The smell makes my stomach churn and prickles the hair on my arms. One whiff, and I'm back in that cell. I switch to breathing through my mouth, which means I can *taste* the mildew, but it does calm my racing heart.

I'd been in no state to examine my surroundings while August carried me out. Now I see that if he hadn't come, I'd have spent a very long time trying to find the correct door, which would have been barred anyway.

I'd envisioned one narrow hallway with the exit at the end. That is a far cry from the reality, which is multiple hallways and over a dozen doors, each as heavily built as the exit.

Is this what befell Charlotte? She escaped from her room only to find herself trapped in this maze of corridors? Alerting members of the staff who were ill-inclined to risk the earl's wrath by helping her escape?

I push off thoughts of Charlotte. I will help her. First, I must find my son.

The men begin opening doors. I dart between them, peeking under their arms, before realizing I'm perfectly capable of opening doors myself. When I start down a side hall, August begins to call to me. Then he pauses and instead only offers me his lamp.

"You keep it," I say. "I can see well enough, and I will be careful."

He nods and continues down his row of doors. I head to the end of my short hall. The first door opens into a storeroom filled with empty barrels. The second seems to contain full barrels by the slight smell of alcohol. The third holds boxes of root vegetables.

As I check rooms, I leave the doors ajar to show which ones have been searched. When I open the fourth door, it is floor-to-ceiling crates. I'm about to retreat when a flicker of blue catches my eye.

"Charlotte?" I whisper, my voice low so that I do not bring August running.

That flicker again, as if she used all her energy appearing to me yesterday and can now only manage that. I grab one stray crate to prop open the door. Then I creep down the narrow passage between stacks, my ears attuned for any sound. When an old board cracks under my feet, I pick it up, the sharp edge a potential weapon.

The contents had looked like stacks of crates with only a narrow passage down the middle, but there are more passages between the stacks. I squint down each and see a bare wall at the end. Then, when I'm almost at the back, the passage to my left is partly blocked by a stack of crates that reach over my head. There is only the thinnest gap between them. Enough for me to pass. Enough for Edmund or Violet to pass.

Through that gap, I spot a bucket, tins of food and a jar of water. Then I see a woman's sturdy shoe. A shoe I recognize.

Mrs. Landon.

I hesitate. I want to throw aside the crates and confront her, armed with my sharp piece of wood. Yes, it is not the best of plans, and it takes me only a moment to realize that. It takes more time for me to force my legs into retreat.

I can see Mrs. Landon, who will know where my son is. If I leave her for even a heartbeat, I'll never see him again.

That's foolishness, of course, but hearts are not the organ of rationality. I must reason with my fluttering heart. I will retreat only to the adjoining hall. There is no way she can escape past me from there.

I remove my shoes to silence my steps. Then I creep backward from the room and sprint to the end of the hall where I collide with August, who is rounding the corner to come see me. The lantern nearly flies from his hand, and I stifle a gasp as I recover myself. Motioning for silence, I whisper into his ear what I've found.

August glances over his shoulder and motions for William to guard this intersection of the hall. Then August and I proceed. At first, he doesn't try to quiet his steps, but I whisper that I do not know whether it is simply Mrs. Landon or also our son. In other words, if we startle her, we put Edmund in danger.

August rolls his steps as we walk. We reach the storeroom, and I gesture for him to enter first. He sets down the lamp so that it will cast as little light as possible. Then I direct him to the spot. He peers along the narrow passage and then nods in grim satisfaction.

August pulls back for a moment to consider. He glances at me for ideas, but I have none. While I could squeeze into that gap, as soon as Mrs. Landon sees me, she could grab Edmund before I could lunge through to stop her. If Edmund is not there, she could attack me while I was trapped in that narrow gap.

Our only option is to use the element of surprise. The boxes are piled up to August's chest. He takes a breath deep enough for me to see the inhalation of his back. Then he removes the top one as carefully as possible.

No sound comes from within. He takes hold of the next box and pulls it out. Then he looks inside.

When he turns to me, he mouths, "She is asleep," and "No Edmund." My heart drops, and I glance away to hide my disappointment.

No, this is still good. We have Mrs. Landon. She will tell us what Violet has done with Edmund.

I look over as August removes one more box. Then he climbs onto the last one, ducking to keep from hitting the ceiling. He leaps down beside the sleeping woman with a shout that echoes through the room. I hurry toward him in case she leaps up and attacks.

Mrs. Landon does not attack. She does not leap up. I scramble over the final crate to see her properly. To see her wide and staring eyes. To see the blood on the back of her head. To see her hands clutched at her throat, where a rope hangs from her neck.

THIRTY-ONE

RS. LANDON IS dead. Hit from behind, like Hugh, and then strangled with a rope while she'd been dazed and unable to fight back. William comes then to see the body, and he surmises she has been dead longer than Edmund has been missing. Dead at least a day.

Killed after she placed me in that room. Killed many hours before I escaped.

Killed before she could call the constable. This is why she did not come for me. While I was sitting on a bed less than a hundred feet away, my captor—possibly the only person who knew where I was—was dead.

Is this Violet eliminating her accomplices after they've served their purposes? First Mrs. Landon, once she'd taken care of me, and then Hugh, after he'd led Edmund to her?

We have begun to believe we were wrong about Hugh, that he is as innocent as he seemed. That he truly did spot Violet dressed as the ghost and ran after Edmund, only to be attacked and left for dead.

And Mrs. Landon? There is no doubt that she locked me in that room. Before I passed out, she said she was putting me somewhere safe for the constable. Is that what she envisioned? Thinking me an imposter, had

she gone along with Violet's plan of locking me up to await justice? Only Violet had no intention of letting me out of that room, and she killed Mrs. Landon once the older woman had played her role.

That is all speculation. Hugh is still unconscious. Mrs. Landon is dead. And we are no closer to finding our son.

We barely make it upstairs before we hear the baying of the hounds. The dogs are here. We already have a piece of our son's clothing from the day before, and August takes it out to the hound master. William and I go with them while Bronwyn stays with Hugh and Amelia.

The hounds find the scent easily enough. It is right there, on the path where we found Hugh. The dogs stop at that point, madly sniffing, following the play of whatever occurred here. Then they are off on a trail into the forest.

The dogs do not go far. Perhaps a couple of hundred feet, and then the trail ends at a road bordering the forest.

Someone met them there. Violet had arranged for a conveyance to take them. She'd have needed it—there would be a limit to how far she could get Edmund on her own. She'd arranged for a pickup at that spot.

We return to the house, and William and August set out on horseback to follow the road and ask whether anyone in the vicinity saw anything. Meanwhile, I search Mrs. Landon's quarters for clues.

The housekeeper's room is immaculate. It is also as impersonal as my own quarters, without a portrait or photograph to be seen.

And who would she have a photograph of? Her family? The Courtenays are her family.

Pity stabs through me. A life in service to a family that is not your own. What happens to a person like that? William may have joked about *Rebecca's* Mrs. Danvers, but the portrait rang true to life in its exaggerated way.

The housekeeper who was devoted to her employer's family. A husband or children would interfere with her work. The same with outside friendships. She might have siblings and nieces and nephews, but as she aged, they would become distant relatives. Her staff could form a

pseudo-family, but Mrs. Landon spent half of her career with Everett, only to be recently brought back to Courtenay Hall, where she'd know no one, and the rapid staff turnover gave no chance to form friendships. All she had was the Courtenays, and to them, she was staff, her manner too cool and brisk to endear her even to August.

Maudlin thoughts, and I dismiss them. This is the woman who locked me in a subbasement. I might forgive her for that if she really had thought me an imposter and a threat. I will not forgive her for my son, though. He is gone, and she might be dead, but she played her role there, and I find what seems like proof of it in her letters. That is all that passes for personal effects here—a neatly bound stack of letters in a drawer.

The letters are from a girl who'd later grown into a woman. Letters addressed to My Dearest Mrs. Landon. They begin twenty years ago, thanking Mrs. Landon for the generosity and kindness she'd shown a stranger, a girl who, as a baby, had been orphaned and adopted by a farming couple. When the letters start, the girl is a maid, a job Mrs. Landon obtained for her. Then, as a teenager, she became pregnant, set upon by her master's son. Mrs. Landon helps again. Sends money. Offers advice. Assists the girl in choosing a husband from several suitors. A daughter is born, and that girl grows into a young woman herself, and Mrs. Landon insists the girl come to work at Courtenay Hall. Mrs. Landon will protect her. She knows a secret that will keep the girl safe.

The girl's name? Violet.

What secret did Mrs. Landon use to keep Violet safe from the earl's lechery? The knowledge that Violet was his grandniece. Oh, Mrs. Landon never says that, but it is obvious enough. The "girl" that Mrs. Landon first helped must be Charlotte's daughter, and here I do indeed feel a stab of grief for the dead housekeeper, for it seems she was that poor girl's fairy godmother.

Mrs. Landon protected the Courtenays, and to her, this baby was a Courtenay. She helped where she could, and then she brought Violet—Charlotte's granddaughter—into the home.

Did Violet realize the truth? She must have. When she did, the scraps Mrs. Landon could scrape together for her would no longer be enough, not when Courtenay Hall was her family estate. She should be an honored guest. Like August. Like *me*. Instead, she is scrubbing out chamber pots for her great-uncles and cousins.

What would that do to a person? From these letters, I know Mrs. Landon had only the best intentions when she brought Violet here. Give the girl a good job where Mrs. Landon can both ease her burdens and protect her from her mother's fate. It had been meant as a kindness.

I could forgive Violet for her rage. I could even forgive her for playing me as a ghost, perhaps to torment August. I know August would have been nothing but kind to Violet, yet in her mind, he'd be part of the family that stole her birthright. Perhaps she even mistakenly believed August knew her mother's fate, a foundling child ripped from Charlotte and cast into the world, denied even her family name.

Yes, for this, I could forgive Violet, and I know August would, too. Had we discovered who she was, even after the haunting, he'd have given her everything Charlotte's granddaughter deserved. I should say that what I do not forgive her for is stealing our child, but her greater crime is killing Mrs. Landon. Whatever Mrs. Landon did to me, she'd been Violet's fierce benefactor and guardian. Mrs. Landon trusted Violet. And for that, the girl killed her.

I continue reading the letters, looking for clues. The mundanity of the details combines with my exhaustion, the mixture a sleeping draft that leads my mind down other paths. I do not fall asleep, but the words swim, and my mind drifts. Where it drifts, not surprisingly, is to the subbasement. It replays that day years ago when August and I had made love in the basement corner and I'd found the subbasement door.

I rouse myself from the pleasant half dream and resume reading, only to fall back into that same reverie again.

Something about that memory is nudging at me, as if there is a reason my mind keeps replaying it.

I'm half-asleep when I bolt upright. In my mind, I hear August's voice from that day.

If you are looking for secret spaces, there is an old poachers' shack at the edge of the forest, complete with a tunnel that may not have completely caved in yet.

The edge of the forest. The far edge, with the tunnel running past the old roadway.

The tunnel running past the road where Edmund and Violet's trail had vanished.

I run to tell Bronwyn what I have remembered. Instead, I find Dr. Cunningham tending to Hugh, who is still asleep.

"Where is Lady Thorne?" I ask. "She was here with her daughter."

He stares at me. Then I remember we haven't met since I returned as Rosalind. Without the wig and contacts and spectacles and makeup, I bear just enough resemblance to Clara Smith to make him stare.

"I am Rosalind Courtenay," I say. "Your father helped tend to my son when he had the croup."

He blinks in surprise. "Rosalind Courtenay? Y-yes, my father said you were an excellent nurse and that your father was a..." His eyes round as the connection hits. "Your father was a doctor."

"It is a very long story, the short version of which is that I am helping my husband find our son. Now, please, Lady Thorne? She was here earlier."

"She took her daughter for a walk. She asked if I knew where Mrs. Courtenay was, and I had no idea who she was talking about, but she left before I could say so. She said that if I saw her—you—I should tell you they are outside and invite you to join..."

He doesn't get a chance to finish. I'm already off and running, skirts hiked up. Behind me, he shouts, "The stables! They were going to the stables!"

I fly straight to the stable, but there is no sign of Bronwyn or Amelia. No sign of anyone. The grooms are out searching for Edmund. Bronwyn and Amelia must have returned to the house, for I see the remains of an apple near their geldings and bits of another caught in the whiskers of Edmund's pony.

I run outside, shield my eyes against the falling sun and search for any sign that my husband and William are returning. Nothing. I see absolutely nothing.

I should speak to someone. Yet there is no one here, and my son is being held in the poacher's old cabin, and I do not know how long he will remain there. I must get to him.

I paw through the tools until I find a stubby pick for prying stones from hooves. I tuck the makeshift weapon into my dress and snatch up a box of matches. Then I run down the row of horses, looking for one I recognize.

I remember the young gelding I always chose. The one I chose the night I rode to Thorne Manor. He died plunging in the sea, and I have not had a moment to mourn him. I still do not have that moment, but I send up a silent prayer for him. Then I spot the mare August rides, a gentler beast than my usual choice.

"Hello, Molly," I say, rubbing her nose.

Her nostrils flare as she drinks in my scent. She gives me what the modern world would call a serious dose of side-eye, as if wondering what I'm doing here after being gone so long. She is a good and docile horse, though, and after a few reassuring words, she lets me lead her out and saddle her up. Then we are off.

THIRTY-TWO

HE POACHER'S SHACK is located inside the forest. To any-one from the modern world, that might seem akin to car thieves setting up a chop shop in the parking lot where they find their targets. Even August and I had laughed at it. The road is less than a hundred paces away. Surely anyone using the shack would be caught.

The truth is twofold. First, it had originally been the gamekeeper's cottage. One of the gamekeeper's main jobs was to scour the forest for poachers. It is ironic, then, that when the position was disbanded and the cottage abandoned, it was claimed by poachers who constructed a tunnel that started beyond the hall's land border.

The road also hadn't existed in those days. It is a recent addition built at the edge of the property, meaning it passes right over the tunnel. While the road primarily serves as a back route to the estate, it also connects two villages, and locals have the right to use it, which means there is enough traffic for poachers to have long abandoned the cabin.

When August and I first visited the shack, we'd found the tunnel in a serious state of disrepair but not yet collapsed. The dogs didn't follow Edmund's scent to the original tunnel entrance, so my assumption is that

there must be a collapse hole now near the road. Violet would have taken Edmund past the hole to the road to lay a scent trail and then doubled back to use the hole as an entrance to the tunnel instead.

I do not waste time searching for that hole. Nor can I risk alerting Violet by riding directly to the shack. I leave Molly at the tunnel's end. Then I open the rotting hatch and descend the rickety ladder into the tunnel.

One must credit the poachers for determination. Digging this tunnel took serious effort, and it is still only a crawlspace, which they had to traverse each time they wished to raid the earl's forest.

I bear no ill will toward these poachers. The earl's forest teems like an overflowing banquet table. Proper conservation would see that game hunted to provide meat for the hungry. Instead, the earl is like an overfed king at his table, picking a sweetmeat here or there and abandoning the rest. When the cook wishes game, someone hunts for it. Otherwise, barring the very rare grouse party, the forest is left with a surplus of fauna.

I thank those poachers of old as I make my way down what is a remarkably well-constructed tunnel. Yes, I'm crawling on all fours, and yes, I do wish I had changed into something different because I'm destroying the engagement dress August had so lovingly preserved. Yet even if I had thought to change my outfit, I'm not sure I'd have spared a moment to do it. This is my son I'm chasing. Once I have him, there will be a lifetime to create new memories with new frocks.

I find the hole. It would be barely big enough for me to squeeze through. I also see footprints and scuff marks in the dirt where someone has come down and then bent to crawl.

Not some*one*. There are two sets of prints, one of a woman's boot and the other...

My heart clenches. The other print is a boot half the size.

My eyes mist, and I blink back tears. I've raced here as if I knew with certainty I'd find my son. I had no such conviction, only desperate hope. That is why I'd made no further effort to locate help or leave a message.

Lacking all other leads, I'd followed this one, half-convinced I'd emerge into the cabin and find no sign of them. Yet here is the sign. Edmund is ahead.

I take a deep breath, and then I continue on.

From memory, I know the tunnel ends in a subterranean room. The hatch into the cabin is hidden, and if the poachers feared discovery, they would climb into the room below to wait until the danger passed.

When the tunnel deepens, and I can walk hunched over, I know I'm nearing that room. There's a door on it, a rough wooden slab with gaps between the slats. I press my eye to one gap, and my heart stops.

Edmund is there. Right there. Not in the cabin proper, but in that crude basement. I see him asleep atop a pile of old sacks. A gas lamp burns nearby.

I take the hoof pick from my pocket and slide the sharp point between my fingers, gripping the handle. Then I peer through various gaps, searching for Violet.

She is not there. My son is alone in the room.

My heart thuds harder, sensing a trick. She heard me coming and snuck up to the shack, where she will fall upon me as I run to my son.

Deep breaths as I stifle that urge. I take the door in hand to open it, and when it does not move, I find a latch on this side. I open it and creep into the room.

It takes all my strength not to run to Edmund. I can see the movement of his chest, and that must be enough. I lift the hatch into the cabin. When it catches, I pause. I try again. There is no latch, just something atop it.

I adjust my grip on the hoof pick, push the fingertips of my free hand against the hatch and shove until something inside gives a clunk. I yank back and freeze, clutching my weapon. The cabin above stays silent.

I slowly lift the hatch to see a stone the size of my head settled beside it. That's what had been on the hatch. A stone big enough that even if Edmund managed to reach the hatch, he'd have been unable to open it.

I keep opening the hatch until I can see into the dim interior. It stinks of rot and must, but there's no sign of anyone in the one-room shack.

I glance down at my sleeping son. Then I climb the ladder into the cottage. I peer around the dim interior. It's a plain wood box, empty save for a broken chair in one corner and some blankets in another.

There's a rotting wooden latch on the exterior door, and I swing that shut. If Violet returns that way, I'll hear her trying the door, which will give me time to escape with Edmund.

Then, my practical mind settled, I give one shuddering exhale and climb back down into the basement. I run to Edmund and lower myself beside him.

I check his vital signs first. He is fine. Just deeply asleep, dark half moons under his eyes speaking to his exhaustion. I ease him up so that his head is on my lap. Then I stroke his hair and sing to him. The words come without me even realizing what I'm singing. The lullaby I'd once used to help him sleep.

I must wake him. I know that. But I do it gently, brushing back his hair, and rubbing his cheek and singing as I lean over his sleeping face. Then, finally, his eyes open, and they stare right into mine.

"Mama?" he croaks.

The tears come. I cannot help it. They come in a flood as I lift him up and hug him tight.

"It's me, Edmund."

He tugs away a little to peer up at me, frowning. "You sound like…"

"Clara Smith?" My lips curve into a wry smile. "Yes, there is a very long story behind that one, and your father and I shall tell it to you as soon as we get back to him. He's looking for you with Uncle William."

Edmund blinks sleepily up at me. Then, in an instant, his face falls, the disappointment shuddering through him.

"I am asleep still," he says.

"What? Oh! You think you are dreaming." I hug him again. "You are not. I'm here. Your mama is here, and your papa is searching for you, and you are safe."

That last word barely leaves my lips before I hear a faint swishing in the tunnel. The swish of skirts being dragged along the dirt. Distant light bobs through the slats in the door.

"She's coming," I whisper. "Shh, now. I'll get you out of here."

I rise as best I can in the shallow room. I lift him up to the hatch, and he climbs into the shack. Then I follow. Below, the scrape of wood tells me Violet is already at the door into the basement room.

I hoist Edmund and run to the door. As the one below opens, I am throwing the latch on this one. Then I put him down and say as I point, "Run that way, Edmund. The road is over there. Run to it, and keep going. Follow it to the house. Can you do that?"

His mouth opens, alarm in his eyes.

"I will be fine," I say. "I must stop her from coming after you. Run, and you will be safe. Can you do that?"

He nods, and I give him the smallest push, and he is off, racing toward the road. From below comes a near-growl as Violet discovers Edmund gone. I slink back against the wall, hoof pick raised. I wait for the first sign of Violet's light hair.

When a dark-haired head appears through the hatch, I must make some noise of surprise, because she turns toward me, and I am staring into the face of a stranger.

THIRTY-THREE

HE YOUNG WOMAN stops on the ladder and gapes at me. I'm about to ask who the hell she is, in hopes my modern language will throw her off her guard. But in her stare, I see more than surprise. I see fear. Then I realize the cause. I am Rosalind Courtenay, in a filthy dress and with wild hair, standing in the shadows as the autumnal sun falls outside.

She thinks me a ghost.

She thinks me the very specter she has been impersonating.

The ghost of Rosalind Courtenay.

"Y-you," she stammers, still on the ladder.

"Why are you surprised?" I say in my most sepulchral tone. "You summoned me, did you not?"

"Wh-what?"

"You impersonated me, and you used that impersonation to steal my son. You summoned me as surely as if you cast a magical spell."

"I-I don't know what you're talking about."

"Oh, come now," I say. "You seem to be a child of some strength. Are you going to shrink into the comfort of lies?"

"Child?" That gets her attention.

"To me, you are a child, Margaret. A silly, inconsequential twit who attempted to steal both my husband and my son. I was ripped from my family. I spent four long years in another world, and I fought daily to return. Did you not think I would find a way to come back? To protect them from one such as you?"

I slide Margaret's name in there easily, as if I know full well who she is. It is a guess. An educated one, though, and she is so incensed by my words that she does not even blink at the name.

"You know nothing about me," she says.

"I need know nothing beyond the obvious. That you are a conniving child who saw a grieving wealthy widower and set her cap on him."

Her face twists. "He needed a wife. Why not me? I come from a family as fine as yours, Rosalind. I am younger, too. I could have provided him with more children, and there is nothing he loves more than being a father."

"And so, to win his heart, you *stole* his child?"

"It was not supposed to—" She bites off the word with a growl. "It was that governess. That new governess."

"Who was not as easily frightened as the others? August hired an older governess, and she saw through your silly hauntings. She realized they were the work of a human. Even that fake journal, which you wrote and secreted in her closet, did nothing to convince her she was being properly haunted."

Again, it is a guess, but the look on Margaret's face says I've struck true. The journal provided the seemingly hardest evidence of an actual ghost, manifesting right in that nameless governess's room. It also did something else.

"You used the journal to blame Mrs. Landon. To make her into a monster who locked the governess in the room right before the poor girl disappeared."

"You think she would not do such a thing? Ask Clara Smith, now trapped in the basement, left there by Mrs. Landon."

The pieces fall together. I remember where we found Mrs. Landon, in that hidden spot with blankets and a bucket and supplies. We thought she'd been planning to hide there. Those items were not hers. They were Margaret's. That's where she has been hiding, her home base for the haunting. That access meant she could sneak into the governess's room. She probably even had a key or knew where to find it.

After killing Mrs. Landon in that spot, Margaret could not return. She's been hiding here—those are her blankets across the room—and therefore does not know that Clara Smith was rescued. That sparks another thought, but I set it aside until I finish with this one.

"I'm sure Miss Smith will be found soon," I say. "Then August will summon the constable as Mrs. Landon intended. That is why you murdered her, is it not? Did she discover your hiding place while she was stowing Miss Smith? Or did you merely use the excuse to kill her while she was down there? Two birds with one stone. Hide the only person who knew where Miss Smith was and set up Mrs. Landon to take the blame for her disappearance?"

Margaret only glares. She does not answer, but nor does she deny the killing.

"And Hugh?" I say. "He was in on your plan, wasn't he? At least the hauntings. But he had a change of heart. You did something that went too far. Killing Mrs. Landon? Planning to kidnap Edmund? Whatever it was, he stopped aiding you. Still, you must have a soft spot for him. You left him alive, unlike poor Mrs. Landon."

"I have no *soft spots*." She spits the words. "Hugh is a fool. A gullible fool and a coward to boot. He took a liking to Miss Smith. Wanted me to stop trying to drive her off. Where did that leave me?"

"Without a plan," I say. "You intended to keep driving off the governesses until August was in such a state that he'd welcome you back. Such a state that if you so much as hinted at leaving, perhaps to start a family of your own, he'd offer to marry you."

"Why not? Edmund is fond of me, and Mr. August would have become fond of me in time."

I laugh. It is not the most ghostly of sounds, but I cannot help myself. "You expected him to marry you after you kidnapped his son?"

She fixes me with a hard look. "He was not supposed to know it was me. He was to think that Mrs. Landon took Edmund and I rescued him and, in doing so, was forced to kill her. But that fool Hugh intervened when I led Edmund away. Came running after him and told him I was not you. Tried to tell him who I was. That's when I struck him. I had to use the sleeping gas I brought for Edmund. I returned to kill the fool when Edmund could not bear witness, but Hugh was gone."

"Such a shame," I say. "All your plans laid to waste."

I take one step toward her, and for a moment, she stands her ground. After all, I'm but a phantom. I can do her no harm. One step. Another. And then she turns tail and scrambles back down the ladder.

I race after her. I catch up as she's opening the door into the tunnel. When I grab the back of her dress, she goes rigid with shock at my unghostly touch, and that gives me the advantage I need. I yank her back and knock her down.

I see the moment she figures it out. The moment she realizes I'm not a ghost. That I'm Rosalind Courtenay. Alive and well.

Her shock coalesces to rage. "You!" she spits as I pin her to the floor.

Something in her snaps. Even before I showed up, her plans had gone hopelessly awry. She'd failed to kill Hugh, who would surely tell everything when he woke. Edmund may not have realized who she was, but he would have realized he hadn't been captured by Mrs. Landon.

Margaret has spent the intervening hours fumbling for an alternate plan, and then I showed up. I freed her captive, unmasked her and, worst of all, dashed all her dreams and schemes with my mere presence, which meant August is not a widower after all.

Something snaps, and she becomes a wild thing, and I'm not prepared for that. Oh, in a modern movie, I would be prepared. I would go from Victorian baker to inhuman fighting machine who anticipates my opponent's every move.

I am not that Hollywood creation, and when she lashes out, clawing and kicking and snarling, it is all I can do to fight her off. Even when I raise the hoof pick, I'm not certain what to do with it. Stab her where? Not the heart or some vital organ. I want to only disable her so that she'll be forced to tell her story and pay for killing Mrs. Landon.

And there, I fail. I hesitate, and Margaret takes advantage. She grabs my wrist, thrusting my hand up, and there is the sick snap of bone.

My hand opens. The pick falls out. When I scramble for it, she flips me onto my back, and before I can even react, she has me on the dirt floor, the pick at my throat.

"Rosalind Courtenay," she sneers. "What happened? Did you run out of money? Did your lover abandon you?" Her free hand touches my short hair. "Or were you locked in an asylum? That must be it. They cut your hair in an asylum."

She leans down to my face. "You should never have returned, Rosalind. All you've done is provide the missing piece to my puzzle. The mad wife escapes the asylum, and the governess stops her before she can destroy her former family. For her pains, the heroic girl wins the lord of the manor."

"August isn't a lord," I say. "He doesn't even own the house. The rest seems a little overwrought. It'd make a good story, though. I think you should call it *Jane Eyre*."

The look on Margaret's face. Bafflement mixed with shock, that I should speak so calmly, glibly even, while under pain of death.

"Perhaps I am mad after all," I murmur. "Or perhaps I'm just trying to—" I slam my hand up, rock clutched in my fist. It hits the side of her head with a satisfying smack. "Distract you," I say as she falls.

I scramble up and grab the pick from her hand. She isn't unconscious, sadly, but I hit her again, and she goes down, dazed. As I pin her as best I can with my broken wrist, footsteps clamor overhead.

"Down here!" I shout, and the trapdoor swings open, and August leaps through.

THIRTY-FOUR

NCE AGAIN, AUGUST'S rescue arrived moments too late to fully qualify as such. Considering that Margaret had bested me once, I'm still grateful that I do not need to subdue and bind her one-handed and then run for help.

It turns out that August had the same flashbulb moment that I did. Something had been prickling at his mind, too, and he'd suddenly realized what it was: that the hounds had stopped near where the tunnel ran beneath the road.

August had turned his horse around and galloped for the cabin with William at his side. They'd spotted Edmund running along the road and stopped just long enough to confirm he was fine and, yes, Mama was at the cabin, and she'd told him to run when his captor came back. August sent Edmund with William, and they headed back only to encounter Bronwyn riding in their direction.

Hugh had awoken, and his first words were to warn that it was Margaret who had Edmund, and she would take him either to the old poachers' shack or her hiding place in the subbasement.

August explains Margaret's "mysterious" disappearance, which had not been mysterious at all to him. She'd tried to seduce him, culminating

with climbing into his bed one night and attempting to force the matter. He'd fired her on the spot, slammed down money from a drawer and sent her on her way. She'd pulled on her clothing and stormed out. When he'd told her to get her things, she just kept going, because really, stopping to pack would ruin her grand exit. That's why he hadn't worried about her departure or sent anyone to search the ponds.

Margaret has now been turned over to the constable, who took all of our statements, with Hugh's being the most important. Yes, he'd helped her in the hauntings. She had seduced him back when he was sixteen and she was first at Courtenay Hall. The affair had been brief, and when she'd sought his help after leaving, he'd wanted nothing to do with her scheme. She'd convinced him that the replacement governesses did not understand Edmund, who needed her, and August just needed to see that.

As naive as Hugh was, he eventually began to question her plan, particularly after I arrived and bonded with Edmund. So she threatened to tell the earl that Hugh had "stolen her maidenhood," and he continued reluctantly helping until August nearly drowned and Hugh realized Margaret was responsible. She was the one—wearing the ghostly disguise—who'd led Edmund from the stable and toward the pond.

And Violet? Violet had nothing to do with any of it. She'd sent August running toward the pond because she'd seen Edmund heading in that general direction, and his mind naturally leaped to "he's at the pond!" The poisoner was Margaret, who'd snuck from her subbasement to taint August's water. When I caught Violet with the tray, she'd been wondering whether anything on it made him sick, perhaps spoiled food.

Nor is Violet Charlotte's granddaughter. The answer is much simpler. Violet's mother has long suspected that she herself was Mrs. Landon's daughter. Apparently, Mrs. Landon claimed that Violet's mother was the daughter of a friend who'd died in childbirth. That friend had been a housemaid seduced by a guest. There was, however, a strong resemblance between Violet's mother and Mrs. Landon, and when Violet's mother

found herself pregnant as a maid, Mrs. Landon's reaction suggested she'd been in the same position herself.

As for the "family secrets" she held over the earl, Mrs. Landon never elaborated, and we now believe she'd known about Charlotte, as she'd obviously known about that subbasement room. Her first name was Matilda, which means she may have been the "Tilly" in Charlotte's letter.

So why had Violet fled? Simple, really. I disappeared, and Mrs. Landon disappeared, and then Violet heard that I'd been imprisoned by the housekeeper and that August was in a fury over it. What if August realized Violet might be Mrs. Landon's granddaughter? What if he at least discovered she'd been closer to the housekeeper than they'd let on?

Violet panicked and fled, and now she has returned to her post, her name cleared, and both August and I are happy to have her back.

Hugh is also back in our good graces. He is not as innocent as Violet, but his crimes were the mistakes of youth, and he'd regretted his involvement before any violence occurred. He is repentant, and we have accepted his apologies.

There is one thing left to do. One piece of the puzzle unsolved. Charlotte.

We send a telegram to Miranda immediately. Bronwyn and William have remained to help with the case against Margaret, and so they are here when Miranda arrives the next day. When she does, I'm in the laneway waiting, and it is as joyous a reunion as I could have hoped for, one completely unhindered by fears of how she will react.

She is Miranda. She is overjoyed to have me back. Someday I'll tell here where I was. For now, I suffered amnesia. That was August's contribution. The man does love his pulp novels, and it seems the world does, too, because no one questions the story.

It has been a few hours since my sister arrived. She has changed, eaten and run around the hedge maze with Edmund, and so she is ready for the séance. We've decided to host it in one of the sitting rooms, and I'm in there, fussing, when Miranda enters. I turn to find her holding the

pirate novel, which I had brought down last evening for while August and I read together.

She waggles the book, her brows waggling with it.

"Whoever might be reading this? Please tell me it is August. I do love the opportunity to torment him about his reading material."

I roll my eyes. It has turned out that while August claimed to "Clara Smith" that he was estranged from my sisters, that was something of an exaggeration. They all lead busy lives and were not as close as they'd once been, but he had not cut them from his life or my son's.

"Yes," I say. "It is August's. Do with that what you must."

Her grin grows, eyes sparkling. "Cross-dressing pirate wenches. August, dear August. Your reading tastes remain unrepentantly questionable."

"It is actually quite good."

She goes still, book in her hand, and in the half light, I can't quite see her face.

"You've read it?" she says.

"I am reading it. It's very well written and quite a thrilling adventure."

"You…like it?"

"Of course." I frown over at her. "What's the matter, Miranda? You seem quite—"

August chooses that moment to barrel in as only he can barrel into a room, and the book is forgotten.

Soon we are all in our places. It is just the five of us. The staff has been sent on various errands to keep them far from this room. Violet and Hugh are with Edmund, proof that we trust them. While Miranda will need to speak to Edmund and teach him about the Sight, this is not something he should witness at his age, especially given what befell Charlotte.

It takes no effort to bring Charlotte to us. Miranda says she'd spotted her earlier, but she seems to have stayed out of Miranda's way until my sister was settled in and ready. Once she is, Charlotte is there.

Charlotte speaks. We cannot see her, and Miranda must communicate on her behalf. By the time introductions are done, I no longer see

my sister in the chair beside mine. I see Charlotte and hear her voice as I might imagine it, light and girlish with youth. Then she begins to tell her story through Miranda.

"I managed to escape that room, as you did, Rosalind," she says. "But I got no farther. I heard someone coming, and I retreated as fast as I could, relatching the door and replacing the stone. It was my father. Tilly swore he was gone, but he must have had some inkling of my plan, for he returned and made certain I knew he was in residence. I should still have left. Taken the chance. But I waited. The baby came several weeks early, and Dr. Cunningham was in attendance."

"A boy," she says, and I swear I hear her voice, the pride in it. "A healthy boy, despite the circumstances of his birth, brought into the world in that terrible place. They tried to take him from me. To the foundling home in York, he'd go. I had just given birth, and I felt as if I could barely move a muscle, but hearing those words, I somehow propelled myself from the bed. I demanded my son. I said I'd take him and leave and Father would never need to think of me again. He said no, and do you know why?"

She doesn't wait for an answer. Doesn't need one. Again, I swear I hear her voice, now in a bitter laugh. "He had already arranged a marriage for me. That's why he locked me away rather than send me to my aunt's. So that I might walk from that room an unsullied maiden. I laughed at him. I could not help myself. I laughed and told him that if he did that, I would tell my affianced that I was not a virgin, having already borne a child. My father exploded. The last thing I remember is him lifting his hand to hit me, and Dr. Cunningham holding my son, shouting for my father to stop."

Silence. Several moments of it before she says, "He must have struck me, and I hit my head on the stonework and died. They put my body in the pond and—" She stops short. "August. Oh, August, I am sorry. I did that entirely wrong. I should have eased into that part of the story."

I'm holding August's hand in my uninjured one as we sit pressed together on the settee. His face is ashen, but he swallows and clutches my hand tighter.

"No," he says. "Do not apologize. It is an old story for you. I only wish I could confront our father with what he did. That I could make him pay for what he did."

"Oh, I have made him pay as best I could. I can summon the energy to appear at least fleetingly, even to those without the Sight. I would take as long as I needed to build up the power for even a moment by his bedside when he woke. Or, on occasion, a moment to appear to Everett, who knew exactly where and why I was being held and never came to my aid. There is a reason both our brother and father came to hate Courtenay Hall."

"As they should," I murmur.

"As they should. And then, to my utter delight, along came little Edmund, who could see me. I played games with him when he was too young to realize I wasn't real. Then, as he grew older, I was not quite certain what to do, so I kept farther away and watched over him. I thought that once he was old enough, I could make proper contact and explain."

She never knew of Margaret then. Never realized the governess was impersonating her, and therefore, she could not warn Edmund. While Charlotte had spoken to Edmund when he was little, she had—as she said—settled for watching from afar these last couple of years. She'd been the one watching at the pond that night, powerless to help. The ghost who whispered to Edmund lately was Margaret, who was also the "phantom" who invaded my room, having a key.

"We will find your son, Charlotte," August says. "We will find him and his family, and they shall get all that they are due."

"My son is gone, August. He passed last year, but I had many years of watching over him. Dr. Cunningham knew where my baby had gone, and when the boy was old enough, he secured him a position here. It was, perhaps, his way of making amends. My son worked here for many years, and along the way, had a son of his own, who is here still."

"Hugh," August whispers.

"Yes, poor sweet Hugh. He has no idea, of course. Nor did his father. Hugh reminds me of you, August. A good and strong heart, if prone to youthful mistakes." She pauses, and in that pause, I imagine a wry smile. "Although youthful mistakes may simply run in the family."

"I will do right by him," August says.

"You already have."

"By letting him clean his family's stables? No. I shall find a way for him to take his proper place and be compensated for it. Everett owes him that much."

"That he does."

"And we owe you your freedom," I say. "Bronwyn told us why you are bound here. You were murdered, and your killer escaped justice. If we name him, you will be free. Is that what you want?"

Silence. Miranda glances over at an empty space, her brow furrowing. Then there is a flicker of blue, and beside me, August scrambles to his feet.

"Charlotte?"

The faint figure moves toward him, embracing him as she speaks through Miranda.

"You've gotten so big, August. You've grown into a good man, who married a good woman and had a delightful, kindhearted son. I could have wanted nothing better for you. Yes, I will have my killer named. First, though, would it be all right to speak to Edmund? I would dearly love to say goodbye to him, as his aunt, if that is all right with you and Rosalind."

We say that it is, and then we go to find Edmund. He meets his aunt properly, and they talk for nearly an hour. Then Miranda says the words that set her free.

"Charlotte Courtenay, I see you, and I name your killer. Your father, George Courtenay, Earl of Tynesford."

THIRTY-FIVE

RONWYN AND WILLIAM left last night. Before they went, they offered to come and stay with Edmund for a few days next week so that we might have at least a brief honeymoon. We can stay at Thorne Manor if we want the privacy. We agree to take them up on the offer later this fall with all the attendant jokes about staying far from the time stitch.

Miranda left this morning. She's returned to London, where she is apparently an early British Nellie Bly, working as a journalist. She did not marry the young man she'd been seeing when I left, thank goodness. As for Portia, she is currently abroad, and as much as I want to know about her life, Miranda cruelly refused to tell me anything, insisting Portia will want to do so herself.

Portia will be home next week, and we shall return to London to spend time with both her and Miranda, as well as gaining access to my belongings, which August stored away in our townhouse.

This afternoon, it is just Edmund and I, baking together in the kitchen. My broken wrist is bound, and he is helping me. We are making jam tartlets, ginger snaps and buttery scones, as if I can roll all my past fantasies into one, introducing him to three different kinds of treat and discovering where his tastes lie.

"Tomorrow, it shall be honeycomb cake," I say. "Since I already know you like honey. Perhaps chocolate-chip cookies, too, as we appear to be out of the last batch. Mice, I think."

"We do not have mice. Surrey eats them all."

"This mouse is slightly larger, I believe. And Surrey likes him far too much to eat him up. He's about this tall..." I lift one floury hand. "He has blue eyes and blond hair, and he is very fond of chocolate. You haven't seen him around, have you?"

Edmund makes a show of scanning the kitchen. "I do not see him anywhere."

"Odd, very odd. We must keep an eye out for him then."

As Edmund giggles, I pass over the bowl for him to mix the dry ingredients.

"So I stir a little or a lot?" he asks.

"For dry ingredients, you mix as much as you can," I say. "It is always a good question, though."

"Because with some recipes, you can mix too much," he says, and my heart swells with pride as I'm sure other mothers' do when their child says his first word.

I kiss the top of his head. "Exactly right. Mix too much, and the end result can be tough. Do you remember why?"

"Science," he says, beaming up at me. "Mix too much, and the liquid acti-acti—"

"Activates."

He nods. "It activates something in the flour that makes the cake chewy."

I kiss his head again, mostly just for the excuse to inhale the smell of him, to brush my lips over his head, to take the time to be in this simple moment that had once been my fondest dream. That's when I see August standing just inside the door, watching us, such a look on his face that my heart swells.

"Your father is spying on us," I whisper. "Making certain we do not overmix the dough."

August comes in and pulls up a stool to the counter. "I am an excellent supervisor."

He watches us for a few more moments. Then he says, "Do you want another bakery, Rosie?"

The words startle me so much that I jump. "What?"

"Another bakery. In York or in London. I know William and Bronwyn are handling the closing of your twenty-first-century one, and I thought perhaps you would like another." He inches his stool closer. "When we married, I expected you to sell the shop. I never thought to ask whether you wanted to. I thought I was freeing you, and now I realize I should have asked whether you wanted to be freed."

My eyes fill, and I walk around the counter. He pushes the stool back and tugs me onto his lap.

"That's a yes, then," he says. "I did make a horrible presumption."

"You made an ordinary presumption, and I was too young and uncertain to speak up. Your family was already loudly disapproving. Imagine if I'd kept working."

"I wouldn't have cared what they thought."

"But I did. The girl I *was* cared. The woman I *am* does not. I'm not sure about opening another bakery, but I would like to bake for others, perhaps as a small business for charity. I planned to ask—to insist—actually. Thank you for beating me to it."

"You need to bake, and not just cakes for your husband. I see that now."

I glance over at Edmund, who is quietly glued to our conversation, even if he can understand little of it.

"Edmund?" I say. "Would you do me a favor?"

"Yes, Mama?"

That word. Oh, that glorious word. I think I could listen to him saying it all day, and it takes a moment for me to remember what I'd been about to say.

"Could you go and tell Mrs. Beechworth that our treats shall be done in time for tea?"

He nods, slides off his stool and runs from the kitchen.

"Excellent distraction," August murmurs. "I do believe you were about to do this…"

He takes my chin in hand and kisses me, a long and slow kiss that I thoroughly enjoy before I say, "Yes, I did want that, but also I wanted to speak to you."

He gives a dramatic, put-upon sigh. "Fine. I presume you are going to ask whether the post brought a reply to my letter?"

"I am."

"Everett has agreed to meet me in London. He is reserving the private room at his club, which seems a suitable location for me to tell him about both you and Hugh."

"Most importantly about Hugh."

"Both are equally important, but I understand you are most concerned with Hugh. I will confront him with Hugh's parentage and our proposition that we name him as Harrison's child."

"Poor Harrison."

"I doubt either of us feels any guilt for that. In death, my brother will do this one good thing, giving Hugh the family name, which will be far less a so-called scandal than admitting my sister had a child out of wedlock. In a perfect world, Everett would be forced to claim Hugh as his own and the boy would become earl one day, but Everett would never go for that, and so Harrison shall be the sacrificial lamb. It's not as if he didn't have affairs before his marriage. Hugh will be the supposed issue of one of them. Does that work for you?"

"It does. But I had another thought, which is why I sent Edmund away. I want Courtenay Hall for us."

His brows shoot up.

I continue, "I know Everett cannot give it to you. The house goes with the title. But we spoke last night about how much we would both like to raise Edmund here. I believe blackmail is the solution."

August's lips twitch. "Blackmail? You are a marvel, Rosie."

"No, I am practical. This was a problem requiring a solution. We wish to raise our family here. We cannot do so while Everett controls the property. Even if he agreed to let us stay as caretakers, he'd wield our tenancy as a weapon against us."

"Mmm. Yes. We'd manage his estate, and he'd treat us like tenant farmers."

"The solution is blackmail. He knew about Charlotte. He will not want Hugh recognized as Harrison's son, but he will want him recognized as Charlotte's grandson even less. Add in the fact that your father killed her? And Dr. Cunningham senior witnessed it?" I shake my head. "Everett hates it here anyway. Let us come to some agreement."

"Where we have a life tenancy and he never sets foot on this property again?"

"It sounds perfectly reasonable."

He kisses me. "It does indeed."

We're still kissing when Edmund returns. I hear his footsteps and leap from August's lap, and Edmund enters to find me back at the counter. As Edmund stirs for me August pulls the recipe between them.

"Tell me what I am to do next," August says.

Edmund's nose scrunches up. "I thought you were sup-supervising."

"I was, but I have decided you do not require a supervisor." His gaze lifts to mine. "And I would really like to learn to bake."